PRAISE FOR THE NOVELS OF
CHANEL CLEETON

"A sexy fighter pilot hero? Yes, please. For anyone who's ever had a *Top Gun* fantasy, *Fly with Me* is for you."
—Roni Loren, *New York Times* bestselling author

"A sexy hero, strong heroine, delicious romance, sizzling tension, and plenty of breathtaking scandal. I loved this book!"
—Monica Murphy, *New York Times* bestselling author

"A sassy, steamy, and sometimes sweet read that had me racing to the next page."
—Chelsea M. Cameron, *New York Times* bestselling author

"Sexy, funny, and heart-wrenching!"
—Laura Kaye, *New York Times* bestselling author

"Scorching hot and wicked smart, *Flirting with Scandal* had me hooked from page one! Sizzling with sexual tension and political intrigue, Cleeton weaves a story that is as complex as it is sexy. Thank God this is a series because I need more!"
—Rachel Harris, *New York Times* bestselling author

"Sexy, intelligent, and intriguing. Chanel Cleeton makes politics scandal-icious."
—Tiffany King, *USA Today* bestselling author

"Fun, sexy, and kept me completely absorbed."
—Katie McGarry, author of *Chasing Impossible*

On Broken WINGS

CHANEL CLEETON

BERKLEY SENSATION
New York

BERKLEY SENSATION
Published by Berkley
An imprint of Penguin Random House LLC
375 Hudson Street, New York, New York 10014

Copyright © 2016 by Chanel Cleeton
Penguin Random House supports copyright. Copyright fuels creativity, encourages
diverse voices, promotes free speech, and creates a vibrant culture. Thank you for buying
an authorized edition of this book and for complying with copyright laws by not
reproducing, scanning, or distributing any part of it in any form without permission.
You are supporting writers and allowing Penguin Random House to continue to
publish books for every reader.

BERKLEY and BERKLEY SENSATION are registered trademarks and the B colophon
is a trademark of Penguin Random House LLC.

ISBN: 9781101987001

First Edition: January 2017

Printed in the United States of America
1   3   5   7   9   10   8   6   4   2

Cover art by Claudio Dogar-Marinesco
Cover design by Danielle Mazzella di Bosco

*To the brave men and women who serve in uniform
and the families who stand beside them*

Thank you so much to everyone who has read this series and supported the Wild Aces family. Your emails and messages mean the world to me. Thanks to my agent Kevan Lyon and editor Kate Seaver for making my dreams come true. I am so grateful to work with such a fabulous team at Penguin—my lovely publicist Ryanne Probst, Jessica Brock, Kim Burns, Katherine Pelz, and the wonderful art department. Thank you to my writing family, especially Lia Riley, Jennifer Blackwood, and A.J. Pine for their friendship and support. And as always, thanks to my family and friends, especially my amazing husband whose love and support makes all things possible.

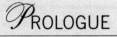

PROLOGUE

DANI

We sat next to each other on the sofa—me and Jordan—
our cell phones clutched in our hands, our gazes glued
to the headline running across the TV screen, willing it
to change, to disappear, for this to be a nightmare we
would wake from. A five-hour-long nightmare.

F-16 Crashes in Alaska.

I'd called the family members on the pilots' emergency contact sheets, letting everyone know we'd had an
incident involving the Wild Aces and were awaiting more
information, waiting for the Air Force to go through the
official notification process. I delivered the message in a
calm tone, pushing back the tremors, the tears, the terror
that crashed into me every time those words ran through
my head.

F-16 Crashes in Alaska.

My husband was flying tonight.

We'd spoken on the phone this afternoon, our last

words him telling me he was getting ready to step to his jet and that he loved me.

He'd said the words out of habit, his mind already on the mission ahead, ending the call the same way we'd ended every single call since we'd first said "I love you" nine years ago. It had been a short phone call—now, my mind foggy with fear, I struggled to remember what we'd talked about, the memory everything as I clung to those words.

I'd told him the dryer was broken. He'd complained about scheduling issues in the squadron he commanded. I'd been irritated about the dryer, cranky because he'd been gone for weeks and I'd just wanted him home. The call had been fine; there hadn't been a fight or anything, but now that those words scrolled across the screen in front of me, I wished I hadn't said a word about the dryer, that the scheduling shop hadn't screwed up, that we'd spent the night on the phone laughing.

What if I never hear his laugh again?

I called him after I first saw the news alert, dialed his number with trembling fingers and the kind of fear in my heart that filled my body with ice. The ring-ring of the phone beat in time with my heart. I prayed over and over again for him to answer so I could hear his voice, even as I knew in a situation like this, none of the guys would pick up; all communication would be cut off until they notified the pilot's family. And still, I called. My heart, my love, my life was somewhere out there, and I couldn't rest until I knew he was safe.

Finally, I heard the sound of his voice, the hint of an accent that came from a childhood in New England, my heart lurching at the sound.

"Michael. Thank God—"

"—I'm not available right now, but if you'd like to leave a message—"

The rest of his voice mail greeting disappeared beneath the sound rushing in my ears. When I heard the beep, I left a message, feeling as though my voice belonged to someone else, as though this night wasn't real and I'd wake up and turn over, rolling into the curve of Michael's body, pressing my lips to his skin, inhaling his scent.

I hung up the phone with a shudder, standing in the middle of our kitchen, no idea what came next.

And then Jordan called, the same fear in her voice that had taken up permanent residence in my gut, and I invited her over, because even though I was supposed to be the strong one, the calm one, buoyed by seven years' experience as a military wife, I couldn't get past the fear dragging me down.

F-16 Crashes in Alaska.

We didn't speak. At some point, Jordan reached out and grabbed my hand. I didn't let go.

I thought of the pilots who were flying tonight. Michael. Easy. Jordan's boyfriend, Burn. Thor. All pilots I'd grown close to, cared about. Men who I'd celebrated holidays with, who had become like brothers to me.

My husband was flying tonight.

I squeezed Jordan's hand a bit tighter, the panic growing with each second that passed. I couldn't sit here and pretend to be calm, as though the worry wasn't ripping me to shreds, as if I wasn't about to crawl out of my skin.

I needed to know he was okay. Needed to hear his voice. It was such a simple thing; how many times had I heard him speak, listened to that husky voice that always filled me with peace? Now I needed it. Needed to cling to the sound as proof he'd survived, that I hadn't lost everything.

Please let him be okay. Please. Please.

The doorbell rang.

We both froze. I'd never thought my doorbell was ominous, but now the sound sent a chill down my spine. Good news didn't come in the early morning, the sun just barely risen. It didn't come wearing service dress. I didn't know if they were here for me or for Jordan, but either way, something inside me shattered.

We both rose from the couch, our lips unmoving, our hands locked. My legs shook, my heart rattling inside my chest. My body aged decades with each step I took, with each step that took me closer to whatever nightmare faced us on the other side of the door.

They say your life flashes before your eyes before you die. And it did.

I saw myself at twenty-one, at a bar in Atlanta, laughing with my friends, my body lighting up with sparks as I made eye contact with the hot guy sitting on a barstool, desperately hoping he'd come over and talk to me. I saw myself in Michael's arms as we kissed for the first time, heard my voice telling my friends I was going to marry him, saw the look on his face as I walked down the aisle on our wedding day. So many moments. His arms around me as we mourned the baby we'd loved and lost after my miscarriage, the way he kissed me each night before he fell asleep. Big moments, small moments, the pieces of a life we'd built together, all the love and hope that had filled me as I envisioned our future, all the things we'd do—the children I'd prayed for, the plans we'd made. My entire world wrapped up in one person.

And then the moments stopped and my mind went blank as I stared at my front door.

I reached out, my fingers grazing the knob, and some part of me wanted to pull back as I hoped, prayed, that *this time* if I called Michael, he'd answer, saying my name in the voice that still put a smile on my face. But I knew. *I knew.* Hadn't I always known we hurtled toward this? That at some point the bill would come due, and eventually he'd go up in the air and the sky wouldn't give him back.

The door opened with a creak. Three officers in uniform stood on our front porch.

It was as though I'd left my body, as if I was hovering above all of this, watching it play out. I couldn't . . . I didn't feel anything. Could barely register the words they said. Jordan, the walls around me, everything disappeared, until there was a hole inside me, around me, swallowing me up.

"Mrs. Peterson, we regret to inform you . . ."

I felt myself falling, taking Jordan down with me as I hit the floor, as I quite simply broke. She was there, her arms around me, but I couldn't feel her.

I couldn't feel anything anymore.

$\mathcal{O}$NE

ONE YEAR LATER

DANI

"Do you want matte or gloss?"

I blinked, the paint cans blurring before me. What type of paint did you use to erase a broken dream?

No fucking clue.

My hands gripped the handle of my cart, filled with painting supplies that had taken me the better part of an hour to assemble. Every time I thought I had what I needed, I realized I'd forgotten yet another thing. Time had ceased to exist here, and I half wondered if I'd finally escape aisle twelve and discover night had fallen and I'd wasted one more day not fulfilling the task I dreaded.

The salesman sighed, running his hand through his hair. I couldn't exactly blame him for the frustration—even with the online research I'd done, it was clear I was pretty clueless on how to repaint an almost-nursery-turned-guest-bedroom in order to make my home more likely to sell.

"What will paint over blue?" I asked.

Air Force blue. Baby boy blue.

There will be another baby, Michael had promised when I'd miscarried. *Let's not change the room.*

So we'd kept it—his way of clinging to hope and my attempt at supporting him.

Of course, now they were both gone, and I couldn't walk into the room without feeling an overwhelming sense of loss.

The salesman's gaze drifted to my left hand, to the diamond engagement ring that sat there atop a diamond eternity band. I couldn't look at either of those things and yet, like the room, I wasn't ready to cast them off. My husband might have died a year ago, but the memory of him still lingered.

"Ma'am, perhaps it would help if your husband came with you. He might have a better sense of what your needs are."

He would have. He would have repainted the room on one of his free weekends and I wouldn't have had to worry about a thing. Which was the problem. I'd always prided myself on having my shit together—being an Air Force wife allowed for nothing less considering how frequently I was alone—but now that Michael was actually gone, I kept realizing how many things I didn't know how to do. And how much I'd grown to depend on him during the seven years we were married.

The paint cans blurred even more, my eyes filling with tears. Oh God, I was going to lose it in aisle twelve.

The thing about being a widow was that you never knew when the tears would come. You could have a string of good days, and then something would set you off—the scent of your husband's cologne on a stranger, the sound of a jet screaming overhead, your wedding song playing on the radio. Apparently mine had come today. I took a deep breath, steadying myself, struggling to push a response out of my mouth when suddenly a large hand landed on my back, palm between my shoulder blades, fingers stroking my ratty T-shirt.

"I got this," a voice rumbled behind me.

I whirled around and came face-to-face with Easy.

As commander of the Wild Aces F-16 squadron, my husband—call sign Joker—had been both boss and mentor to the twenty-something pilots who had flown under his leadership. I'd gotten to know all the guys and their families pretty well, but there was no doubt that out of all of them, my favorite was Alex "Easy" Rogers.

There were many things to love about Easy—the contagious smile on his face, the compassion in his eyes, the memory of how he'd comforted me when I'd miscarried and Michael had been halfway across the country, how he'd stood next to me at the podium while I delivered Michael's eulogy, the way he'd always treated me with indulgent affection. He'd been one of my husband's best friends, so for that alone, I'd always love him. But it wasn't just that. He was a big kid with a wild streak ninety percent of the time, but the other ten percent of the time he was one of the best men I'd ever known. He was also one of the last people Michael had spoken to when he was alive—a voice over the radio in their formation of four jets right before Michael was lost to us forever.

I struggled to get my tears in check as Easy spoke to the salesman, and then the guy was gone and I was staring up into Easy's blue eyes.

"You okay?"

"Just trying to pick out paint."

"What do you need?" he asked, his expression solemn, the usual swagger and amusement drained from his expression.

It had been a rough year for everyone.

"I'm trying to repaint the guest room." *Do not cry.* "The one that was going to be the nursery." The rest of the words came out in a whoosh of pain. "The Realtor thinks the house will be more marketable if the rooms are neutral. It's been on the market six months now and we still haven't gotten any interest."

I still hadn't gotten any interest. When you'd been a "we" for seven years, it was hard to switch back to the singular.

The days after I'd received the knock on my front door, after the casualty officers had notified me that Michael's F-16 had crashed in Alaska—that he was *gone*— I'd walked through a nightmare. When the official military events had ended, I'd gone home to Georgia to grieve in private. But at thirty-one, living at my parents' had begun to feel cramped, so now I was back in Oklahoma, waiting to sell the house I'd lived in with Michael, trying to figure out the next step.

Easy looked down at his feet, his big body hunched over, and then his gaze was on me again. "I can do it."

"No. Thanks for offering, but it's too much. I'm fine on my own."

The squadron was deploying to Afghanistan in a month. No way I wanted Easy working in his final weeks before he went to war.

"I can hire someone to do it. Which I probably should have done all along," I admitted.

Michael's life insurance took financial worries off

my plate for a few years, but thanks to seven years of moving all over the world, my résumé wasn't exactly impressive. Luxuries like hiring someone to paint felt irresponsible until I found a job. Although if the house didn't sell . . .

"I'll do it." He nudged my shoulder, positioning his big body between me and my cart, studying the items I'd collected so far.

"You have the deployment—"

"It's no big deal," he answered. "It'll take a day. I can come over tomorrow and work on it, if it's okay with you."

It hadn't escaped my notice that the squadron had begun stepping in to help out, although I hadn't seen Easy for a while. I guessed this was his way of doing the right thing for a buddy's wife, and as much as it made me feel guilty, I couldn't argue with a military man's sense of honor.

"Okay. That's so sweet. I really appreciate it." I smiled. "I'll make you a thank-you dinner."

"You don't have to," he mumbled, a slight flush covering his cheeks as soon as the word "sweet" fell from my lips.

"I want to."

I hated eating meals alone; half the time I couldn't even be bothered to cook for myself and I ended up eating cereal for dinner. And there was something about Easy that always seemed to need taking care of. He was a confirmed bachelor to the extreme and while I'd seen him with plenty of girls over the years, I couldn't remember the last time he'd had a girlfriend or anything close to it, had never seen anyone take care of him.

He nodded in response, his Adam's apple bobbing.

His hand left my back, running through his thick, blond hair. He looked tired and I wondered how he was really doing. All the guys who'd been in the air with Michael when he'd died had struggled in the past year.

Easy turned, his face in profile as he scrutinized the paint cans. And what a beautiful face it was. He was teased mercilessly because he looked more like an underwear model than a fighter pilot—high cheekbones, full lips, long eyelashes, the kind of blue eyes people tried to replicate with color contacts.

Hell, I was a little jealous of how pretty he was.

"So what else do you need?" he asked, his gaze still on the shelf.

I handed him my list; the words scratched there might as well have been a foreign language. I'd always handled the finances, but anything related to the house had been Michael's domain.

"I got most of it," I answered. "I've never painted before beyond my college dorm room, and I figure this needs to look good if it's going to impress buyers."

He nodded again, and I realized this was the most economical I'd ever seen Easy be with his words. Since Michael's death, things had been . . . strained. He was polite, still willing to offer a hand if I needed it. But the friendship we'd built years ago seemed to have been replaced by the guilt he felt over the accident.

"How have you been?" I asked, trying to pull the conversation out of him, realizing how much I'd missed our friendship. "I haven't seen you in months." I thought about it. "Since Thanksgiving?"

Had we really let five months slip by? I'd e-mailed him on his birthday in February and he'd responded, but we hadn't seen each other—

"I saw you at the squadron in March. You were leaving with Jordan."

Surprise filled me. "I didn't see you. Why didn't you say hi?"

He shrugged. "You guys were talking; I didn't want to interrupt you."

Could this be more awkward? Did I remind him of Michael's death? Was he just uncomfortable around me?

I'd been walking through a fog for the past few months, and somewhere along the way I'd missed that we'd gotten to this point. And it wasn't just Easy; I'd been so consumed by my grief that life had passed me by. Friends' lives had changed, they'd moved on to other things, and I'd stayed rooted in that day in May, in the loss that defined and overshadowed my world. I'd lost touch with people, simply stopped trying, and I'd given up more than I'd realized, and suddenly, I wanted to make up for it, needed to fix the gap between us.

"Hey." I laid a hand on his arm and his entire body stiffened. A pang hit me, and then another one, piercing the numbness shrouding me.

My voice cracked. "I miss him, too. If it's too weird to be around me or if I remind you of everything that's happened, and you need to take a step back, I understand. I know it's been hard for you guys to move on from the accident, and I don't want to make it worse. But if you need someone to talk to, I'm here. I miss our friendship. I miss you."

EASY

Fuck.

I closed my eyes for a beat, trying to drown her out, to throw the wall back up, attempting to push her out of the cracks and crevices of my heart where she'd snuck in and taken up permanent residence in my chest.

She smelled like apples. Forbidden-fucking-apples. She looked . . .

My eyes slammed open and my gaze slid over her. I blinked, not sure if it was the scent of apples or the sight in front of me that made me so fucking hungry.

She wore a pair of white shorts that showed off surprisingly tanned legs. A faded T-shirt that likely harkened back to her days as a cheerleader at the University of Georgia. Her red-gold hair was up in a loose braid, her green eyes staring up at me.

I'd been in detox, hoped the months apart would cure this ache inside me every single fucking time I saw her.

They hadn't.

If anything, the time apart had only made the ache worse.

I fisted my hands at my sides, looking away from her again, her words cutting through me as I focused on the paint cans as though my life depended on it. And then I couldn't take it anymore, and my gaze slid down to the spot where she touched me, where her fingers rested on my bicep, her skin a few shades paler than mine.

I swallowed, trying to drag more air into my lungs, her hand suddenly as dangerous as a deadly spider.

I had a pretty solid you-can-look-but-you-can't-touch policy where Dani was concerned. There had been moments when I bent the rules a little bit, like a few minutes ago when I'd seen her standing there amid all the painting supplies looking so lost, as though she was drowning and needed a life raft to pull her to shore, but I paid for every fucking moment in spades.

"You don't make it worse," I lied, answering her original question, hating that I'd given her a reason to worry about anyone other than herself. She had more shit on her plate than most people could ever deal with, and the last thing I wanted to do was add to it.

I shoved my hands into the pockets of my cargo shorts, breaking the physical connection between us, still not quite able to meet her gaze. Her eyes could bring the most resolute man to his fucking knees.

I swallowed again, wondering if my voice sounded as strained to her ears as it did to mine. "It's good to see you again."

Heaven and hell rolled into a knot in my stomach.

I'd had it bad for her since the first moment I saw her, but as guilty as I'd felt wanting my friend's wife, the desire inside me now for his widow was infinitely worse.

I would have given everything I had to trade places with him, so he could have come back for her.

She smiled, a real smile, one she rarely doled out anymore. "You, too."

Her gaze drifted past me, her smile deepening, and she stepped forward another foot, close enough so her side brushed against mine, warm and soft, the apple smell filling my nostrils once again. It had to be her shampoo. Her head barely came to my chin, her scent wafting up at me. I bent my head just an inch, barely resisting the urge to inhale, drowning in her, the warmth from her body—

"You have admirers," Dani commented, her teasing voice breaking me from my stupor.

I blinked, following her gaze.

Two girls stood at the end of the aisle—college girls by the look of the youthful glow they sported and the sorority letters stretched across their tits—staring at us, wide, curious smiles on their faces. They both blushed as they caught me staring back, exchanging whispers behind cupped hands.

Dani nudged me, the touch sending another jolt through my body. I was hard as a fucking rock in a home improvement store and it had everything to do with the scent of apples and the allure of soft curves against me, and nothing to do with the sorority girls.

She gifted me with another smile, this one brighter than the last, filling her gaze and spilling over into my heart.

My mouth went dry.

"You can go work your magic," she teased, her words jolting me back to reality. "I'm fine here."

The only thing worse than being utterly and totally in love with the one woman who you absolutely could not fucking have, who saw you more as a brother than a man, was having the same woman, the one who'd ripped your heart out of your chest time and time again, try to set you up with someone else.

I was pretty sure there was some bitter fucking irony here considering my rep, but with my heart lying in the middle of aisle twelve, gushing blood, I wasn't much for humor.

I shook my head, turning away from the girls, Dani once again all I could see.

"I'm okay."

"You sure? I really don't mind. Think of me as one of the guys. Hell, I can be your wingwoman."

"I'm sure," I croaked, pretty sure she'd just slayed me—death by well-meaning matchmaking and the thrust of a sharp blade that accompanied every one of her words.

I tilted my head, staring back at the girls, wondering if it would help if I did go over there, if I lost myself in two hot bodies. In my younger years, I probably would have gone for it. Now it would be another meaningless fuck in a string of them. And I didn't want that anymore. I'd watched two of my closest friends—Noah and Thor—meet women and fall in love this past year. Noah was now married with a baby on the way, and Thor was engaged to the girl he'd loved, and lost, and somehow regained. So yeah. Maybe I couldn't have Dani, but that didn't mean I didn't want to meet a woman I could love, who would love me in return. At thirty-three it might have taken me a while to get here, but I was ready for something more. And if my perfect woman bared an uncanny resemblance to Dani, whatever.

Some women slid under your skin so deep, you couldn't carve them out no matter how hard you tried.

$\mathcal{T}$WO

DANI

I met up with a very pregnant Jordan for dinner at our favorite barbecue restaurant in town that night. Of all my friendships, ours had probably grown the closest in the aftermath of Michael's death. Maybe it was that we'd been together when the casualty officers had arrived at the house; experiencing something so devastating had bonded us together.

But even as I loved her, as I knew she understood as best as she could, I would have been lying if I didn't admit there weren't still moments when it was hard, when I felt the same disconnect from her I experienced with everyone else around me. She had the family I'd always wanted, and even as I was happy for her, I couldn't deny there was a part of me that was angry—at God, fate, the Air Force, the fucking F-16, whatever it was that decided to take my husband and the future we'd imagined away from me.

This was one of the places where the ghost of him

lingered, a restaurant we'd gone to so many times over the years, where we'd sat and laughed with friends. It was crazy, but I swore I could feel his arm draped across the back of my chair, the heat of his leg pressing into mine. I pushed back against the tears pricking behind my eyelids.

"When does Noah's flight get in?" I asked.

Jordan was two weeks away from her due date and her husband, Noah—known to the Wild Aces by his call sign, "Burn"—was coming back from Korea for the birth of their first child. They hadn't seen each other since he'd returned to the U.S. in November and I knew how much she missed him.

"Saturday afternoon."

I grinned at the way her face lit up when she said it. Their one-year anniversary was a couple weeks away, and despite the distance between them, she still had that "newlywed glow" about her.

"I'm so happy for you guys."

"Thanks. I can't believe everything is happening at once. It feels like I've been pregnant forever, and now the baby's almost here. And I'm so excited to see Noah and have him home with us for a while."

"How long will he be here for?"

"A month. He's using this as his mid-tour leave. He'll go back to Korea for his final month and then he'll be back for good."

They'd been lucky enough to get Bryer as their next assignment, so they'd be in Oklahoma for another three years.

"How are things going with you?" Jordan asked.

I shrugged between mouthfuls of brisket. "Good, I guess. Nothing really new."

My life had become a cycle of wake up, run errands, occasionally read, fall asleep, and repeat. Sometimes I hung out with friends, but since Michael died I found myself narrowing my social circle. People meant well, but sometimes it was harder to be in social settings. I didn't fit. Not anymore. I could laugh, could find reasons to smile. I could be happy . . . ish. But no matter how hard I tried, or how much time passed, there was a hole inside me; a piece was missing, gaping open, edges ragged, and I hadn't a clue how to fill it. I tried. I tried so fucking hard. And still, the pain beat inside my chest, my future a yawning void without the one thing I'd built my life around.

I'd had interests when Michael was alive, friendships, things that had kept me busy during the long stretches when he was away from home. But the heart of everything, what had given me a purpose to throw myself into every day rather than going through the motions had been the life we'd built. I'd spent so much time focused on our marriage, dreaming about our future, the family we were building, envisioning us growing old together, that he had simply become part of me. And now he was gone, leaving me fractured and alone, and the other stuff didn't matter anymore. Everyone had a suggestion for how I should deal with my grief, and they meant well; they loved me and wanted me to be happy, but I couldn't yoga my way through widowhood. I hadn't achieved anything beyond coping, wondered if that was too lofty a goal.

"How are things with the house?" Jordan asked.

"We've had a few showings, but nothing solid. I spent the week doing home improvement projects—planting flowers and organizing the garage. Easy's actually coming over to paint tomorrow."

"Easy's doing manual labor?"

I laughed. He was Noah's best friend, and he and Jordan definitely had a sibling-like relationship where they ragged on each other constantly.

"Yeah. I ran into him while I was shopping for paint and he was nice enough to offer to help."

"Speaking of Easy," Jordan said. "I was talking to Noah, and we thought it would be fun to do something as a squadron before the guys deploy. Would you come?"

The Wild Aces continued to include me in squadron events. I tried not to overstep too much since I didn't want to make the new squadron commander's wife feel as though I was usurping her position, but there were enough people I cared about, so I went to the important ones.

"Yeah, I would. Thanks for inviting me."

"No problem. Everyone would love to see you there."

I missed feeling like I belonged. I hadn't loved everything about military life, but the friendships I'd built meant the world to me. We'd been a family when the strain of the lifestyle took your biological family away from you.

"How's Becca doing with the deployment coming up?" I asked.

Becca was the newest member of our military family. She'd just gotten engaged—or re-engaged—to Thor, one of Michael's buddies and the fourth member in the formation when he died. Thor had struggled with PTSD in the months following Michael's death, but he seemed to be doing a lot better now, and reconnecting with his high school sweetheart had definitely played a huge role in his recovery.

"She seems okay. A little stressed, but doing her best

to be strong for Thor. She's worried about how he'll handle the deployment with his PTSD, but she said it's really important to him to be there for the squadron."

The buildup to a deployment, especially your first one, was always the worst. This horrible event loomed large, and each day took you one day closer to the thing you dreaded most. The month before my first deployment with Michael had been one of the most difficult times of my life. Well, until now. I remembered the fear that had clawed me as I'd said good-bye to him, as I'd wrapped my arms around his body, trying to memorize the weight of him, the shape of him, trying to hold him to me and keep him close enough to weather six months apart. The fear had pummeled me wave after wave—that our relationship would flounder, that he would change, or I would change, and then of course, most of all, the fear that was my constant shadow. That this would be the last time I held him, the last time I saw him, kissed him.

And for all those times I'd tried to keep the image sharp, after a while, the years ran together and you adjusted to the life, to the TDYs and deployments, and you forgot how scary their job was. You grew used to hearing about the dangers they faced each time they flew, even when it was just a training mission, and you loosened your grip each time.

I'd taken Michael to the squadron to fly to Alaska on a Tuesday. I remembered snippets of our conversation in the car, his fingers entwined with mine as I drove him to work, Tom Petty's "Learning to Fly" playing on the radio, and Michael turning up the dial and singing along in his off-key tone.

I played that song at his memorial service.

When I thought of him now, when I clung to the memory of him, it was the image of saying good-bye to him in the squadron parking lot that always stuck with me—the last moment I'd seen him alive. It had faded with time, with the year that had gone by, like a worn photograph, and sometimes I woke in the middle of the night, panic flooding me at the possibility that I'd forgotten some detail, some moment, that eventually the memories of him would fade away, too, and I'd really be left with nothing.

"I'll talk to her," I offered.

Being a fighter wife was a sisterhood of sorts. Nothing could prepare you for it, not entirely, at least, but it helped to have someone to talk to who'd gone through deployments and TDYs, who'd lived with the fear of loving someone with such a dangerous job, who understood in a way those unconnected to the military simply couldn't. I wasn't as close to Becca as I was to Jordan, but we'd hung out a few times over the past few months and I really liked her. After everything he'd been through, it was good to see Thor so happy.

"Thanks," Jordan answered. "That would mean a lot to her. She's planning their wedding so that'll probably help her stay busy, but I imagine it has to be tough, especially since she struggled so much with his job."

They'd been engaged when they were in college, but broke up when Thor went to Texas to start pilot training. Ten years later, they'd run into each other in their home state of South Carolina. Fast forward a few months, and they were engaged again, adorably in love, planning their wedding.

Jordan took anther bite of her brisket, a nervous expression on her face I recognized all too well and had seen directed my way countless times, so much so I'd termed it the "Widow Look" in my head. We were headed somewhere into the murky territory of talking about either Michael's death or my widowed status. It wasn't her fault; *everyone* got that look on their faces, as if they were afraid their words would break me.

I didn't know if it would make them feel better or worse if I assured them nothing they said would *really* make a difference. I was already shattered inside.

"What would you think about going to dinner with someone?"

I froze, my fork hovering in midair. The words pushed out with a squeak. "You mean, a date?"

Jordan winced—another gesture I'd gotten used to in the last year—her expression suggesting she'd kicked a kitten.

"Nothing serious. Just for fun."

I couldn't think of much that sounded less fun.

"He's my doctor and he's really nice. Mid-thirties. Divorced. Cute."

"I—"

Am so not ready.

Apparently, the one-year mark was when people started feeling comfortable saying stuff like that to you. I wasn't sure I would ever feel comfortable hearing it. I still wore my wedding rings. Still considered myself married. Jordan wasn't the first person to suggest I try my hand at dating, but each time I heard it, it sent a knife through my heart. I wasn't ready to move on. I didn't *want* to move on. Moving on meant Michael wasn't coming back, and while I knew it, I didn't want the reminder in my face every single fucking day.

I opened my mouth and closed it again.

Do not cry. Do not cry.

I took a deep breath. "I don't know. I don't think I'm there."

Sympathy filled her gaze. "Do you need more time?"

Time was the last thing I needed. Time was my enemy now . . . when I looked down the long tunnel of my future, fifty-plus years of being alone, of mourning my husband, stared back at me.

"Maybe," I lied.

"'Maybe' sounds like 'no.'"

It was hard to fool the people who knew you best.

I sighed. "It might be. It would take someone pretty incredible to make me want to be in a relationship again. Michael was a wonderful husband. And he loved me. Really loved me. I don't see myself settling for anything less, can't imagine going through dating and more if it isn't someone really special. And it seems too much to hope I could get so lucky twice in my life. I'm okay on my own."

At least, as "okay" as you could be in a situation like this.

Jordan reached out and squeezed my hand. "Yeah, but *you're* really special. And I hate the thought of you alone all the time. You're getting through this as best you can, but I love you, and I want you to be happy again. I'm not saying this has to be anything serious, but go and give it a chance. Worst case, you gain a friend."

"It's been almost ten years since I dated. I don't know how to go through that again. It was a lifetime ago."

I still couldn't wrap my head around how I'd gotten to this point. I was supposed to be a mom by now. We were supposed to be a family. Instead I was talking to Jordan about going out on dates.

Why me? Why him? Why this?

"Isn't it harder going through this alone?" she asked.

I wasn't sure I had an answer to that one. It was hard no matter what. I was lonely, I couldn't deny it, but at the same time, the answer wasn't to shuffle some guy into the spot Michael had occupied. It felt disrespectful to everyone involved, and even more, like I'd told Jordan, I didn't see how it could work. There was no way anyone could replace what he'd been to me, what he was to me, and I'd never love anyone as much as I'd loved him. I didn't *want* to love anyone as much as I'd loved him. Not again.

I forced my lips into an approximation of a smile. "I know you're trying to help, and I appreciate it, I really do. And I'm sure your doctor is a really nice man, but . . ."

"What's the worst that could happen?"

I didn't know anymore. My worst thing had already happened. Nothing else came close. But that wasn't exactly true. The new worst thing that could happen—my new reality—was my fear that if I went out on a date with another man, I was closing the door on my relationship with Michael. I was giving up on him, on us. Even though he was already gone.

"It seems like a betrayal," I finally answered.

"Dani." The compassion in Jordan's eyes sent another pang to my chest. "He loved you. So much. He would want you to be happy."

I nodded, the tears building now. "The logical part of me knows you're right. But it doesn't make it easier. I still feel guilty, every time I move on. When I took his clothes out of our closet and donated them to charity, when I got rid of his car, selling our house." The tears came now, and nothing I could do would hold them back. "I see him in everything and it hurts so much, and at the same time, the thought of losing those pieces of him hurts even more. I don't know how to move on. Or if I want to."

I held on to my grief now that I had little else left to hold on to.

"I can't take my wedding rings off. I've tried and I just can't. I'm not ready to be single again. It's too much like I'm erasing him, as though we never happened."

Jordan's voice trembled. "That's okay. I'm sorry I pushed. So sorry."

"No. It's not your fault. I'm not mad at you, only at the situation. You're right. I can't stay like this, can't live like this; it's choking me and I can't breathe. I keep trying to come up with a plan for what I'm going to do after the house sells, for what job I'll have and where I'll live, and I keep trying to envision this life I'm apparently building without Michael, and I can't see it. I spent the last nine years envisioning myself somewhere completely different and I have to adjust, but I'm falling apart instead."

Jordan wiped away the tears that had fallen down *her* cheeks. I really was an uplifting dinner companion.

"You need to go out. You need to start putting yourself out there, even if you don't want to, because you have to find some way to move forward. And I know it's tough, can't imagine how you're dealing with this, but you have to have faith and give yourself a chance to be happy, even if it won't look exactly how you envisioned it. None of this is fair. And I'll never understand why this happened, but you have to try your best to move forward, because you can't stay stuck in your pain forever. I know it's easy to say, and I have no idea how you're handling this. I only want you to be happy."

I hated the words falling from her lips, felt an irrational, horrible flash of anger that she sat there, with everything she wanted—the husband, the baby—and told me to move on. I wanted to scream that I couldn't move on. Wanted to rail at the injustice of it all, that we had been happy and it was all ripped away from me.

I hated when everyone told me I would be "happy." They meant well, hoped I'd find solace in their words, but if anything, the promise of "happy"—the lie of it— almost made things worse. Grief didn't allow for "happy," instead it yanked the rug from under your feet and knocked you on your ass until you were drowning in quicksand with no one there to pull you out.

"Happy" only made me angry.

The anger snuck up on me at the most inopportune times, turning me into someone I'd never been, someone I didn't know how to handle. I met with a grief counselor regularly, and I knew these emotions were part of the process, and yet, they threw me for a loop every single time. I'd read the books in the self-help section; had done everything I could to try to learn how to get through this, but it never got any easier. With each day I lost a piece of myself, the woman who stared back at me in the mirror becoming someone I didn't even recognize, a shell of the woman Michael had loved.

That shamed me, too.

"I'll go out with him."

The words escaped in a whoosh, and as soon as they did, I was overwhelmed by the urge to take them back, to get up and leave and go sit in my house and hide away from all the things I had no desire to face.

I'd always prided myself on being a strong military wife. I'd definitely had my moments, the times when I found myself sick with worry or angry with Michael when he had to work late and didn't come home yet another night, but he'd pretty much been my hero, and I'd worked hard to be a wife he could be proud of, who could weather anything thrown her way. I needed to get my shit together, needed to find some way to get through this. I couldn't afford to keep floundering.

"Are you sure?" Jordan asked.

"Yeah. As long as he knows this is only casual. Maybe you could explain things to him."

"I already mentioned you," she admitted. "He remembered . . ."

She didn't finish the sentence, but she didn't have to. There'd been a lot of local media attention and even some national press when Michael died, and the local community had definitely rallied around Bryer. Nearly one thousand people had shown up for his memorial service.

I barely remembered that day. Barely remembered the speech I'd given, what people had said about him. It was all a horrible blur I wished I could completely erase. Of all my memories, I'd happily cast those off.

"Is it okay if I give him your number?" Jordan asked.

"Yeah."

"His name's Paul. And he's cute. Really cute. He's been through a lot with his divorce, so he's looking for someone who wants to take it slow, too." She smiled. "He has a really calm personality, and he's honestly a good guy. I promise I've thoroughly vetted him."

I laughed even though I wanted to weep. Apparently, I was dating now.

$\mathcal{T}$HREE

EASY

I showed up at Dani's house Sunday afternoon, question-ing my sanity for the hundredth time since I'd agreed to paint her spare bedroom the day before. The past few months hadn't been so much out-of-sight, out-of-mind as much as out-of-sight, out-of-trouble, and I'd figured the best way to keep things from becoming awkward be-tween us was to avoid her, period. Except—

She'd looked so lost in the paint aisle, standing there by herself, and if I had an Achilles' heel, she was it.

I knocked on the front door, shifting my weight back and forth. I was way too excited to see her. Excited and dreading it. And then Dani opened the door, a smile transforming her mouth as her gaze settled on me, and I braced myself—

She stepped into me, wrapping her arms around my neck, her body pressing against mine.

Her hugs weren't casual; no, she hugged you as though she meant it, and I couldn't resist the urge to let her hold me close, for my palm to rest on her back as I inhaled the scent of her shampoo. Her hair was silk against my face, a strand brushing across my lips. She wasn't curvy, but she was soft, her body the kind you wanted to curl up against. The height difference between us was significant enough that she felt tiny in my arms, and the familiar need bubbled up inside me—to protect her, love her, worship her.

I took a step back.

"Thank you so much for coming over."

The hint of her accent sent a pull low in my belly, and an ache even lower. I swallowed, my mouth dry, giving her a nod, not sure I trusted my emotions enough to speak.

I followed her into the house, my gaze drifting over the swaying copper-colored hair, the loose top, the denim shorts, the bare legs. There was a rhythm to her walk, one I'd memorized.

Fuck.

I forced myself to look away, the sight of the pictures on the wall—her and Joker on their wedding day—obliterating my body's reaction faster than a bucket of cold water could have.

She led me into the room they'd planned for their nursery, the one I'd helped Joker paint blue what seemed like a lifetime ago. A whole other host of emotions hit me as I remembered that day, the two of us sharing a beer, talking about flying, about him becoming a dad.

He'd been the weapons officer at my first F-16 assignment, and despite the years between us, we'd struck up a friendship. He wasn't defined by his rank; he didn't use it to set himself apart. He was nice to everyone, approachable, genuinely cared about the people in his squadron. He'd been a bro. We'd kept in touch over the years, run into each other at various assignments, our paths crossing as they so often did in the small community of F-16 pilots. When I'd heard he was going to be the squadron commander of the Wild Aces, I'd been thrilled. He was the kind of guy you wanted leading, who was destined for great things. We hadn't been as close back then, but I'd admired him, respected him.

The first time I saw Dani was at a squadron Hail and Farewell—a party to celebrate the pilots and families leaving the squadron and those coming in. I'd been standing at the bar, talking to Noah, and all of a sudden, I'd looked up and I swear to God, I fucking fell.

She'd been standing behind the bar with one of the wives, wearing a pink dress and a smile on her face that lit up the room. Her eyes fucking sparkled. And I wasn't a guy who thought shit like that. At all. But the second I saw her, any hope of game disappeared. I had to talk to her. I'd taken the first step, and Noah had nudged me, and then I'd watched, the dream of her sliding away, as Joker took her into his arms and pressed his mouth to hers, my gut twisting as something inside me that had sprung to life simply died.

I wasn't someone who messed around with married women or the kind of guy who would ever move in on a bro's girl. There was a code to this stuff and it was the same code that made us willing to die fighting to protect the guy at our side. I'd vowed to put her out of my mind, that whatever I'd felt in that moment, or thought I'd felt, wasn't real, didn't matter, had to be forgotten at all costs.

Two years later, I was still trying.

"—I set everything up," Dani said, and I realized she'd been speaking this whole time, and I'd been somewhere else entirely.

A smile played at her lips. "Are you okay? Rough night last night? Do you want me to make you coffee or something?"

There was no censure in her voice, merely affectionate amusement. I knew the reputation I had in the squadron—player, asshole, manwhore—and I couldn't care less what people thought about me. Hell, I'd worked hard to cultivate that reputation and had a pretty damn good time doing it. As fucked up as it was, in my world you got ahead by being the flashiest guy in the group, by having a larger-than-life personality that translated to how you handled yourself in the jet. Ours was not a profession for the meek or humble. There was an arrogance to what we did, an absolute belief in yourself that often meant the difference between life and death, a need to be the biggest, baddest motherfucker in the sky and on the ground.

And at the same time, I couldn't stand the idea of her seeing me through that lens—all swagger and no substance.

"No. I stayed in last night. Sorry. Distracted."

I forced a smile, wishing I could relax around her. It hadn't been this hard before, but now there was too much there, too many things twisting me up in knots, so much guilt washing over me that I was drowning.

I was here and Joker wasn't.

"Are we okay?" Dani asked, her voice going quiet.

The worry in her voice added another layer to the guilt.

"Yeah, of course."

"Are you sure? Because you seem different with me. You said everything was fine the other day, but it doesn't seem fine."

I ran a hand through my hair. Of all the emotions running through me, I picked the easiest one to address. We'd spent enough time together that she knew me well, and I figured my act wasn't really fooling anyone.

"I'm sorry. I miss him. It's weird being here again." I took a deep breath, releasing some of the pressure from my chest. "I'm still . . ." My voice trailed off.

"Getting used to him being gone?"

"Yeah."

"Me, too." Her gaze surveyed the room before settling back on me. "Can I ask you something?"

"Of course."

She bit down on her lip, worry in her eyes. "Jordan wants to set me up on a date."

My gaze was so focused on her mouth, on all that pale pink, that I didn't hear what she'd said, and then her words registered and they hit me like a fucking truck. Was Jordan trying to kill me?

"What?"

"Jordan wants me to go on a date with her doctor. I guess he's divorced or something, and she said he's really nice . . ." Dani swallowed, her face pale. "It's weird. Michael's gone, but I feel . . . guilty. You were one of his closest friends, and I guess I want to know . . ."

Was she really asking my permission to go on a date? If I thought her husband would be okay with her dating now? I experienced a momentary stab of anger at Jordan for wanting to set up Dani, for injecting some fucking doctor into this mess. I wasn't waiting in the wings, but—

I moved away from her, needing to put distance between us.

"You think it's a bad idea, don't you?" she asked. "I did, too. I was worried it was too soon."

"No." I took a deep breath, steadying myself, trying to be the man she deserved, a better man than I'd ever been. I turned, fixing my gaze to a point over her shoulder. It had been what, a year now? "It's not too soon." I'd seen what she'd been through. The losses she carried with her. She deserved to be happy. Deserved to have a good life, a stable life, deserved a guy who would love her and treat her right. For all she'd loved Joker, she'd never had stability, had come second to the military, and I wanted that for her now. A doctor could give her that. And Jordan loved Dani. She wouldn't have set her up with anyone who wasn't good for her.

"You should go out with him."

Surprise filled her gaze. "Really? You're not just saying that?"

I would have been lying if I didn't admit it hurt to get the words out, but it was the right answer.

I forced a smile. "Yeah. You deserve to be happy. Joker loved you with everything he had, everything he was. When you love someone like that, you want what's best for them. He would want you to be happy."

I wanted her, had always wanted her, would always want her. But more than anything, I wanted her to be happy. I would have gladly given up everything to remove the pain she'd experienced, for things to have ended differently. I lived with that moment in my head constantly, plagued by the question of why it had gone down the way it did, why the spatial disorientation had hit him and not me, why I'd returned home in a jet and his remains had come home in a coffin.

DANI

I messed around in the kitchen while Easy painted the nursery, the remnants of our conversation lingering in my mind. I still wasn't entirely comfortable with the idea of going on a date, but I did feel better after talking to him. On the surface, Easy didn't seem like the deepest guy; he embodied the stereotypical image of the fighter pilot who partied hard, fucked harder, and lived on the edge. But I'd learned throughout the years that there were layers there, and he could be a rock when you needed him to be. So I took his advice and I trusted him, not only because he'd mattered to Michael, but because he mattered to me.

I worried about him. I'd watched Noah and Thor take time to recover from the accident, had seen them lean on the people in their lives to get them through their loss. Easy didn't really have anyone. Noah was his closest friend, but he had his hands full with Jordan's pregnancy and managing their life apart. Easy and Thor hung out socially, but I couldn't quite envision them having deep heart-to-hearts. Couldn't really envision Easy having that with anyone. I'd tried reaching out to him a few times over the past year without much success. Maybe it was time for me to make more of an effort.

I pulled the roast from the oven, letting it cool for a few minutes, walking over to the dining room to set the table. There was something both comforting and sad in this ritual, too. Another piece of myself I'd lost somewhere along the way since Michael's death. I'd taken these moments for granted when he was alive, relegating them to the mundane, but now these were the things I missed the most. I blinked, imagining Michael sitting at the head of the table, in his usual seat. An empty space greeted me instead.

When the table was finished, I walked back to the bedroom to tell Easy the food was ready.

The smell of fresh paint hit me first, and then I walked over the threshold to my now-beige guest bedroom, and stopped in my tracks at the sight before me.

I'd heard the guys' jokes about how fanatical Easy was about working out and eating healthy; even in a squadron where most guys had made CrossFit their own personal religion, he had a rep for taking it a step further. And holy hell, it showed.

At some point he'd clearly gotten hot, his T-shirt now tucked into the waistband of his cargo shorts . . .

I swallowed, my gaze riveted to the sight of those muscles, *so many* muscles, the tan skin, the indentation above the back of his shorts that dipped beneath the fabric. I swallowed. It was so wrong to perv on *Easy* of all people, and then he turned and whatever I'd been prepared to say dried up in my throat.

I didn't even bother trying to hide my reaction, because there hardly seemed to be a point. I doubted I was the first, tenth, or even hundredth woman to lose her shit in the face of Easy's body.

I swallowed again, not meeting his gaze, lost somewhere in pec-land. And then I went lower.

Defined, tan abs gave way to indents on either side of his hips. He was tan and smooth, his skin . . .

Jesus.

No wonder he had so much success with women. If this was what came of hitting the gym and eating healthy, maybe I needed to rethink my life choices.

Say something.

The words tumbled out. "So that working-out thing is working for you, huh?"

I did not just say that.

A moment passed and then he let out a strangled laugh. "Something like that."

I forced myself to look higher, staring at his stomach, those pecs, his neck, that angular jaw, until our gazes met. His eyes were wide, and if I hadn't known how confident Easy always was, I'd almost have thought he was embarrassed.

I was ready for a hole to open in the ground and swallow me up.

And underneath it all, the thing that shocked me the most was that for a moment, I hadn't thought of Easy as my friend, but as a guy. A hot guy. The sensation inside me—it wasn't arousal or attraction, but it was something—a feeling I'd thought I'd lost. I hadn't appreciated male beauty in a long time. That it was Easy made the whole thing weird on so many levels.

"Sorry," I mumbled, my face on fire. "I didn't realize you'd taken your shirt off." I was a grown woman, not some innocent virgin, but damn nothing had really prepared me for *this*. In all the years we'd known each other, I'd never seen him shirtless. It was like seeing a Renoir for the first time.

A flush settled over his cheeks. "Yeah, sorry, I got a little warm."

Me, too.

I took a deep breath, maintaining eye contact and mentally dressing him, which I was pretty sure *was* a first with someone who looked like Easy.

"No, it's fine." I forced myself to act like an adult and

not dissolve into awkward giggles. "I wasn't expecting all that." I made a waving motion in the general direction of THE SIX-PACK. "I mean, go you. Clearly the kale and wheatgrass and those weird little smoothies you drink are working their magic."

This time his laugh came out full-bodied and warm, his lips curving into a smile that was quintessentially Easy, that reminded me of the side of him I hadn't seen in a long time.

"Thanks, I think."

Silence settled between us and I remembered why I'd come back here in the first place. "So dinner's ready."

"Perfect timing. The room's finished."

So it was.

I looked around at the beige-colored walls, another knot forming in my stomach, and suddenly I couldn't be in this room, didn't want to acknowledge that my life was moving on, that Michael and I would never have a baby.

I took a deep breath, and then another, the room blurring together as I struggled to adjust, to keep moving forward, when all I wanted was to fall to the floor and give in to the emotions ripping me to shreds.

Grief was a sneaky bitch.

And then Easy was there, wrapping his arms around me, pulling me in close as the tears began to fall, stroking my back, telling me it was going to be okay over and over again, his voice so determined even I almost believed him. And as much as it should have felt awkward crying in a half-naked man's arms, it didn't because it was Easy. There were very few people I was comfortable showing this side of my grief, but he was one of them. He'd seen me with my walls down.

I'd never forget how he'd stood beside me when I'd

faltered at Michael's memorial service. There was something about him—as if a switch had been flipped—transforming him from the cocky guy who seemed to sail through life without taking anything seriously, to a rock.

My rock.

"Thank you," I whispered, the sound muffled by my face buried against his chest.

He stroked my hair. "It's okay. You're going to be okay."

I nodded, reaching between us to wipe at my face. I let myself linger there for a beat, and then another, enjoying the solace I found in his arms until his grip on me loosened, and I took a step away, missing the comfort of his body.

My hand came to rest between my breasts, the heel pressing into my skin as though it could erase the permanent ache in my heart.

"Sorry. It hits me sometimes. I figured doing the room would be hard, but I wasn't prepared for it."

"I know."

And he did. When I'd miscarried, Easy had been the one who took me to the hospital and stayed with me until Michael arrived. Some of the wives had shown up, but I'd never forget that he'd stayed, holding my hand when the doctors gave me the news, after I'd been inconsolable. For that alone, I would forever love Easy.

He reached out and hooked his arm around me, pressing a kiss to the top of my head.

"Come on, let's get out of here and go eat."

I nodded.

He let me go, reaching down and grabbing his shirt, pulling it on over his head.

He walked behind me, his hand at the small of my

back, his touch gentle but steady, as though he knew I needed the extra support. It was nice to have someone to lean on, even for a little bit. Felt good to not be so alone. That was another thing I hadn't been prepared for—how lonely I would feel now that I was on my own. Not even lonely—it was more than that—I'd simply disappeared, had gone from someone who was loved, who experienced affection, to someone who wandered an empty house alone. I missed the physical affection I'd almost taken for granted when I was married, the little signs that let me know someone was thinking of me, caring for me. I felt like a plant that had gone without sunlight or food for a year, and this little bit of kindness from Easy was needed more than I'd realized.

We took our seats at the dining room table, the food already spread out.

He smiled at me, a beautiful, blinding curve of his lips. "This looks amazing."

"Thank you. It's the least I could do for how much you helped me today." A wave of emotion hit me as I looked at him. "I don't know what I'd do without you. You've been such a good friend to me these past few years, and if there's ever anything you need, I'm here for you."

He looked down at his plate, and I wondered if I'd gone too touchy-feely, but then he looked up at me and the emotion in his gaze staggered me.

"I'll always be here for you, Dani. You . . ." He trailed off, staring down at his plate once again. "I care about you, too. I always will."

I reached between us and took his hand, lacing my fingers with his, and squeezed, trying to give him some of my strength, just as he'd so often done for me.

FOUR

EASY

Seeing her cry earlier, how fragile she looked—whatever I felt for her, however badly I ached, I couldn't keep putting distance between us. I'd hoped it would help, that I could force myself to get over her, but I'd have been lying if I didn't admit I'd thought of her constantly. I'd missed her, and now, even as much as it hurt, there was something about being around her. I loved her, and loving someone was more about them than you, so it didn't matter what I wanted. If she wanted me around, if she wanted to be friends, then I'd give her that. I'd give her everything I could.

We ate in silence, and then slowly eased ourselves into conversation, past the emotions throbbing at the periphery of the dinner.

"When do you leave for Afghanistan?" she asked.

"Four weeks."

In the past ten years, I'd deployed to the Middle East five times. Considering I was single and rented my house, deploying was little more than packing some bags and heading out. The living situation usually sucked, the food and not being able to drink alcohol sucked more, but it came with the territory. And it definitely felt good to do the mission we spent so much time training for. I was one of those guys who got a little restless if too much time passed between deployments, if I didn't get to do what I'd been born to do.

"Are you doing better with experience in the squadron?" she asked.

Dani hadn't just been the squadron commander's wife; she'd been tapped in to the day-to-day operations. She'd been part of the F-16 community for long enough; she understood the nuances of what we did and what it took to manage a squadron.

"Yeah. We got three new pilots in who are all IPs, so we should have the instructor problem sorted. We have two guys going through the FLUG now, so that'll help to have more pilots who can lead sorties."

I was the assistant director of operations in the squadron, which meant manning issues slowly trickled down to be my problem. Our director of operations, the guy who was second in command, was uncharacteristically laid-back for the job, so he tended to delegate a lot to me. Which I fucking loathed. I loved to fly, but the rest of it? Hated it with the fire of a thousand suns.

"That's good. Jordan mentioned you guys were doing a big send-off before the deployment."

"Yeah, I heard something about that. Are you going to come?"

She nodded. "I think so."

"Good."

For the first time it hit me that she might sell the house

while we were gone, and I could return to Oklahoma and never see her again. As much as I'd miss her, it would be good for her to move on, to start her new life, away from the squadron and the memories of Joker. She thought of us as a family, but it also hadn't escaped my notice that she was basically in the same place she'd been before he died.

I took a deep breath, steeling myself. "Okay, so tell me about this date."

She made a face.

I could do this. We just needed to keep things friendly and casual between us.

"Come on, it'll help to talk about it. Besides, Jordan wouldn't set you up with anyone terrible. And the guy's a doctor, right? That's good."

What did I know? Women were probably into doctors. They made good money, and saved lives and shit.

"What, are you playing matchmaker now?" she asked, her tone incredulous.

I coughed, choking on the beer she'd poured for me. What a fucking joke. "God, no."

"'Cause it sounded like it."

"I wasn't playing matchmaker; I'm just saying it might not be bad." I swallowed, the beer bitter on my tongue. Or maybe that was just the words coming out of my mouth. "And if you go into it with a good attitude, you might be surprised."

Where did I come up with this stuff?

"Maybe."

"Come on. You might enjoy yourself."

He definitely would.

I bet she was fun to go on a date with, could too easily imagine taking her out to a nice dinner or hanging out at a bar somewhere. That was one of the things I loved most about Dani—how proper and elegant she could be one moment—utterly untouchable—and the next she was joking around, completely at home with a rowdy group of fighter pilots.

She groaned. "I doubt it. I didn't really date before I met Michael. I mean, a little bit, but nothing serious. And I never really liked it. It always felt awkward sitting across from someone playing twenty questions."

"You have a point there." I hesitated, not entirely sure I wanted to go down this path, but unable to resist the urge to know more about her past, about *her*. "You were young when you guys met?"

Joker had been older than Dani—we'd celebrated his fortieth birthday right before he died—but I didn't know much about their relationship. Joker had been a great guy, but he wasn't one to talk about emotional shit.

"I was twenty-one. He was thirty." A smile played at her lips and I realized she was somewhere else entirely. "My parents freaked out. A thirty-year-old fighter pilot? I was in my last semester of college and trust me, Michael was not what they had in mind."

That wasn't shocking. I'd known Joker when he was younger; Dani had definitely mellowed him out.

"How did you guys meet?"

I wanted the image in my head of her when she was younger, of her happy. It was another piece of her to add to all the other ones I'd collected throughout the years.

"We met at a bar after a Georgia football game. He was there doing the flyover; I was out with friends. We locked gazes across the room and that was it. He walked over and introduced himself, and I knew my life was about to change."

The expression on her face—

Her smile was blinding.

"I never talk about him anymore. Everyone's so afraid to upset me that they avoid mentioning him as much as possible. And sometimes it is hard to remember—sometimes it hurts so much—but other times it feels good. I've missed talking about him. Sometimes I'm afraid if I don't talk about him, if I let these memories fade, I'll forget them all."

"You won't." I reached out and squeezed her hand, her skin smooth beneath mine, the ban I'd made on touching her obviously obliterated. "You can always talk to me."

The smile she sent my way had my heart tumbling in my chest.

"Thank you."

I nodded, my voice hoarse. "Anytime."

She released my hand, going back to her food. "Enough about me dating. What about you?"

"What about me?"

"Are you seeing anyone?" she asked. "It's been so long since we've caught up."

"Nah, not really."

This year had been rough on every level. Joker's death had messed me up too much to consider seriously dating anyone and honestly, I couldn't muster up the enthusiasm. There'd been a few nights I could barely remember, even more nights searching for peace at the bottom of a bottle, but I'd learned pretty early on that screwing pain out of my system never quite did the trick. And I'd also figured out that as much as I wanted to get over Dani, it wasn't fair to someone else to use them as a placeholder for the woman I really wanted. I wasn't a saint; I still had sex once in a while, but lately those times had become few and far between. Maybe I was finally growing up, or maybe I'd tried all the tricks in the book to get over her and finally come to the irrefutable conclusion that I was one of those poor bastards who was done for once he gave his heart away.

I settled for the politic answer rather than spilling my guts.

"I'm not looking to date right now."

She smiled. "Just wait. Love will knock you on your ass when you least expect it."

Oh, the irony.

"I'm not really in a place where I'm up for a relationship. Work's taking up my focus right now."

Not entirely true, but she understood better than anyone the level of sacrifice that came with being a fighter pilot's wife.

"Are you ready for the deployment?" she asked, putting us back on safer ground.

"As ready as I'll ever be. Being away will suck, but at least it's not too long. And at this point, there's so much buildup that I'm ready to leave."

Our dates had shifted a few times, the length changing from four months to three, and now I was ready to go, do what we needed to, and get home. And yeah, it helped that I wasn't leaving anyone behind who'd miss me while I was gone. In my younger years, I'd had a few girlfriends through deployments and the separation was tough. It was easier when you were on your own.

"Becca's having a hard time with the lead-up to you guys being gone. I told Jordan I'd talk to her," Dani commented.

"Yeah, Thor's a little worried about it, too."

"How's he doing?"

"Better. He's looking forward to getting out and joining the Guard."

"Have you ever considered it?"

"Getting out and joining the Guard?"

She nodded.

"After I retire, maybe. I haven't really thought about it, to be honest."

I'd made the decision to stay active duty until I was eligible for retirement in seven years, pretty fucking pleased with the fact that I'd be receiving a pension at forty-one. I hadn't been tapped by the Air Force brass for leadership, though, which was fine with me; guys like Noah and Joker were groomed early on. I was a damn good pilot, but I didn't have the patience or finesse to play the game the way I needed to in order to get ahead. Flying was all I really cared about.

"What about you? Have you considered going back to work?" I asked.

"Sort of. My Series 7 license lapsed a few years ago so if I go back to working as a financial advisor I'll have to retake the test."

"How bad is it?"

"It was okay the first time around, but that was when I was straight out of college. Now it's like my brain's been asleep for years. I'm not really sure I'll pick up the material as quickly." She shrugged. "The other problem is that in order to get licensed you need to be employed by a financial services firm, and I've filled out more job applications than I can count, and still nothing."

"It's gotta be tough after moving around so much."

"It is. With all our overseas assignments I didn't really work much, at least not the type of work experience that's helpful now. I can explain the gaps in my employment history, but it's hard enough to get a job." She took a sip of her beer, her tongue darting out to catch a stray drop of liquid that landed on her bottom lip. I forced myself to look down at my plate, to concentrate on something other than her mouth. "Plus we got married so young that I didn't have a lot of time to build much work experience."

"Are you okay with money? If you need help . . ." I figured Joker had the same standard life insurance we all did, but I'd never been in the position to worry if it was enough to take care of a wife. Mine would go to my parents in the event something happened to me.

"I'm fine, but thanks. I'm just trying to find out what happens next."

"You will."

"Sometimes it doesn't feel like it. It's been a year."

I'd never imagined it was possible to feel someone else's pain, but hers was a knife in my heart.

"That's right. It's *only* been a year. You need time. You don't need to have all the answers now and no one expects you to."

I didn't know where these words came from, didn't even know I had them inside me, just that I had an overwhelming need to make her feel better. Maybe that was what drew me to her—the way she made me want to work to be a better person, to be more than I'd ever thought I could be. Flying came easy; the rest of it? Not so much. Maybe that's why it mattered more, why I felt more like a hero when she swept those green eyes my way than I ever did in the sky.

We made small talk for the rest of dinner and then I helped her clean up, having more fun hanging out in the kitchen with her than I'd had in a long time. So much so that I didn't want to leave to go back to my empty house.

I hovered in the doorway, the dishes cleaned and put away. I shoved my hands in my pockets, feeling like I was in high school again, lingering on a doorstep after a date, saying good night to a girl I crushed on.

Dani stood in front of me, tugging yellow rubber gloves off her hands, an apron tied around her waist.

Fuck me—I didn't know why it was hot, only that it was.

"Thanks for dinner."

She grinned. "Thanks for painting. I really appreciate it."

"No problem. If you need anything else done before we go, let me know. I'm happy to help out."

"Thanks. And if you want another home-cooked meal, you're always welcome. I had fun tonight."

I nodded, the curve of her lips doing funny things to my heart. I'd had plenty of women in my life, but I wasn't sure I'd ever known anyone with a smile like hers. She was so expressive—when she smiled, I swore it set something inside me on fire, and when she was sad, my heart broke.

I didn't move. Neither did she.

"I should probably get going."

"Night's still young?" she teased.

"It's a Sunday."

"I seem to remember a Sunday Funday, or two, or twelve throughout the years."

I laughed, embarrassment filling me. "Not too many of those anymore. I'm old now. I usually limit my partying to one night a week."

If even.

"So no big plans?"

I shook my head. "I'll probably just go home and watch TV or something."

Sundays were always the worst days when you lived alone. Everyone was with their families, and I usually ended up sitting home alone and bored. Now that Noah and Thor were in relationships, there were only a few of us single guys left in the squadron, and I'd lost my two best wingmen.

"Do you want to watch TV here for a bit?" She looked a little nervous, and that tugged at my heart, too. "If you don't have anything else going on."

How had I missed that she was lonely? She had friends here—people like Jordan and Becca—but it was tough when everyone else around you had families and lives of their own.

"I would love to watch TV with you," I answered honestly.

I followed her into the living room, a rush of adrenaline similar to the one I got in the jet hitting me as I settled onto the couch next to her, careful to put some distance between us. This whole day had been exquisite torture, no more apparent than sitting next to her now, the scent of her perfume clinging to me. I shifted, trying to adjust my arousal without her noticing—the odds of her staring at my crotch were blessedly low—willing myself to think of the least sexy thing I could.

"What do you want to watch?" she asked.

Considering how much I was struggling to concentrate on something other than her, it didn't really matter. "Whatever you want."

She flipped the channels for a bit until she came to a home improvement show. "Does this work?"

"Sure."

The couch shifted next to me, and I stared at the screen, not allowing my gaze to drift in her direction. The last time I'd felt like this—hell, I was having some serious flashbacks to being fourteen and sitting next to my first girlfriend, Casey, too shy and awkward to make a move. Except I wasn't fourteen anymore, and I knew exactly how good it would feel to have her beneath me, or on top of me, or against the wall . . .

Out of my periphery, I watched Dani bring her bare legs up to the couch, tucking them to the side so she was curled up in the corner, the hem of her T-shirt raising a hair and exposing the tiniest sliver of skin, her shorts exposing a whole lot of leg.

Fuck me.

I wanted to take her into my arms and settle her into my lap, wrapping my arms around her, pressing my lips to her hair. That was the thing about Dani—it wasn't only that I wanted to be inside her; I wanted to hold her hand. That alone, the simple gesture of her fingers linked with mine, would be everything.

The show went by in a painful half hour. I couldn't focus on anything besides Dani sitting next to me on the couch, looking so soft and warm, while I sat there, my body stiff and aching. The credits rolled and I waited to see if she'd say something, if she'd get up, but instead she shifted to the other side, another hit of her perfume wafting over me.

Another episode started, and she began making small talk—how she would have chosen a different paint color or commenting on how difficult the couple was. I wasn't a big fan of talking when the TV was on, and I definitely didn't give a shit about home improvement, but I found myself relaxing with each of her comments, laughing along with her. Maybe we could do this. I'd been her friend for years; it hurt, but having her in my life as my friend was better than not having her at all. Not to mention, she seemed happy having me around. Lighter.

Another show started and she got up, grabbing a blanket from a basket next to the TV.

"Are you cold?"

The fan was going overhead, the A/C was on, I was wearing cargo shorts, and I was on fucking fire. But even as I told myself we were going to be friends, the devil on my shoulder answered for me.

"A bit."

My heart hammered as she sat back down on the couch, closer this time, wrapping the blanket around her legs and handing me the rest so I could cover myself as well. I took it from her, her fingers brushing mine in a tantalizing tease. The blanket wasn't quite long enough to cover both of us, and she moved a little closer, her leg settling against me, suddenly making touching calves seem erotic.

Jesus.

"Better?"

I nodded, not sure I trusted myself to speak. I was rock hard, need pummeling me like a prizefighter.

Another episode started up, and I sat there pretending I was riveted, pretty sure nothing in the fucking world would get me to move off this couch. This was heaven and this was hell, and I swallowed up every single moment.

DANI

I settled into the curve of Easy's body, barely resisting the urge to lay my head on his shoulder. I couldn't remember the last time I'd been this relaxed, my mind, for once, quiet. These were the moments I'd missed, the times I ended up talking to myself while I sat alone.

I missed cuddling. Missed the sensation of having someone close by, of feeling a little less alone. I wasn't necessarily physically affectionate by nature, but there was something about Easy, a bond that had been forged long ago that made me more comfortable with him than I was with anyone else. He'd held my hand—held me— through so many of the toughest moments in my life, that now it was the most natural thing in the world to curl my body into his.

I snuck a peek at his profile, wondering if he minded. I couldn't see his eyes, his gaze focused on the show, could barely make out the edge of his strong jaw, the curve of his full lips.

His head cocked to the side, his blue eyes connecting with mine. "You okay?"

I nodded. "Is this okay?" I made a face, trying not to laugh. "The cuddling, I mean?" I doubted many women said the word "cuddling" to Easy. Likely, if they found themselves in my position, there were a lot of other things they'd do instead.

He was quiet for a moment.

Oh God, had I made him uncomfortable? I was so used to being myself with Easy, I hadn't even considered . . .

I pulled back, but he caught me mid-motion, his arm

coming around my waist, tugging me toward him until my body curled up against his side, my arm draped over his waist, my head leaning against a monster bicep. He adjusted me for a second, his big hands coming under my calves, his fingers grazing the back of my knees, pulling my legs across his until they rested just above his knees.

"Better?" he asked.

It really was. My body went limp against his, my limbs boneless. I sighed and nodded against his shoulder, completely and utterly content.

We watched three more episodes with me wrapped around him, my legs in his lap, until my eyelids started fluttering, sleep beckoning.

He nudged me gently with his shoulder. "Why don't I go and let you get some sleep?"

I nodded, too tired to say much of anything. I released him, my body reluctantly rising from its position on the couch. I walked him to the front door, hiding a yawn behind my hand. He caught that, too, smiling down at me.

"Get some sleep, okay?"

"I will. Thanks for hanging out tonight."

His smile deepened. "My pleasure."

I expected him to turn and walk out, but instead he took a step toward me, wrapping his arms around my waist and pulling me in for a hug. His lips ghosted across the top of my head and something inside me swelled with the sweetness of the gesture, with the way he looked at me, the kindness in his voice.

He really was an amazing friend.

He released me, but I reached up, placing my palm on his face, my fingers skimming his cheekbone.

"Thank you," I whispered, and by the look in his eyes,

he knew I wasn't just talking about the painting, or even tonight, but how much he'd been there for me these past few years. I couldn't imagine what I would have done without him.

He nodded, his jaw clenching against my fingers. "Sweet dreams, Dani."

I let my palm fall, watching as he turned and walked to his car, all long-limbed grace. I stayed there in the doorway, waiting until he got in, and then it was clear he was waiting for me to close the door before he'd drive away, so I did, locking up and walking into the bedroom.

A few minutes later I was asleep, and I didn't wake until morning.

$\mathcal{F}$IVE

DANI

Doctor Paul called me on Tuesday and asked me to dinner. The conversation was okay, and thanks to Jordan's prodding and my own desire to be proactive—whatever the hell that meant—I agreed to meet him at my favorite Italian restaurant on Friday, figuring worst case, I'd get some tiramisu out of it. Now, fifteen minutes into the date, it was obvious the tiramisu would be the highlight of my evening, and even the promise of really good dessert wasn't making this worthwhile.

Jordan was right—he was a nice guy. And he was cute—dark hair, brown eyes, decent build that probably would have been more impressive if I hadn't spent most of my adult life hanging out with fighter pilots who treated working out like a religion. The conversation started out polite and stilted, but the evening quickly devolved into a dissertation of all the things that were wrong with Doctor Paul's ex-wife. I sat there, beyond uncomfortable, wishing the night would end.

Poor guy. His ex-wife had obviously hurt him when she left, and he definitely wasn't over it, but he was looking for someone who would identify with what he was going through, someone he could commiserate with, and that wasn't me. I was on my own now, too, but I couldn't relate to the stories he told or the anger inside him. I supposed I was angry in an abstract way—not at Michael, but at life. Being a widow was a different manner of loss entirely.

By the time dessert came around, not even the prospect of tiramisu could make me want to extend the date.

"Are you sure you don't want anything?" he asked.

"That's okay. Thanks, though. I should probably get going. It's late."

He shot me a look of disbelief, which I'd probably earned considering it was barely 8 p.m.

When the check came, I split it with him, beyond guilty over my lack of interest. I'd tried. I really had. I'd asked him questions, I'd made polite small talk, I'd even dressed up for the occasion. I didn't feel anything. At all. And no amount of loneliness would ever convince me to settle for anything other than love, not after what I'd had with Michael. And even as I felt guilty being on a date with someone else, he wouldn't have wanted me to settle, either.

Doctor Paul and I said good-bye outside the restaurant, neither one of us bothering with the façade of making plans for another date, and then I was sliding into my car, grateful I'd decided to meet him there rather than have him pick me up at home.

I called Jordan.

"How did it go?" she answered instead of a normal greeting.

I laughed at the eagerness in her voice. Bad date and all, I appreciated her attempt to help.

"I hate to break it to you, but I don't think we'll have a repeat performance. He was nice, but not for me."

"Ugh. I'm sorry."

"Don't be. I appreciate you setting me up." The truth was, even though the date was a bust, it was nice to get dressed up, to put on makeup and do my hair. I couldn't remember the last time I'd made an effort with my appearance—not since Michael died, at least—and it felt good to be me again.

"Did you get your tiramisu, at least?"

"Ha. No. By the time dessert rolled around, I was ready to get out of there."

"Well, don't go home. I'm at Charley's with Noah, and Easy's meeting us here. Why don't you join us?"

Charley's was a bar on the right side of the line away from seedy, a favorite with the Wild Aces, an unofficial second home of sorts.

I looked at the clock on my dashboard. It was early, and I wasn't really in the mood to go home considering I was all dressed up. This was good. This was what I needed to be doing—reintegrating to normal life. I couldn't hide in my house forever.

"Okay. I'll be there in fifteen."

"Excellent. See you soon."

We hung up and I drove down Memorial, turning into the familiar parking lot, spotting Noah's SUV. I didn't see Easy's car.

I parked and walked into Charley's, saying hi to one of the waitresses I recognized, my gaze running over the crowd, searching for Noah and Jordan. I found them at a table by the bar, water in front of Jordan, a beer in

Noah's hands. I hadn't seen him since he'd gotten back from Korea earlier this week, and I gave him a hug, nostalgia stinging the back of my eyelids. He'd been close with Michael, had been flying with him when he died, and was one of those guys I could count on for anything.

"It's good to have you back." I released him, and gave Jordan a quick hug, the bump between us, before sliding into the empty seat next to her.

"It's good to be back," he responded with a grin. "How have you been? You look great."

"Thanks. I've been doing well."

We chatted for a few minutes while they caught me up on what had been going on since he'd returned. They seemed a little frazzled, an air of nervous excitement about them; Noah was only here for a month, and Jordan was due next week. They both looked like they were ready for the baby to come at any moment.

"And how are you feeling, mama?" I asked her.

"Ready to meet her," Jordan answered with a wry smile. "I haven't seen my feet in months and I'm running out of clothes that fit."

"Soon."

She groaned. "Not soon enough."

"Well, you look beautiful. And you totally glow."

Noah grinned, leaning over and pressing a kiss to his wife's cheek. "I told her the same thing."

Jordan made a face. "Glow or not, I'm *really* ready for this baby to come out."

I laughed. "Fair enough." I scanned the crowd. "Where's Easy?"

"He's on his way," Noah answered.

Jordan frowned. "He should have been here by now.

He was only five minutes away, and I talked to him right after you called."

I searched the sea of faces again, but no sign of Easy.

"Do you want a drink?" Noah asked me.

The bar was slammed and all the waitresses seemed pretty busy. The downside of coming to a place like Charley's was that they were usually packed on weekends.

"Yeah, but I'll go to the bar and get one."

"I'll get you a drink," Noah protested.

"You stay with your wife. I'll be right back." I got up before he could protest. "Does anyone else want anything? Jordan, water?"

"I'm okay, but thanks."

I headed to the bar, fighting my way through the crowd. A few guys stared at me, but I ignored them. Finally, a bartender came and took my drink order.

There was something about the energy in the bar tonight—you could feel the excitement and flirtatiousness—perhaps a tinge of desperation—coming off everyone as they looked for love, or in some cases, entertainment for the night. I felt out of place here among the single and hopeful, pretty sure that particular emotion had run out a long time ago. What would it be like to be one of those women—hell, to feel like a woman again? Tonight when I'd stared at my reflection in the mirror, it had taken a moment for me to adjust to the woman staring back at me, for the first time in the past year actually feeling pretty. I'd lost weight, way more than I probably should have, and I couldn't deny some of the shine had worn off—the twenty-something-year-old girl who used to smile back at me had been replaced by someone older, her optimism replaced by shadows, and lines, and sadness.

But something about tonight—putting on makeup and a pretty dress—had me slowly returning to the land of the living, and while the guilt was still there, this was a good thing. I was getting somewhere I desperately needed to be.

By the time I got my drink, I spotted Easy sliding into the seat next to Noah.

He looked good. Really good. His usual style was normally pretty casual, but today he'd clearly dressed for a night out—expensive-looking jeans and a T-shirt that hugged his body in all the right places and looked way cooler than a normal tee. His gaze scanned the crowd, and then it settled on me. For a second, he looked at me like he saw me, but didn't recognize me; he didn't smile or wave, he merely stared. I looked down at my dress, more than a little self-conscious; maybe I'd gotten the outfit wrong, or it was too sexy, or something, but when I looked back up, the glint in his eyes was gone, and instead I saw the smile I typically associated with Easy.

He stood as I approached the table, the smile growing as he put an arm around me, tugging me against his side.

"You look gorgeous," he whispered in my ear.

I felt my cheeks heat. He was probably saying it to be nice, but at the same time there weren't many girls who wouldn't feel a sense of satisfaction at hearing someone who looked like Easy compliment them.

"Thanks. You, too." I elbowed him in the side playfully. "We've been waiting for you for a while now. What happened, hair emergency?"

He laughed, the sound husky and low. "Not exactly."

He reached for a white box on the table and handed it to me. "I heard you missed out on tiramisu."

Ohmigod.

The smile slid from my face. I stared down at the white box in my hands, feeling more than a little silly at the overwhelming urge to cry.

"You went to Carmine's and picked up tiramisu for me?" I squeaked.

He nodded.

"How did you even know?"

"I talked to Jordan, and she mentioned your date didn't go so well. I know you; it's your favorite. I figured you could use some cheering up."

It was. I was surprised he even remembered, that he cared enough to go out of his way to do something to make me smile. This had to be the sweetest thing anyone had done for me in a really long time.

I fought back tears, not wanting to embarrass him or myself. I leaned up on my toes, pressing my lips to his cheek.

"Thank you."

His cheeks turned pink. "Anytime."

EASY

The look on her face had me determined to bring her tiramisu every single day. When I'd first walked into the bar and saw her . . .

She was beautiful and sexy no matter what she wore; tonight she'd turned the volume all the way up.

It was hard to imagine her dressed like that for some guy, and all day and night I'd been wondering about her date, torn between wanting it to go well for her and dreading it with every fiber of my being.

When I'd talked to Jordan earlier tonight, she'd been apologetic about the setup, my feelings for Dani the awkward subject everyone danced around. I'd told her not to worry about it, and I'd meant it. I wasn't pissed she'd set Dani up on a date, just selfishly relieved it hadn't worked out, and even more pleased to have Dani sitting next to me in that dress, a smile on her face as she ate the dessert I'd brought her.

I avoided Jordan and Noah's pointed looks; as far as I was concerned, they might as well have not been at the table. We slid into a conversation about Korea, and thanks to my two tours there, it was one I could participate in while still sneaking glances at Dani. I draped my arm around the back of her chair, the devil in me unable to resist the urge to send a couple fuck-off glances in the direction of a few guys who leered too hard. Dani seemed oblivious to all of it, but Noah shot me more and more curious glances until finally he kicked me under the table and told the girls we were going to get drinks at the bar.

"What the fuck is going on?" he asked as soon as we reached the bar.

"Nothing."

"Nothing? Are you kidding me? Why don't you pee on Dani? At this point, that would be less fucking obvious."

"I'm not doing anything."

"Not doing anything? You have your arm pretty much around her—"

"On her chair."

"You keep glaring at anyone who comes near her."

"Those guys are being dicks, staring at her tits."

"You're staring at her tits."

"I'm really not in the mood for a fucking lecture," I snapped.

"Tough shit, you're getting one. I thought the plan was for you to stay away from her."

"It was."

"This isn't staying away from her."

"You told me it was a terrible plan when she first came back to Oklahoma. You told me she needed me. That I should be there for her. Yeah, it took me a few months to realize you were right, but that's what I'm doing—being there for her."

"It looks like you're doing a hell of a lot more."

I ran a hand through my hair. "What do you want me to do? I avoid her and you tell me I'm being an asshole. I try to be her friend and you act like I'm trying to get her to go to bed with me."

"Aren't you?"

"Fuck no."

Fine, maybe he was right; I was basically marking her. And yeah, for all my feigned altruism, I didn't want to see her with some guy. I'd never had this problem before; when she was with Joker, I'd accepted that she wasn't mine, that she loved him, that she wouldn't see anyone else that way. She'd picked Joker, and considering he was one of the best guys I'd ever known, I was okay with it. It made sense. But for some reason, the idea of her moving on, of letting a guy into her life and still not choosing me, hurt in a completely different way and I couldn't turn it off. It was the fact that she still didn't see me; married or single, I still wasn't someone she could love as anything other than a friend, and that fucking burned.

My gaze swept the crowd, settling on a group of girls eying us.

Fuck this.

"You want me to stay away from Dani; fine, I'll stay away from Dani."

Noah followed my gaze, a frown settling on his face as he realized my intentions. "That's not what I'm saying, okay? I'm not saying that at all. Believe me, no one's happier than I am to see you whoring around less. This isn't about you; it's about Dani. I don't want you to fuck with her feelings; she's been through enough."

He was my best friend and one of the few people whose opinions mattered to me most, so his words were a knee to the balls.

"You really think I would hurt her?"

"No." He sighed. "I don't know, man. I don't think you'd hurt her intentionally, but you're in a different league than she is. She's spent most of her life married. She's not up for the game. She's lonely and she misses Joker, and she's been through more loss in the past two years than most people experience in a lifetime. I care about her, just like I cared about him, just like I care about you. We all do."

I knew he came from a good place, but that didn't make hearing it any easier. We didn't normally talk about our feelings, but losing Joker had changed all of us. We'd watched one of our bros crash, heard the last words he'd ever uttered, the static over the radio his final good-bye, so yeah, there was more sharing in the Wild Aces than normal.

"I don't want to see either one of you get hurt," Noah continued.

"I know."

"Then be careful, okay? With her and with yourself."

I nodded. On some level, he was right. I'd been indulging in a fantasy, imagining she was mine, even for a moment, and the truth was, she never would be. I was being the possessive asshole he'd claimed, and I didn't have a good defense. If I loved her, really loved her, then I'd put her first and that included encouraging her to move on with someone who made her happy and gave her everything she wanted. She should be meeting guys and going on dates, and I should be the type of friend who supported her, not secretly thrilled because her date had blown.

I ordered a beer, self-loathing swirling in my gut as I looked over at the table of girls. My dick was a wet noodle, but I forced my lips into a smile I'd perfected over the years, pushing off from the bar. We—I—needed better boundaries, and the best way to accomplish that was to move the fuck on.

"I'll be back in a little bit."

Noah grimaced, his gaze sliding from the girls back to me, the faint hint of disapproval stamped all over his features. "You sure this is how you want to play this? Just because things won't work with Dani doesn't mean you don't deserve to find someone to love."

For a moment I stopped pretending everything was okay, that loving her wasn't broken glass slicing through my veins, leaving me bleeding out, that the sheer fucking torture of wanting someone I couldn't have wasn't a constant ache that brought me to my knees and made me feel as though I'd broken an unspoken promise.

"Don't you get it by now? There is no one else. There never will be anyone else. There's just her."

"I'm sorry."

I ignored him; the words escaped me now, the effort of holding them back breaking down with each moment that passed. "I don't know what to do anymore. She needs me to be her friend; I can't stay away from her. And I can't stop loving her."

The sympathy in Noah's eyes hurt more than any condemnation could have. I had no shot in hell with Dani and we both knew it.

I headed toward the table of girls, fighting the urge to look over at our table, over at her. He didn't try to stop me.

DANI

I turned in my seat, the sound of Easy's laughter distracting me from the conversation. He stood holding court a few tables away, surrounded by beautiful women who ate him up with hungry eyes. One woman in particular kept touching him, her hands running over his muscular arms, her body brushing against his side.

I'd been out with Easy enough times that the sight of him chatting up girls was definitely nothing new—hell, I'd heard the story of where his call sign came from and the women who'd inspired it—but something about tonight—

He'd been over there for thirty minutes now, and I had a feeling he wasn't coming back.

Disappointment filled me.

I didn't know why it bothered me, especially given his reputation, but it did. Maybe it was how much I'd been looking forward to hanging out with him, and the feeling that he'd found someone more interesting who he'd rather spend time with. It was stupid, but that didn't mean it didn't still sting.

I forced a smile at Jordan and Noah. "I'm going to head out."

Noah's gaze darted behind me, then settled back on me, concern flickering in his gaze. "Are you sure?"

I nodded as I stood, grabbing my purse from the back of my chair. "Yeah. I'm getting tired. It's been a long night."

I leaned forward and gave Jordan a quick hug. "Thanks for inviting me tonight. I had fun."

"Do you need a ride home?" Jordan asked.

I shook my head. I'd had two glasses of wine, but I was okay to drive.

"I'll walk you out," Noah offered.

"I'm okay, but thanks. I'll call you guys later and check in on baby-watch."

I left them sitting at the table and walked toward the exit, unable to resist a glance at Easy's table. He still stood next to the same blonde, a laugh escaping at something she said. Even across the room, I could tell his laugh wasn't genuine. Not really. It was the one he put on sometimes, the one that made it appear he was having more fun than he really was, not the real one that reached his eyes and made his body shake.

I loved his real laugh. There was something comforting in it, something that reassured me that everything would be okay. It was like being engulfed in a bear hug.

Easy froze mid-laugh, his gaze connecting with mine across the crowded bar. His brow quirked, his expression searching, and I pasted a smile on my mouth, the move stiff and unnatural. I considered going over there and saying good-bye, but I couldn't muster up the desire to deal with Easy and his women. Not tonight. Suddenly, I hated it here—the people, the loud music, the bodies brushing up against one another. I wanted to go home, crawl into bed, and stay there. It was stupid of me to come out, to put on this ridiculous dress, to curl my hair. Those days were so far behind me, and I didn't belong here. There was a lightness to these people and I was fettered by the weights dragging me down.

Tears rose and I realized I was thisclose to losing my shit. I headed for the door, pushing through the crowds of people.

I'd nearly reached the exit when a warm hand touched my back, above where my dress met skin. I turned and bumped into a hard body. I looked up. Easy stared down at me, his blue eyes filled with worry.

"Are you okay?" he asked, his palm pressing into my skin, his voice louder than normal to be heard over the music.

I nodded, even though I wasn't. All I wanted was to get the hell out of here without talking to anyone.

"Are you leaving?"

I nodded again.

"You weren't going to say bye?" His expression looked vaguely hurt by this.

"You seemed busy. I didn't want to interrupt."

He jerked back a bit, surprise etched across his features.

I closed my eyes, a headache coming on. "Sorry. That sounded way less grumpy in my head."

I opened my eyes in time to see his lips curve into what was definitely his real smile.

"You're fine." He stood there, smiling down at me, until I realized we were blocking the exit, his hand splayed on my back. My gaze narrowed as I studied him. Guys weren't supposed to be beautiful, but he was. His eyes were an ocean shade of blue, made even more impressive by how tan his skin was. His shoulders were so broad he blocked out the rest of the club, his body towering over me. No doubt, he'd make one—or more than one, if the rumors were true—of those girls at the table very happy tonight.

I swallowed, the image of Easy in bed with two girls rearing its ugly head. I'd hung around the guys enough to know shit happened, and it had never bothered me before, but for some reason the idea of Easy in a threesome made me feel a bit ill . . .

I took a step away from him, averting my gaze.

"It's time for me to head home. I'll talk to you later."

"Are you sure you're okay?" he asked.

"Yeah. Just tired."

"Come on, I'll walk you to your car."

"You don't have to." I peered around him to the table of girls watching us with avid interest. "Seriously, I don't want to take you away from anything."

He didn't bother answering me. He reached down between us, taking my hand and tugging me toward the door.

We walked in silence, his grip firm and steady. There was something about Easy, the way he held on to me as though he wouldn't let me ago, how he scanned the parking lot as if I was someone he wanted to protect, that gave the impression bad shit didn't go down on his watch.

With each step, the tension drained from my body, my earlier unease disappearing. This was what I'd been looking forward to the whole evening—the simple enjoyment I got from being in his company.

Our steps slowed the closer we got to my car. He released me when I took my keys out of my purse.

I stood there awkwardly, clutching my keys, the little F-16 keychain I'd had for years digging into my palm. I'd been ready to go, but now I was reluctant to get into my car, to go home to my empty house, to the bed I slept in alone. When I was with Easy, it was one of the few times when I experienced some semblance of peace, when I could be myself, and I wasn't alone.

I wished he'd never gone over to that table, that we'd spent the evening like I'd originally envisioned—just a couple of friends hanging out.

"Are you sure you're okay?" he asked, his voice barely audible over the sounds spilling out from the bar, the noise of the traffic on the street.

"Yeah. Sorry. I'm off tonight. It's been a weird day."

I didn't want to tell him the rest of it, felt silly admitting he'd hurt me tonight when he'd abandoned us to get laid—abandoned *me* to get laid.

His expression changed, his voice growing rougher, his gaze flickering over me. "The date?"

I felt my cheeks flush, choosing the easiest answer over the whole truth. "Yeah. Everything is happening a little quickly for me. It was a big step forward—one I'm not entirely sure I was ready to take."

He was silent for a beat. "Jordan said it didn't work out with that guy."

"It didn't. He was nice and everything, but there wasn't any chemistry. I didn't feel anything, you know?"

"Yeah, I do."

For the briefest of moments, he reached out and his fingers ghosted across my face, skimming my cheekbone, and I leaned forward, taking the affection he offered.

And then it disappeared.

His hand fell away, the cool night air a slap in the face, swallowing up all the warmth as he stepped back, his expression impossible to read.

The instant his fingers left my skin, my body protested their absence. That sick feeling rolled around in my stomach again, a lump growing in my throat.

Neither one of us spoke.

I felt off-kilter, my emotions all over the place, the weight of tonight overwhelming me.

"I should go."

Easy jerked his head in a nod, his gaze still hooded, stepping back while I opened the car door and climbed in. I opened my mouth to say something, but no words came. I settled on offering him a small smile and a little wave, my hands trembling.

Easy stood there while I locked the doors and turned on the ignition, was still standing there after I waved again and pulled out of the parking lot. I kept my gaze on him standing behind me until he was little more than a speck in my rearview mirror.

$\mathscr{S}$ix

EASY

I didn't talk to Dani all week. I'd pulled out my phone a few times to text her, but each time I'd lost my nerve. Friday night had been weird. The whole time I'd been talking to those girls, I'd felt guilty, as though I'd done something wrong, and when I'd caught up with her walking out of the bar, the expression on her face had been wounded—like I'd hurt her feelings. And then in the parking lot . . . I hadn't meant to touch her, honestly I hadn't, but as always, all it had taken was one look and I hadn't been able to resist. I'd spent thirty minutes with a group of gorgeous women who'd flirted with me and felt nothing; I touched Dani's cheek and I felt too much.

The image of her in that dress, her hair flowing in the breeze, entered my mind.

I kicked up the speed on the treadmill, my legs pumping, body aching, sweat dripping down my face as I pushed myself harder than normal. I hadn't gotten laid in what . . . three months? Four? My hand wasn't cutting it anymore.

The treadmill beeped, indicating my time had expired, and I slowed to a walk. My phone pinged with an incoming text message, and I picked it up, grinning at the picture that flashed on my screen. Julie Ann Miller was born on Wednesday morning. She had a full head of dark hair like Noah, Jordan's eyes, and was easily the cutest kid I'd ever seen. Noah had been texting me photos nonstop since she was born.

My phone pinged again with a message from Noah.

You still coming by the house to meet the baby?

I stopped the treadmill, shooting off a reply.

Yeah, leaving the gym now. I'll be there in an hour.

I headed to the locker room, taking a quick shower and throwing on a pair of shorts and a T-shirt before grabbing my gym bag and heading to the car. I drove off base, the stuffed animal I'd bought for the baby on the passenger seat next to me. I probably looked like an idiot driving around with a larger-than-life-sized bear next to me, but I didn't give a fuck. I was looking forward to being Uncle Easy and spoiling the kid rotten.

I couldn't quite envision myself having kids—getting married was a pipe dream—so my friends' kids were the closest I'd ever get to the real thing. And considering Noah was more brother than friend, his daughter felt very much like the niece I wouldn't have otherwise.

I pulled up in front of Jordan and Noah's place, nostalgia wafting over me. I'd lived here until Noah and Jordan got married, and Noah and I'd had some good times in that house.

We'd become friends our first year at the Air Force Academy, had bonded through basic training, roomed together for three years of college, kept in touch when we both went to pilot training, through our Air Force careers. There was a bond between all of us, forged in combat, solidified by the lives we lived, the understanding of what it took to constantly hover on the edge, a step away from losing control. We walked a tightrope between pushing our limits and taking it too far, and sometimes you needed a bro you could trust to pull you back.

Noah would always be that for me.

I got out of the car, walking around to the passenger side to get the baby's gift, and my gaze settled on a silver sedan parked in the driveway.

Dani's car.

My heartbeat kicked up a notch, a kind of nervous energy pulsing through me.

I shifted the bear in my arms, knocking on the door, lips twitching at the note written in Noah's messy handwriting, taped where the doorbell used to be.

Sleeping baby. Don't ring the fucking doorbell.

A minute later, Noah swung open the door. His gaze swept over me and he laughed.

"Nice bear."

"Nice note."

I crossed over the threshold, giving him a one-armed hug and a pat on the back.

"Congrats, man."

He fucking beamed back at me. "Thanks."

"Fatherhood looks good on you. You look grown-up, and responsible and shit."

He laughed again. "Something like that."

I shifted the bear on my hip. "Is she awake?"

"Yeah, she's with Jordan and Dani. Dani brought a bunch of clothes, so they've been trying outfits on her."

I followed him through the house until we reached the bedroom that had been mine and was now a nursery. The dark walls had been repainted a pastel pink, filled with dainty white furniture, pictures of F-16s replaced by paintings of flowers and princesses.

Noah grinned. "No worries, we had it thoroughly disinfected after you moved out."

I flipped him off.

"Hey, no teaching the baby bad habits," Jordan teased, turning to greet us.

I started to respond, but the words got clogged in my throat as my gaze settled on Dani sitting in the corner, the baby in her arms.

Dani looked up at me, surprise on her face, her attention obviously utterly consumed by the baby she held. And then her lips curved into a blinding, heart-clenching smile, her eyes shining.

Most beautiful fucking thing I'd ever seen.

I stood there, bathing in her glow, corny as that sounded. And then the words came, pouring out of me, crashing against the barrier that kept them from escaping my lips.

I love you. I love you. I love you.

I settled on "hi" instead.

"Hey," she whispered, her voice lowered as though she didn't want to wake the baby. "Do you want to hold her?"

I looked to Jordan and Noah for confirmation. The baby was so tiny, her face scrunched up, her little fist moving . . .

"I don't know," I confessed. She seemed so fragile, so utterly breakable.

Jordan grinned. "You'll be fine."

I hesitated, my gaze on the baby. How did Noah do it? How could he manage to not be utterly terrified all the time? If she were mine, I'd constantly be scared shitless.

"I can see her from over here," I protested.

Dani grinned. "Come on, don't be a baby." She stood, cradling Julie, and walked toward me. She was right in front of me before I realized it, before I even had a moment to react, and then I found myself putting my arms out, taking the baby from her, my heart racing, some part of me recognizing that in some fucked-up, impossible way, we were playing a parody of everything I wanted—Dani, a child, the family I'd never have with the woman I loved.

There was something about this, the baby passing between us, that was as natural as breathing.

"She's gorgeous, isn't she?" Dani asked, her voice little more than a whisper, the thread of wonder there audible.

I could barely speak, couldn't look anywhere but at her, at the glimpse of what she'd be like as a mom. "Yeah, she is."

I forced myself to avert my gaze to the baby, settling there, registering her features—I didn't know much about kids, but she had to be one of the cutest ones I'd ever seen—feeling a tug in my chest at the knowledge that my oldest friend was a dad now. I couldn't be happier for him.

The lump in my throat grew.

I turned my attention toward Jordan and Noah.

"She's amazing. Congrats, you guys."

They both looked as though they were about to explode with pride.

Dani stood next to me while I held the baby, her joy a palpable caress, and at the same time, because I knew her as well as I did, had spent so much time picking up on the subtleties of her moods, the lingering sadness hit me. She was genuinely happy for Jordan and Noah, and she did a great job covering it, but I'd been there. I knew. There was nothing she'd wanted more than to be a mom, and I would never forget the look in her eyes or the heartbreaking cry that had escaped her lips when the doctor told her she'd lost the baby. She'd reached out for me in that moment, and I'd wrapped my arms around her while she'd buried her face against my chest, sobs racking her body, my shirt damp from her tears, my own falling down my cheeks.

I'd cried twice in my adult life—that day with Dani, and after, when we lost Joker.

Our gazes locked, Julie between us, and I saw the emotion there, and it was as though an entire conversation passed between us, her eyes answering my unspoken question.

Are you okay?

Yeah, I am.

And then Dani surprised me, wrapping her arm around my waist, leaning into me as though she wanted me to take some of the sadness from her, a burden I'd gladly bear.

We stood still, our bodies fused together, staring down at the baby, until Julie started crying and Jordan swooped in, announcing it was time for a feeding. We said goodbye, following Noah out of the nursery, leaving Jordan with her daughter.

I didn't even realize it, but somehow my hand found

Dani's, our fingers locking together. She squeezed mine as she tilted her head up to face me, a soft smile playing at her lips. "Nice bear."

I laughed. "Thanks. Noah already gave me shit about it. If I can't spoil my honorary niece, who can I spoil?"

"Goddaughter and niece," Noah corrected.

I froze. "Seriously?"

"Yeah. There's no one else I'd rather have. Jordan agreed."

My voice came out rough. "Thanks, man. I'm honored."

"Us, too."

He walked us out and we said our good-byes. I let go of her hand, and Dani and I stood in the driveway, staring at each other, keys in hand, lingering there. I didn't want to go home and eat dinner in front of the TV by myself. I wanted—

"Do you want to come over? We could order dinner or something. Watch a movie."

She hesitated for a second, and I wondered if I'd misread her mood, and then she nodded, that simple gesture suddenly everything.

"Yeah, I'd like that."

"Do you want to follow me to my house?"

"Sure."

DANI

I followed Easy into his house, sidestepping a pair of flight boots in the middle of the entryway.

He grimaced, bending down to pick them up. "Sorry. I wasn't expecting company."

"No worries. Believe me, I'm more than used to shoes strewn about."

For some reason, flight boots never made their way into a closet. It was one of those annoying-but-endearing fighter pilot traits I'd grown used to over the years and now missed.

"What do you want for dinner?" Easy asked, setting his gym bag down on a bar stool in his kitchen.

"I'm up for anything."

"Pizza?"

"Yeah, pizza sounds good."

He pulled his phone out of his pocket and dialed the number from memory.

"Mushroom and sausage, right?"

I nodded, surprised he remembered my favorite pizza. How the hell did he keep all this stuff straight?

He placed the order and then hung up. "Do you want a beer?"

"Sure."

He gestured toward the living room. "Make yourself comfortable. I'll bring the drinks."

I turned down the hall, sitting down on the giant sectional. He had the stereotypical guy living room—sparsely decorated, big-ass couch, bigger TV, expensive stereo system. Various flying plaques and squadron photos sat on different ledges of the mammoth entertainment center, several F-16 signed lithographs from various assignments on the walls.

A minute later he walked in, carrying two beers, and handed one to me.

I took it from him, placing the cool bottle to my lips, talking a long pull. He stayed standing for a moment, almost as though he didn't know where to sit. Finally, he moved forward, and I shifted to the side, making room for him next to me.

He hesitated for a beat, and I wondered if I'd made a mistake, if it was too weird to assume he'd want to take the same position we had the last time we'd watched TV together, but his big body settled down next to me, his leg pressing against mine. His arm came around my shoulders, gathering me close, and for the first time all day, I relaxed.

Today had been rough. As much as I'd loved spending time with Noah, Jordan, and the baby, I'd ripped the Band-Aid off a wound that would never heal. I didn't want to be this person, to have this ugliness and anger swirling inside me, and yet, no matter how hard I tried, there was a part of me that couldn't understand why life worked out the way it did, how some people ended up with their happy endings, and others had everything taken away from them. I didn't understand what I'd done, what it had been about me and Michael that had tempted fate. And even worse was the baby we'd lost months earlier, the last link I'd had to him, who now lay buried next to his father.

One loss was difficult enough; two were nearly unbearable.

Sometimes I was convinced I'd done this; that we'd been too happy, had too much, that you were only ever entitled to just a sliver of love and then your quota was used up. Other times I saw what happened to Michael as an accident, a matter of timing, a shift in moments that meant the difference between life and death. It was the utter unpredictability of it all that terrified me—the idea that at the exact moment he'd crashed, I could have been in our beautiful home, thinking about how lucky I was, a room full of hope for the baby we'd eventually have, not knowing I was about to lose everything. It was the fear that it didn't matter how tightly you held on, how hard you prayed, or how badly you yearned, some omnipotent and unseen force could still come in and tear everything away.

What was the point of putting yourself out there, of taking a risk, of rolling the die if you faced such unbeatable odds, if the house always won? Better to play it safe, to hold everything inside, than let love in and end up with a broken heart and a wound that wouldn't heal.

It was hard being around other people, normal people, people who didn't walk around with a gaping hole in their chest where their heart used to be. Easy got it. I didn't have to pretend with him, didn't have to be someone I wasn't anymore. He'd seen the flash of pain when we were at Noah and Jordan's, and I loved him because I didn't have to explain, he'd just understood, and been there for me when I'd needed it. There were very few people who wanted to be around you when you were at your worst; that was Easy for me. I was never more myself than I was with him.

He grabbed the remote, flipping channels, and told me to tell him to stop whenever I found something I wanted to watch.

We finally settled on the same TV show we'd watched before, the routine of it making me smile, and I wrapped my arm around his waist, leaning my head against his chest. He felt good—solid—his heart beating steadily beneath me. He smelled good, too—like he'd just gotten out of the shower. The rest of the tension simply drained out of me, an overwhelming sense of contentment filling me.

"This is nice," I murmured, the sound muffled against his shirt-covered pec.

"Mmm hmm." His fingers stroked my hair, skimming along my scalp.

God, that was amazing. I lay there while he held me tight, playing with my hair, each touch melting me. He was so sweet when he wasn't the guy who walked around full of swagger, when he was the version of himself he was with me. I liked the other guy—he was fun to hang around with, guaranteed to make you smile and laugh, but this guy was something else entirely. I loved this guy. He was so sweet, I ached.

We watched TV until the food came, and Easy got up to pay the deliveryman. He returned a minute later with paper plates and pizza.

He grinned, his expression sheepish. "Sorry. Single guy. I forgot to run the dishwasher."

I laughed. "No worries."

We ate in silence, nursing our beers, the show playing in the background. When we'd finished, he took everything to the kitchen and sat back down next to me on the couch.

We shifted positions, until I was lying across him again, our limbs tangled.

And promptly fell asleep.

I woke sometime in the middle of the night, sprawled across something big and hard. For a moment I thought I was dreaming, my mind struggling to catch up, and then my eyes adjusted to the dark, a crack of moonlight filtering in through the blinds, and I realized I was lying on top of Easy.

I sat up, gently untangling myself from his body, trying not to wake him, my heart pounding. We'd left the TV on and the glow from the set was enough that I paused, unable to resist staring at the sight that was Easy sleeping before me. He looked softer in sleep, younger . . . more human, less sex god . . . more like the sweet version he was with me.

My breath hitched.

I reached out, my hand hovering in midair, the fog of sleep still covering me, my fingers twitching. Later I told myself it was the hair—lustrous and thick—that practically screamed, "Pet me." I closed the distance between us, not sure what I was doing, but unable to resist.

My knuckles grazed his skin, and then the tips of my fingers threaded through his hair as my heart skipped and stuttered in my chest.

A voice inside me screamed—

What are you doing?

Easy sighed in his sleep as I stroked his forehead, and something tumbled inside me—a boulder rolling off a cliff. My hand stilled, my entire body frozen as I waited to see if he'd wake up.

He didn't.

I should go. This felt like a line I was crossing, somewhere outside the bounds of normal friend behavior.

There was that voice again—

What the hell is wrong with you?

Moments passed, but I didn't move, didn't get off the couch. Didn't stop touching him.

I didn't want to leave.

I wanted to curl back around him and fall asleep again, enjoying the kind of deep sleep that didn't bring bad dreams and didn't have me tossing and turning. I wanted the weight of his body next to me, giving me something to hold on to.

And that freaked me the fuck out.

Because I didn't feel that way about Jordan, or Noah, or Thor, or any of my other friends. They'd been there for me after Michael died, but I hadn't leaned on them, hadn't found a place where I wanted to settle.

Easy was different and I wasn't sure why.

I pulled my hand back, balling my fingers into a fist, sliding off the couch, trying not to wake him, pretty sure I couldn't handle facing him right now. I felt naked, open, raw, as though I'd let him in somewhere I shouldn't have, like something had shifted in an already fucked-up world and now when I reached for something—someone—to hold on to, I came up empty. Because suddenly, I didn't trust Easy—or more accurately, I didn't trust the way Easy made me feel—the need and the unmistakable ache at the possibility of him being yanked away from me, if one day he took off and didn't come home.

I wanted to hold on to him, and if life had taught me anything, it was that the things you clutched to your chest were the first things to be ripped away from you.

EVEN

EASY

How's your week going?

I hit "Send" on the text, staring at the screen, waiting for Dani to respond, my gaze glued to the little message box on my phone.

Dani had left at some point in the middle of the night, after we'd fallen asleep together, and I'd woken up the next morning, my body stiff and my heart sore. The truth was, us falling asleep together hadn't exactly been accidental. I'd watched her eyelids flutter, had heard the heavy sound of her breathing as she slept on, and instead of waking her and moving her, I'd been all too happy to lay there with her in my arms, indulging in a fantasy I'd had for years, only to fall asleep myself and wake to an emptiness I couldn't erase.

That was four days ago. I hadn't heard from her since.

Did we take things too far? Had I freaked her out? It had felt so good to have her in my arms, and I'd thought she needed it, wanted it, but now I worried we'd crossed an invisible line she regretted.

My phone pinged. I stared at the words across the screen, my heartbeat picking up as I offered a silent prayer of gratitude to the heavens.

Good. You?

It wasn't much, but it was everything. My fingers shook a bit as I typed my reply.

Busy with work. Getting ready for the deployment. Flying my ass off.

I waited a beat, and then sent another text.

Thor was talking about going boating this weekend. Becca will be there. Want to come?

It was one of my last weekends before we left for the deployment, and I wanted to spend it with Dani.

Sounds fun. I'm in.

Thank God. My fingers flew over the keys as my heart raced, my lips curving into a broad smile.

I can pick you up Saturday at eight in the morning.

She texted back.

Sounds good. See you then.

The week flew by in a blur of briefs as we geared up for the squadron to head to Afghanistan. The work kept me busy, and more importantly, kept me from obsessing about Dani. I drove to her house Saturday morning, two cups of coffee sitting in the console next to me, a carton of donuts on the passenger seat. I had a cooler full of beer in the trunk, gorgeous weather, and I was spending the day on the lake with some of my favorite people—and my favorite girl. I couldn't have asked for a better deployment send-off.

I pulled into her driveway, and before I could kill the engine, she bounded out of the house, dressed in a pair of white denim cutoffs and a sheer white long-sleeved top that flowed around her in the breeze. Her hair was back in a long braid, a pair of gold aviators on her face.

I didn't bother fighting the smile that took over my face as I got out of the car and grabbed the canvas bags from her hands. I leaned down and pressed a kiss to the top of her head. She smelled like suntan lotion and her usual perfume.

"Morning."

"Morning," she echoed with a smile.

"Why do you always smell like apples?" I asked.

She tilted her head. "Apples?"

"Yeah. You always make me think of pie."

She grinned, her cheeks going a little pink, her lop-sided smile tugging at my heart. "I use apple-scented body wash and shampoo. I'm surprised you noticed."

She had a freckle below her right knee, was allergic to pears, and she was right-handed, but held her fork in her left hand.

I'd noticed.

Whatever worries I'd had that things would be un-comfortable between us fell away. The day was too beau-tiful for things to be awkward, and she seemed to be looking forward to it as much as I was. I walked to the backseat and dropped off her bags while she slid into the passenger side, grabbing the donuts. I joined her, putting the car in reverse and backing out of the driveway.

"Did you get—"

"Iced with sprinkles," I answered with a smile.

She grinned. "You're the best."

It was seriously adorable that her donut of choice was

a favorite among the under-twelve set. I'd gone one step further and bought pink frosted donuts with little heart-shaped sprinkles. I'd probably abdicated my balls somewhere along the way, but I honestly didn't give a fuck.

Dani was happy; I was happy.

She opened the box, a hum of pleasure escaping her lips. I might have abdicated my balls, but my dick still grew hard at the thought of hearing a sound like that while I thrust into her, her nails digging into my skin, legs hooked around my waist . . .

Fuck.

"I got coffee, too. Hazelnut," I added, my voice strangled as I adjusted in my seat.

"Seriously. How do you always know all my favorite things?"

I shrugged, more than a little embarrassed and still more than a little aroused. "I pay attention."

She reached out and squeezed my hand, her palm cool against mine, her skin like silk.

I shifted in my seat.

"It's really sweet. And I appreciate it. More than you'll ever know."

I could actually feel my cheeks heating. The guys would totally give me shit if they saw this. And yet . . .

I snuck a peek at her face.

Yeah, still no fucks to give.

I turned the radio up as we pulled out of her neighborhood, switching to a classic rock station. "Jack & Diane" came on over the speakers, the loud beat hitting us, the lyrics putting another smile on my face.

Perfect.

The sun shone bright in the sky, the air still breezy and cool. Perfect fucking day.

"Windows down okay?" I asked her.

She nodded.

I opened the windows and sunroof, grinning when she turned her face to the open air, her braid blowing crazily in the wind. She looked a decade younger, the sadness that cloaked her cast off for the moment.

As much as I'd wanted today, she'd needed it. She'd always had so much responsibility on her shoulders as Joker's wife—the need to navigate the world of Air Force politics as his wife, to be there for everyone in the squadron when they required it, to weather the ups and downs and daily stresses of being a military spouse. The past year had been hell in an entirely different way. It was good to see her taking care of herself and enjoying life. She looked so happy, and it was the best feeling in the world to play some small role in that.

It was a trek to the lake, but the time flew by as we drove with the radio blaring, singing along to the classic rock songs that came on. I was a terrible singer, Dani only marginally better, but neither one of us cared. We joked around, mixing up the lyrics and singing off-key with gusto. The more time I spent with her, the more the nerves disappeared, the more tension gave way to the comfort that had always existed between us, despite whatever feelings got in the way.

We met up with Thor and Becca at a gas station a few miles away from the lake and caravanned over in a line of vehicles. The group had grown when people heard about our plan to go boating, and there were eight of us total in two boats. Thor brought his, pulling it behind his truck, and Merlin brought his—a flashy boat that looked wicked fast to ski off of.

We made it to the lake a few minutes later, parking

the cars and loading all the food and beer on the two boats in preparation to launch them. When I turned back to the parking spot—

Holy fucking hell.

Dani was deep in conversation with Becca, dressed in a bright blue bikini that showed more of Dani than I'd ever seen before . . . and there was a lot of good stuff to see. I told myself to look away, honestly I did, but my eyes didn't get the memo. My gaze drifted from the curve of her tits—the perfect size to fit in the palm of my hand—to her tiny waist, down past her hips, to her long, slim legs and the freckle near her knee that I could barely make out from here.

I was instantly hard, fantasizing about reaching out and tugging on those ties, letting the triangle top fall, cupping her tits in my hands, rubbing my thumbs across her pretty nipples, bending down, taking one into my mouth, running my tongue over her . . .

Fuck.

I prayed my swim trunks were baggy enough to hide my erection, that my tongue wasn't hanging out of my mouth, that I didn't look like a horny virgin, even if I felt like one.

Becca had an amused smile on her face, and Thor was outright fucking smirking, so I doubted I'd fooled anyone.

"Dude."

"Not a fucking word," I muttered to Thor.

He shook his head, that same stupid smirk playing at his lips.

I left him there, heading toward Becca and Dani. I made a concerted effort to look at anything but Dani.

"Do you have everything you need?" I asked her.

"Yep."

"Sunscreen?"

She grinned. "Yes, Mom. I'm all lathered up."

Jesus.

There were so many places my mind could go with that one, but I fought the good fight. Mostly.

"Do you have a hat?"

"No hat. I meant to bring one, but I left it on the counter."

I took my baseball cap off and reached over, setting it on her head, tugging the bill down so it covered her brow.

Fuck, she was cute.

Dani tipped her head up at me, a smile playing on her pink, glossy lips. "What about you? Now you'll burn."

I put my arm next to hers, my skin a golden tan against her pale coloring.

She grinned. "Point taken, Malibu Barbie."

I laughed. "I think you mean Malibu Ken."

"Touché."

God, she was adorable when she gave me shit. I couldn't resist. I pulled her into my arms, reaching out and tugging on the cap, enfolding her in a quick hug. She leaned into me, her breasts brushing against my side, her body warm from the sun, her skin smooth.

Thor and Becca were watching us, but I didn't have it in me to care.

"Ready?" I asked, my throat tight.

Dani smiled up at me. "Yep."

"Okay, I'm going to go help them launch the other boat. Are you sure you don't need anything else?"

"I'm good, but thanks."

I left her there to go chat with the guys in the other boat, and then I helped Thor get us launched.

Dani and I ended up with Thor and Becca. The girls sat in the back of the boat chatting while Thor drove. I relaxed in the seat next to him, a bottle of beer dangling between my fingers and the Eagles playing over the boat's stereo speakers.

Thor glanced back at Becca and Dani deep in conversation, and then turned to me, his voice low.

"Okay, give. What's going on between the two of you?"

I took a long pull of the beer, wishing I could avoid this conversation. For all we were badasses in the sky, we gossiped like nobody's business. Then again, when you lived in a world as small as ours, privacy and boundaries didn't really exist. It was a tight, incestuous community and little was off-limits.

"We're friends."

"Bullshit."

"Good friends," I amended.

The hum of the motor mixed with the song streaming from the stereo, filling the silence between us.

I lifted the bottle of beer to my mouth—

"She's different with you now."

My hand froze in midair. My heart thumped. "What's that supposed to mean?"

"She looks at you," Thor answered.

Suddenly, my throat felt really fucking dry.

"She watches you," he continued. "That shit with the hat? Be careful with her."

I barely heard his words over the hammering in my heart. I tried to formulate a response, but I couldn't make my lips move, so instead I sat there like an idiot, trying to fight the hope his words inspired. I'd always been good with women, could read when a woman wanted me, but

I might as well have been robbed of all my senses when it came to Dani. I had no clue what she thought, what she wanted. We were close, she enjoyed being around me, but she'd always felt that way, and she'd definitely never seen me as anything other than a friend when she was married.

I couldn't feel the shift Thor described, unless you counted that we were spending more time together now. And the thing was, there was absolutely no way I could make a move. She still wore her wedding rings, still grieved, and the last thing I wanted to do was take advantage of her when she was vulnerable. Besides, if she wasn't interested in me, if she really did see me as a brother, as one of her husband's closest friends—*Jesus*—then there was no way I was going to risk our friendship by hitting on her. I didn't want to lose her, and I'd rather have this, even when it was fucking torture, than have nothing at all.

DANI

I sat next to Becca in the back of the boat, nursing a beer, admiring the view. And not the one provided by the blue water or the clear sky.

Maybe it was the cool beer sliding through me, or the sheer perfection of the day around me, but I didn't even have it in me to feel guilty, because there was no fucking way any woman could have the view before Becca and me and not appreciate the man candy.

Thor looked like Prince Harry with more muscles, and Easy . . .

Easy looked like he should be in an underwear ad.

He wore a pair of navy swim trunks slung low on his hips, a pair of aviators, and a smile. Hell, if I had a body like that, I'd walk around without a shirt all the time. He'd put on suntan lotion before we got on the boat, his body golden and gleaming, muscles rippling . . . Dear God, I was overheating and I couldn't even blame it on the sun.

Becca snuck a glance at me and grinned. "No one should be allowed to actually be that hot. I mean, really? Does he have any flaws? Any body fat?"

Not from where I sat.

I laughed, taking another sip of my drink. "He definitely won the gene lottery; plus he's actually a really good guy. Some people have all the luck."

I couldn't figure out why he didn't have a girlfriend, why he wasn't married with three little Easy kids running around. I'd seen him with Noah's daughter, the ginormous bear he'd bought for her—pink and fluffy—and I'd been on the receiving end of Easy's kindness—he'd be an amazing dad someday.

I'd always told Michael that I wanted to set Easy up with someone, but I'd never come up with anyone who was good enough for him. I was protective of Easy, much more so than anyone else. He was special and he deserved someone equally special in his life.

"Hey, Easy?" Becca called out.

He got up and walked toward us, and I lost myself a little in the V framing his magnificent abs. I was just tipsy enough to not bother hiding my admiration.

"Do you have any brothers?" Becca asked, a smile on her face.

He gave her a wolfish grin that I'd seen him share with

countless girls, but never with me. It was too smooth, too practiced, too *easy*, and it was another piece of the facade rather than genuine, but my knees still felt a tinge weaker. Yeah, that smile was a deadly tool in his arsenal.

For a moment, my mind drifted and I wondered what it would be like to be the object of Easy's interest. Hot. And fun. From what I'd seen of his relationships, he didn't stick around for long, but I didn't doubt the women had the time of their lives for as long as it lasted.

"Sorry to disappoint. It's just me." He jerked his head toward where Thor stood driving the boat. "You ready to get rid of this guy and run away with me?" he teased.

"We're getting married in six months," Thor complained, a mock-frown on his face as he turned back to face us.

He leaned forward and jabbed an elbow into Easy's pecs. Nary a ripple.

Becca laughed. "Sorry, but he needs me."

"That's right, I do. Don't be fooled by princess over here."

I snorted. The guys were forever coming up with nicknames for Easy and it was pretty much a miracle that he hadn't ended up with a less flattering call sign. I had a feeling he'd had many nights drinking off bad call signs at namings.

"Actually, I thought he looked more like Malibu Barbie," I confessed.

Thor cracked up and I felt a slight twinge of guilt at the gleam in his eye.

Easy groaned. "Fuck me. You know better than to give them ammunition. Do you know how much shit I'm going to get at the next naming?"

I grinned at the boyish expression on his face. "I do.

I'm sorry. You know we're just jealous, right?" I gestured in the general direction of his abs. "That's a pretty impressive arsenal you have going on."

He laughed, the sound warm and full, and slightly smug. "True."

I stepped forward, wrapping my arms around his waist and giving him a quick hug, my lips brushing the top of his pecs. He stiffened for a moment and then his whole body relaxed, his arm hooking around my side, leaning into the embrace.

"Sorry in advance for the next naming," I murmured.

"Mmm hmm." He pressed a kiss to the top of my— *his*—hat and released me. "You're forgiven, although I might call on you for hangover food if I have to drink off Malibu Barbie."

I grinned. "Deal."

The sound of hoots and catcalls filled the air, and I turned in time to see Merlin and some of the newer—and younger—members of the squadron—guys who'd recently graduated from the F-16 Basic course and were going through their first Viper assignment, gearing up for their first deployment—speed by in their boat. They'd picked up some girls along the way, and by the shit-eating grins on their faces, I could tell they were in the mood to push it up.

Thor and Easy exchanged looks I knew all too well, proving it didn't matter how long you'd been flying or how old you were—being a fighter pilot meant living on the edge constantly and loving it. They shouted for us to hold on, and then we were tearing across the lake after them.

I grabbed the hat, my braid flapping around me, my body jerking as we hit the waves with a series of hard bumps. Easy turned and glanced back at me, shooting me a thumbs-up sign, and I had no doubt that if I didn't return it, he'd tell Thor to slow down.

But I didn't want to slow down.

I'd spent so much of my life playing it safe, not taking risks, and right now I wanted to recapture being young and free, to not worry about anything and let go.

I sent him a thumbs-up back, and he gave me a gorgeous smile before turning toward the front and yelling something to Thor.

"Are they always like this?" Becca shouted over the loud roar of the engine.

She and Thor had only been back together a few months, and since she lived in South Carolina, she didn't spend a lot of time hanging out with the squadron. I remembered what it had been like in the beginning, how intimidated and overwhelmed I'd been when Michael had first brought me around the guys. Oh, how times had changed . . .

"Honestly? This is tame." I made a face, my gaze settling on the other boat, wincing as one of the guys appeared to be seriously contemplating doing a flip off the edge of the boat while it was moving. "I hope no one gets injured today. Or arrested. Especially with the deployment coming up."

"Seriously?"

The lawyer in her sounded vaguely appalled.

I couldn't resist. "Hey, Easy," I called out, my voice playful. "Becca can't believe anyone in the squadron has ever been arrested. Would you have anything to add to that?"

"Not funny," he grumbled, walking to the back of the boat and sitting down next to me, unfolding his long legs until he slouched in the seat. "If anything, it was all Noah's fault. I just got roped into it. And for the record, I still have no idea where the pig came from."

I laughed. "I'm pretty sure that's his line, except the roles were reversed."

"What happened?" Becca asked.

I grinned, reaching out and rumpling Easy's hair while he made a face next to me. "Public intoxication in Florida. There might have been a loose farm animal involved. Michael had to go pick them up from jail."

"Was he pissed?" Becca asked, her voice scandalized.

Easy shook his head. "Nah. He was more relieved he didn't get arrested, too. It was that kind of night."

I laughed. "Somehow he left that out."

Michael had always been good about hanging with his guys, wanting to make sure they saw him as part of the squadron, as someone they could trust, someone who had their best interests at heart. He'd had enough leaders in his career who he'd seen walk all over their subordinates to get ahead, and I'd always respected how much he cared about being a good commander.

Easy nudged me, mock-hurt in his eyes. "Why you gotta hate on me and bring that up?"

I grinned. "Poor baby."

He made a face, this new playful side of Easy tugging at my heartstrings.

"I am a poor baby," he teased.

He sprawled out on the bench of seats next to me, laying his head in my lap, his hair brushing against my skin, his lips close to my raised knees. I could feel Becca's gaze on us, a funny sensation rolling around in my stomach, but I ignored it, concentrating on Easy.

He reached up, sliding my sunglasses off my face, his

fingers grazing my temples, his touch warm and soothing. He stayed there, looking up at me, his gaze obscured
by his dark-tinted aviators. But even though I couldn't
see his eyes, I still felt the heat of his stare on me. I
wanted to look away, wondered how I looked through his
eyes, worried what he saw was somehow cracked and
tarnished. He was so bright, so full of life, even now,
even after everything he'd been through, and I was faded
and pale in comparison.

"What?" I asked.

He shook his head, a smile playing at his lips. I stared
down at his mouth, fighting the ridiculous urge to reach
out and trace the curves with my fingers.

You can look, but you can't touch.

"It's good to see you like this," Easy answered. "You
seem happy." He leaned up and tugged on the edge of
my braid, running my hair through his fingers and then
releasing me. A shiver slid down my spine.

I swallowed, surprised by my answer and the strange
sensation in my body. "I am."

His smile deepened, and then I had to look away,
because something about that gesture sent my insides
tumbling around, my heart bouncing and jerking in my
chest like a Ping-Pong ball. A familiar pull settled low
in my belly.

I looked out over the water, at the boats beyond. What
was happening to me? In my periphery, I watched Becca
get up and go sit next to Thor, leaving Easy and me in
the back.

Was it weird that we were sprawled out together? Was
it wrong for this to feel as good as it did? Were Becca
and Thor judging us? Had we made them uncomfortable?
Should I be uncomfortable? And if so, why wasn't I? I

didn't know where the lines were, what was appropriate and what wasn't. I wasn't married anymore and we were close friends, but if I were married, if Michael were still alive, I definitely wouldn't have been *this* affectionate with Easy. Did that make it wrong? I considered not saying anything, but it was Easy, so I found myself telling him anyway. I didn't know how to hold back with him.

"This is okay, right?" I asked.

His body tensed. "What?"

My cheeks heated, the curse of pale skin and freckles.

"How physically affectionate we are with each other. It's just . . ." I struggled for the right words, a difficult task when I didn't even know how I felt. "I'm really comfortable with you, and we're close, and I don't want anyone getting the wrong idea."

And I didn't want to make him uncomfortable, either. At the same time, he'd come back here and laid down in my lap, so I figured he was as comfortable with it as I was, but I still worried.

He tensed beneath me. "It's fine."

Was it, really? Did he say that to make me comfortable or did he really think it?

"Shh," he whispered, raising a finger to my lips before letting his hand fall back to his side.

I sucked in a breath. "I didn't say anything."

He smiled. "You were worrying. I can hear you worrying all the way down here. We're friends. Don't overthink it."

It was silly, but hearing him say it deflated the tension in my chest.

"Yeah?"

His answer was a husky whisper. "Yeah."

My fingers found their way to his forehead, stroking

the skin there, gliding through the strands of hair. He let out a happy sigh, and a few minutes later I heard the softest snore, watching as his chest rose and fell.

There was something about him sleeping in my lap, something that made me want to protect him, something that sent a sharp barb of terror to my heart when I remembered where he'd be in a few weeks, that we wouldn't see each other for months, the danger he'd face.

The possibility he wouldn't come home.

EIGHT

DANI

I didn't see much of Easy in the lead-up to the deployment. He was busy making sure his life was in order, getting the squadron ready, but we texted throughout the week, and on Friday night he picked me up to take me to the Wild Aces' farewell party at Charley's.

He opened the door for me and I slid into the passenger seat, waiting while he came around to the driver's side and got into the car. He leaned across the armrest and kissed my cheek, the scent of his cologne filling my nostrils, his clean-shaven cheek brushing my skin.

"You look beautiful tonight."

I hadn't realized how much I cared what he thought until he said those words. "Thanks. You look pretty great yourself."

He'd dressed casually in pair of nice jeans and a T-shirt, but he could have worn anything and rocked it.

"How was your week?" he asked, pulling out of my driveway.

"Good. Quiet. The Realtor showed the house a few times, but nothing came of it."

I was beginning to wonder if our house would ever sell, torn between the desire to get rid of it so I could try to move on to the next chapter in my life, and terrified that one day it *would* sell and I'd lose another link to the life I'd had with Michael. My fingers went to the bands on my left hand instinctively, twisting them around my ring finger, the weight of them more comforting than any security blanket.

"Did you get any useful feedback from the showings?" Easy asked.

"Not really. One person hated the color of the granite in the kitchen. The other wished the backyard was bigger. Not exactly things I can change. I'm pretty sure the others were just curious neighbors."

"I'm sorry."

"Thanks. It'll sell eventually. Hopefully. How about you? How was your week? Ready for the deployment?"

The word tasted funny coming out of my mouth and evoked a sinking feeling in my stomach. The deployment was probably not more dangerous than any of their other regular training missions, but there was something about him being far away, about the uncertainty of it all, that filled me with worry.

"Sort of," he answered, his voice as calm as though we were discussing something mundane like the weather. I'd learned a long time ago that deployments weren't something the guys stressed about. "It's only a few days away, but it still seems far away. Too much to do before."

"Do you need help with anything with your house?"

"Nah, one of my buddies in the eighty-ninth is going to check on it while I'm gone."

I looked out the window, watching as the traffic on Pennsylvania Avenue passed us by.

"It'll be weird when you're gone."

My words sounded hollow to my ears, and I wondered if he could hear the sadness and worry there.

I turned to look at him.

He was silent for a beat, and all I could make out was his profile, the hard line of his jaw, a faint tightness around his lips.

"Yeah, it will. I'm going to miss hanging out."

I nodded, the lump in my throat growing. "Me, too."

"If you need anything while I'm gone, you can always e-mail me. I'll try to find out a phone number you can call. We haven't heard much about the communication situation over there."

I'd heard a similar answer so many times before.

"Okay."

"And if you need anything, Noah will be here for another week and then he's back for good a couple months after that. And there are always the guys in the other squadrons. I can—"

My heart clenched. "Easy?"

He jerked his head toward me. "Yeah?"

I reached out and took his hand, linking my fingers with his and squeezing. "I appreciate you worrying about me, but you don't have to. I'll be fine. Worry about doing whatever you need to in order to come back safe. Please."

He didn't answer me, but he squeezed back, his touch gentle, and something about the gesture had another lump rising in my throat.

I stared out the window, the scenery blurring. I took a deep breath, rubbing my breastbone with the heel of my hand, trying to steady myself.

"Let's not talk about the deployment tonight, okay? I just want to have fun and not worry about stuff."

I wanted another day like the one he'd given me out on the lake, when all the sadness that had been dragging me down had disappeared for a few amazing hours. I wanted to spend time with him and feel the happiness he always evoked in me.

"Okay," he answered.

EASY

We walked into Charley's and I felt an overwhelming urge to turn around and go home with Dani, to take her somewhere we could hang out together without the distraction of twenty-something fighter pilots and their significant others. I'd sensed the sadness coming off her in waves on the car ride over, and all I wanted to do was take her in my arms and tell her everything was going to be okay. Except I wasn't sure I was in much of a position to tell anyone that considering the ache in my chest at the thought of being away from her and coming back to the possibility she'd be gone for good.

I tried to tell myself we'd always keep in touch, always be friends, but I wasn't sure I believed it. Eventually, she'd move on; her life couldn't remain here forever. Hell, when I returned from Afghanistan I'd get another assignment and move somewhere else. And yeah, we were friends, but she'd meet other people along the way. One day she'd go on a date with a guy and it would be better than the one with Jordan's doctor, and then what? What role would I have in her life? Maybe this was for the best.

Maybe I needed to accept that the closeness we'd developed was a temporary thing, a reaction to her grief and loneliness, convenient, impermanent.

"Are you okay?" Dani asked, nudging me with her shoulder, a worried look on her face.

"Yeah. Sorry. I got distracted. Do you want a drink?"

"Sure."

We walked over to where the squadron was gathered and I left her with Becca while I went up to the bar to get our drinks. It was packed tonight, and I exchanged greetings with a few regulars, making at best a half-assed attempt to be social. I turned as Noah walked up to me.

He jerked his head toward the bar. "What are you drinking?"

"Beer for me. Cosmo for Dani."

"I got it."

I started to protest, but it was one of our traditions on the eve of a deployment, and you didn't argue with tradition.

"How are you doing?" he asked.

"Fine."

He followed my gaze across the room to where it rested on Dani and Becca.

"She'll be okay," Noah said.

I wasn't surprised he got to the heart of what was bothering me.

"Yeah. She will."

She'd survived losing her husband; there was no question in my mind she could handle my deployment. What I was less sure of was whether *I* could handle it, and my fear of how much would have changed by the time we got back. That was the thing about going to war—we found ourselves in our own world, cut off from reality, from the things happening back home. Our lives became bombs and targets, and it was easy to lose touch with the people we left behind, for the experiences we went through in between leaving and coming home to change us so irrevocably that those connections were forever severed. It wasn't as bad for us as pilots—we weren't on the ground, and there was a level of detachment we experienced in the air—but the stakes were as high, the threats as real, and our focus so single-minded that it was easy to lose our grip on normal.

"That's not true," I admitted. I needed to get this off my chest and Noah was the only person I could confide in. "I'm worried about her being by herself, worried she'll be gone when I get back."

Worried I'll lose someone I don't really have.

"What if she is gone when you get back?"

"Fuck if I know."

"Dude, what are you going to do about this?"

"What do you mean?"

"It's been years; it doesn't seem to be going away. You have to move on, have to focus on your own life instead of living yours for her." His gaze darted over the crowd. "Have you considered talking to her?"

"Are you joking? You were the one who told me I needed to lock this shit down."

"Yeah, I did. But you're terrible at it. At this point, I don't know how she hasn't realized you're in love with her."

"She doesn't see me like that," I muttered.

"Then maybe it's best she isn't here when you get back. You deserve to be happy, man."

"I am happy."

Ish.

Maybe this was enough. Hell, the pieces of her were more than I'd ever had from anyone else.

"It's not real," Noah countered.

"It is to me."

"Yeah, but it's not to her. Don't you think you deserve a woman who loves you? Don't you want to settle down eventually? Have a family?"

Annoyance filled me. "You were right there next to me at the clubs a little over a year ago. Don't act like you've been a fucking saint your whole life, like you weren't taking it where you could get it."

"Yeah, I was. And even then, before I met Jordan, I wanted more. And then when I met her, I realized nothing—not flying, partying—mattered more than she did."

"And I'm happy for you," I shot back, realizing I sounded anything but. "I am. You guys are great together and the baby's adorable. But don't think because it happened for you, it's going to be the same for me. I've dated. I've tried to get over her, and no matter what happens, I always end up back here. There isn't anyone else."

Merlin came up behind us, slapping me on the back.

"What are we talking about?" he asked, his words slurring together a bit; he was already more than a little drunk.

He was a strong IP, the other ADO in the squadron, and a bro. Now that Noah and Thor had women, I found myself going out with Merlin and some of his friends more and more, although even that had been less frequent lately.

Since I started hanging out with Dani.

Noah shook his head as though he was frustrated with the conversation and likely me. "Nothing." He jerked his head toward the rest of the group. "I'm going to go say bye to everyone and then I'm going to head out. Jordan's at home with the baby, and I don't want to leave her for too long. I'm still taking you to the squadron when you guys fly out, right?"

"Yeah, thanks."

He walked off, leaving me at the bar with Merlin.

"You okay?"

I took another swig of beer. "Yeah."

He grinned. "Good, then come be my wingman."

"Wingman" came out missing a few letters.

"Dude. Not in the mood."

I craned my neck, trying to catch a glimpse of Dani. The crowds had shifted, blocking her from my view.

Merlin shot me an incredulous look. "We're going to be away from women for three months and you're not in the mood?" He nudged me. "See the girls over there?"

I followed his gaze to a group of four girls who looked to be either in college or recent graduates.

"I'm going to talk to the blonde. You chat up her friends."

"Seriously. Not up for it."

"What's the problem? Her friends are cute."

I glanced over there. Yeah, they were.

Merlin nudged me again. "How long has it been since you got laid?"

Too long.

"I'm just saying," Merlin continued. "If you're passing up an opportunity like that . . . think of the pick-up potential. All you have to do is lead with our upcoming deployment and you'll be fighting them off with a stick."

Yeah, I'd done this before. So many times. And the old leaving-on-a-deployment line was usually lucky for me—ninety percent success rate of a woman's clothes hitting the floor.

I didn't want to be an asshole anymore.

"I brought Dani here. I don't want to leave her."

"She doesn't care; she's talking to Becca."

She doesn't care.

The words stung. Fuck. Noah was right. She would always be out of my reach, and I was kidding myself if I thought we were anything more than friends. I'd let myself get so caught up in having her around this past month that I'd let myself want things I had no business wanting, things she definitely didn't want.

I was a single thirty-three-year-old fighter pilot and it was time to stop moping around like a pussy and start acting like it. I gave the waitress Dani's drink order and asked her to deliver it to the table.

I turned toward Merlin. "Lead the way."

DANI

"How are the wedding plans going?" I asked Becca from our vantage point near the bar.

"Good," she answered. "I have the venue lined up and I found a dress. I'm working on invitations and flowers now."

"That's exciting."

I'd had a blast planning my wedding. We'd ended up with a small destination wedding in the Bahamas and it would always be one of the happiest memories from my life with Michael. I'd never forget how excited I'd been walking down the aisle, our future an adventure spread before us. I'd been young and in love, and while I hadn't imagined how much that love would grow after we married, I also hadn't imagined myself ending up where I was now. Hadn't truly fathomed the life of a thirty-one-year-old widow. I missed the hope most of all, the feeling that the world lay before me, my future shiny and bright.

"It is," Becca answered. "Plus it helps to give me something to focus on while the guys are deployed."

"Yeah, that'll make the difference in how quickly it goes by. It really helps to keep busy. Of course, you have work, too, so that'll probably take up a lot of your time."

"Yeah, it will."

"If you need to talk or anything, or if you need someone to listen, you can always call me. I know how hard it can be."

She smiled. "Thanks. I'll probably take you up on that. It's been tough lately."

"If it makes you feel better, the first one is always the worst. And the build-up sucks, but once they actually leave, you'll be surprised at how quickly time passes. There will still be hard times—days when all you'll want is to see him, nights when you feel really alone, but find a way to do little things to pamper yourself and try to talk to him as often as you can. That helps a lot. Michael and I came out of deployments stronger and more connected than we went into them."

"Thanks. I really appreciate hearing from someone who has been in the trenches, so to speak." She sighed. "I'm hanging in there. Trying, at least."

"No problem. We need a handbook or something. The Official Guide to Surviving Life as a Fighter Pilot Wife: The F-16 Edition."

She laughed. "God, yes. It's as though I'm in a foreign country or something. Does that ever go away?"

"Not a chance. You pretty much are. They create their own world with their own set of rules, and in doing so they have the power to live their lives however the hell they want. You eventually learn to go with it, or at least, find a way to happily coexist."

"That's the goal now."

The irony was that in my case, I had learned to mostly embrace the lifestyle, but now it was gone, and I found myself floundering, unsure of how I fit in with the world I'd created for myself if I *wasn't* a fighter pilot's wife. Tonight made the contrast even more stark—all the times I'd come to these types of gatherings as Michael's wife and now here, as what exactly?

I scanned the crowd, looking for Easy, and froze.

He and Merlin stood in a circle of girls, talking and laughing, making animated gestures with their hands I recognized from years of hanging out with the guys—they were talking about flying, looking to get laid, and using the fighter pilot card to do it.

The lump in my throat dropped to my stomach.

Becca followed my gaze. She opened her mouth as if she wanted to say something and then closed it again.

Finally she spoke. "I don't get his deal."

"Easy?"

She nodded.

"Easy's . . ." I struggled for the right words, tearing my gaze away from him, not wanting to watch what was about to go down next. "Easy's complicated," I finished.

"I guess that's the thing. He doesn't seem complicated. He seems like—"

"A manwhore?"

Becca looked embarrassed, but she nodded. "Basically. He and Thor are close; I guess I have a hard time understanding why the guys respect him so much."

"Loyalty," I answered automatically. "Easy's the most loyal person I've ever met. When he takes your back, he has it forever.

"When Michael died, I went to greet the jets coming back from Alaska. It was something I needed to do, to represent him and what the squadron had meant to him. I saw Easy when he landed, and the look on his face when he saw me." I swallowed. "There isn't a question in my mind that if he could have traded places with Michael, he would have. He would die for any one of these guys, no questions asked. That's the type of guy Easy is. That's why they love him.

"He's smart, too," I continued, not sure why I felt this overwhelming urge to defend Easy, to show her the side of him I knew and loved. "He was an engineering major at the Air Force Academy. He's funny and he's an amazing pilot. He can be thoughtful, too. He's always remembering what I like, bringing me my favorite things. He can come across as arrogant, and yeah, he is, but he definitely doesn't take himself too seriously. He knows when he's being full of himself.

"And he's fun. He's always up for anything and if you're down, he's the best person to cheer you up. He's like a big kid most of the time, and I mean that in the best possible way. But when you need him, he really steps up and becomes a rock. He's stood by me for the most difficult moments of my life and I can't imagine how I would have gotten through them without him."

A smile played at Becca's lips, but I only caught a

glimpse of it because my gaze had already returned to where Easy stood.

"You guys are really close, aren't you?" she asked.

It hadn't hit me until now how *much* I relied on him, how much he'd changed my life.

"We are."

Maybe that's why it burned so much to watch as he essentially blew me off when the whole point of the night was for us to hang out before he left, to see him hitting on the girls on one of the last nights we had together before he deployed. I didn't necessarily blame him for choosing orgasms over friendship, but that didn't mean it still didn't hurt.

Becca looked like she wanted to say something else, but she didn't. Instead she continued to stare at Easy and Merlin.

My gaze drifted back to the girl closest to Easy. Would he take her home tonight? She leaned in closer to hear something Easy said, and I knew she could smell the scent of his cologne, knew how firm his jaw would be against her face, could easily conjure up the sensation of how hard and big his body would be as he loomed over her.

I'd gotten used to the physical closeness of him in the last month and found myself needing that connection— my hand in his—as much as I enjoyed his company.

My breath hitched.

His hand rested on her back, right at the base of her spine, his fingers idly stroking there as something clenched in my stomach. Having him there would make her feel safe, cherished; she wouldn't be able to resist the urge to lean in to him. Right now she was probably wondering what he looked like under the thin T-shirt, imagining how it would feel to dip under the fabric, to put her hands on his abs, to stroke lower—

Oh God.

"Are you okay?" Becca asked.

I tore my gaze away from Easy, my body warm and achy, my head a mess.

"Yeah. Why?"

I told myself I didn't sound defensive, that I hadn't imagined Easy, *my* Easy as a man, a man I could want, a man who could make my body yearn for things I hadn't felt in a long time.

"Your face—you seemed upset."

I started to tell her no—*deny, deny, deny*—but something else came out instead.

"I hate when he does this."

My gaze drifted back to Easy and the girl, watching as she tossed her hair back, as he smiled down at her—

"The girls?"

I nodded, unable to speak.

It had never bothered me before—well, besides the last time we were here, but even that had been different. As foolish as it had been, my feelings had been hurt then. Now other parts of me ached—dull, throbbing, constant. I wanted to go over there and break them apart. It took effort to hold myself back. I wanted him to look at *me* like that. I wanted . . .

The girl leaned into his body and kissed his neck, and suddenly it crashed into me, like learning a new word, the sound of it alien, but the moment it entered my head, I knew, just fucking knew—

I had a crush on Easy.

Panic hit me, followed by guilt, so much guilt that I found myself gasping for air as I drowned in it. What kind of person developed a crush on one of their dead husband's best friends? What was wrong with me? The time we'd spent together, the touching, all of it—

Fuck.

It was so obvious, and the only excuse I had for why I hadn't realized it sooner was that I hadn't had a crush on a guy in a decade, didn't even remember this sensation, had honestly never imagined feeling this again. The sheer agony of it—

Awful. It felt fucking awful.

I stared down at my wedding rings until they became little more than a blur, losing myself in the diamonds, in the memories they contained, in the feeling of Michael's fingers skimming my skin as he slid them on my fingers, until suddenly that was ripped away and replaced by the memory of my hand intertwined with Easy's.

"Are you sure you're okay?" Becca asked. "You look really pale."

I was so far from okay it wasn't funny. It had always been Michael for me. Always. Sure, when I'd been married I'd appreciated the occasional movie star or something, but I'd never wanted anyone else, fantasized about anyone else. Never been attracted to anyone else.

Why Easy?

"Are you okay?"

This time it wasn't Becca's voice that greeted me and I froze at the low rumble behind me, at the sound that sent a tingle down my spine. I turned and came face-to-face with the last person I wanted to see.

$\mathcal{N}$INE

EASY

Whatever Dani and Becca were talking about, it had definitely upset Dani. She'd gone pale, and even now, she wouldn't meet my gaze.

I looked at Becca, a moment of panic hitting me, wondering if Thor had told her about my feelings for Dani, if for some reason she'd told Dani, but I didn't see guilt when I looked at her, only worry.

"Do you want a glass of water or something?" I asked, turning my attention back to Dani.

Fuck Merlin and his stupid wingman needs. I shouldn't have abandoned her. It made sense that tonight would be hard for her, that she'd be missing Joker, surrounded by the Wild Aces, and I should have stood by her to help her get through tonight.

Dani shook her head, still not meeting my gaze.

"Do you want to go? I can take you home if you're getting tired."

"No. I'm fine." This time she did look up at me, more

force behind her words, and the smile that greeted me was Dani, but not Dani, some version of her that seemed stilted and fake, so different from what she usually gave me. "You don't have to hang with us. I'm sure you want to get back."

I followed her gaze to the group of girls, trying to read the emotion in her voice. She sounded like she wanted to get rid of me, almost as though the thrust of her words could propel me away.

"Are you sure? I don't mind. I want to spend time with you tonight."

I hadn't meant to leave her for as long as I had, but I'd kept an eye on her. She'd seemed fine, and then all of a sudden, she hadn't.

"Seriously," she replied. "It's fine. Go have fun. You should be chatting up girls, not hanging out with a bunch of old married ladies."

I opened my mouth to explain about Merlin needing a wingman, started to tell her that hanging out with her was all I'd wanted to do tonight, that I would rather spend the evening with her than with anyone else, when she shot me down.

"Come on, she's cute. I know you—you don't want to miss out on a chance to get laid."

She delivered the line casually, as if she didn't realize the power it had, that she'd effectively sliced me open, her words shattering something inside me. Noah was right; I was an idiot. We were friends. That was it.

How could she love someone she thought so little of?

Dani took a sip of her drink, the diamonds on her finger sparkling in the light, dimming something inside me, and suddenly I had to get away before she saw the truth in my eyes, the love I feared was etched all over my face. Becca saw it. The sympathy in her gaze hurt like hell.

"I'll see you later," I mumbled, not waiting for her to answer. I needed to get the fuck out, now.

DANI

My face felt hot as he walked away, as I choked back unshed tears.

"Why did you do that?" Becca asked.

I had no clue how to answer her. I needed Easy gone, somewhere far out of reach, somewhere where I wouldn't be tempted by anything other than friendship. Because I was so fucking confused I couldn't think straight. For years I'd seen him as nothing more than a friend, and suddenly, someone entirely different stared back at me.

"I don't know," I whispered. God, I'd basically told him to go fuck that girl. What the hell was wrong with me? It was the last thing I wanted, and now I had a different image in my head of Easy naked, sliding over her body . . .

I wasn't emotional by nature, had always managed to tuck my feelings into neat little boxes, but now the lid had sprung open, the contents spilling out, and I was on my knees in the middle of the bar, rushing, panicking, trying to scoop everything back inside me again.

"I'm going home."

I'd officially reached the point in the evening when no good could come out of me staying out, and more than anything, I wanted to retreat to the one place where my life had made sense, where I'd been happy.

"Do you need a ride?" Becca asked. "We're about to head out, too."

"That would be awesome, thanks." I didn't allow myself to glance back at Easy. "Are you sure you're ready to go home? I feel bad making you guys leave early."

"No worries. Honestly, I'd rather spend time alone with Eric. I'll go find him and let him know we're ready to leave."

"Thanks. I'm going to say bye to a few people. I'll meet you by the entrance."

I said good-bye to some of the guys, exchanging hugs and telling them to be safe. When I'd finished, I hesitated, wondering if I should go say something to Easy. I really didn't want to interrupt what he had going on, but at the same time, I couldn't imagine not saying good-bye to him before he deployed. I knew better than anyone how final "good-bye" could be.

I took a deep breath and headed toward his table, my heart racing with each step, my legs wobbly. Everything had shifted between us, and I would never look at him the same way again.

Easy laughed at something Merlin said, and then he turned his head to the side and caught sight of me. I watched as the smile slid off his face and his gaze narrowed, his entire stance changing as though he braced himself for an invisible blow.

I couldn't meet Easy's gaze as I offered a halfhearted wave to the girls, as I gave Merlin a quick hug and wished him good luck, but I could still feel the weight of his stare on me, could sense the anger emanating from him. I forced a smile on my face, stepping into his body, giving him a little half hug, all too aware of the beautiful girl who stood next to him.

"I'm heading out." Thanks to our height differences, I didn't even have to look into his eyes. "Be careful, okay?" I swallowed, my eyelids stinging, unable to believe this was it. "Take care."

I pulled back, the tension building in my chest, unable to meet anyone's gaze, when suddenly a hand touched my shoulder.

I didn't need to look to know it was Easy's fingers pressing into my skin.

"Can I talk to you for a second?" he asked, his voice so low I had to strain to hear him, his lips brushing against my ear in a move that had a shiver sliding down my spine. A shiver that had never been there before.

I nodded.

He said something to the group, his words obliterated by the white noise rushing in my ears. I expected him to let me go, but he didn't. Instead he took my wrist, tugging me forward so I had no choice but to follow, leading me to a quiet corner near the entrance.

I stepped back into the corner and my back hit the wall as I tried to put some distance between us, to give my body much-needed space and a chance to cool off. It felt like the flu, this sensation coming on strong, hitting me hard, and leaving me staggering and delirious in its wake.

"Why are you leaving without me? I gave you a ride here; I'll take you home."

I looked everywhere but at him.

"Don't worry about it. Stay and have fun. I'll catch a ride home with Thor and Becca."

"What's going on with you tonight?"

He leaned forward, bracing his arm above my head, his scent surrounding me, his giant man-bicep inches away from my lips, and I realized my crush was a little worse than I'd thought. A *lot* worse than I'd thought.

I wanted to lick him there, wanted to suck on his skin. That someone else probably would was nothing less than utter torture.

"Nothing," I snapped, realizing I'd gone full-on unhinged but lacking the ability to reel myself back in. Something had been unleashed inside me, and I found myself lashing out, the calm, rational, adult side of me standing outside my body, looking on, wondering when I'd lost my mind, while this other side of me took over.

"That right there. I'm not stupid. You're pissed at me."

"I'm not pissed at you."

"You are. You've been distant since we got here. Why did you come if you didn't want to be here?"

"I'm surprised you noticed, considering how little time you've spent with me."

His gaze narrowed, and he shifted forward, getting even more in my space, his presence sucking up all the air around me. In the years I'd known him, I'd never seen him lose his temper, and had definitely never seen him be annoyed with me.

"Are you pissed because I was talking to those girls?" he asked.

Maybe he sounded harsher than he'd intended, but his words scraped over me, peeling off a layer of skin.

I opened my mouth to say something, closing it almost immediately. There was nothing to say, no explanation I could give, other than the absolute truth.

Yes.

"You practically threw me at them when I came to talk to you," he added. "I wanted to spend the night with you. I wasn't out looking to get laid."

"When are you not looking to get laid?"

I heard the words leave my mouth, and as soon as they exploded between us, I knew I'd fucked up. Bad.

Easy's arm left the wall, dropping away from me. He took a step back from me as though I'd hit him, his expression shuttered.

The hurt there—I *never* wanted to hurt him.

"I'm sorry. I didn't mean it like that—"

My throat closed up, the words clawing at me.

I'd spent the night defending him to Becca; there was so much more to him than his call sign and his rep with women, and yet I'd said the words without thinking—no, that wasn't true. I'd wanted to hurt him, to push him away, and now that I had—

"No, you meant it exactly how it sounded." His voice dulled, all the anger filtered out of him. His hurt was so much worse than the anger had been and it shamed me. "I'm the guy who fucks anything that moves, right?"

"Easy—"

I reached up, my fingers closing around his arm, trying to bring him closer to me, hating the distance between us, but he shook me off with no effort at all.

"There hasn't been anyone in months."

I froze.

"It doesn't matter, though, does it? You're always going to see me as the guy who's screwing his way through life, who thinks with his dick and doesn't care about anyone but himself."

The pain in his voice pushed me out of my momentary stupor.

What had I done?

"No. I'm sorry for what I said. It was stupid and thoughtless. I don't think that. I'm so sorry."

He shrugged me off. "It doesn't matter."

But it did. Because the affection that was always in his eyes when he looked at me had completely disappeared.

"I'm sorry," I whispered, tears in the back of my throat. "So sorry."

"I'm going to head back." He shot me a twisted smile that wrenched something in my gut, shooting up to my heart. "After all, I have a big night ahead of me."

He didn't bother waiting for me to respond, just turned on his heel and left me standing there, gaping after him.

Becca found me a moment later. "Eric's almost ready, he's. . ." Her voice trailed off. "What happened now?"

Somehow things had exploded, and I had no idea how we'd even gotten to that point. I should never have said what I did, but at the same time, I'd never expected him to act that way. The Easy I knew was good-natured and took his reputation in stride. I'd never seen him lose his temper, never imagined a comment about his women would set him off.

I wanted to cry.

"I don't know. I got into a fight with Easy."

"Seriously?"

I nodded, trying to swallow past the giant lump in my throat.

"I'm sure whatever it was, he'll forgive you," Becca replied, her voice kind.

My gaze followed him through the crowd; it took everything I had to keep from going after him.

"I don't think so. I really hurt him."

And as the words fell from my lips, as he became a smaller and smaller speck in the distance until he disappeared completely, I felt like I'd lost something I'd never recover, something—someone—I couldn't live without.

EASY

I didn't go back to the group. After everything with Dani, the last thing I wanted was to be around other people. I hit the bar instead, ordering a shot of Jeremiah Weed. It was standard fighter pilot fare, and right now I needed the hard stuff.

Someone came up behind me mid-shot.

"Hey, I'm going to head out . . ." Thor's voice trailed off, a look of censure that definitely wouldn't have been there a fucking year ago stamped across his face. "You're getting drunk tonight?"

"Apparently."

I definitely wasn't getting laid. I didn't think my dick would even work after Dani had essentially shamed it into submission.

"Thanks for taking Dani home, by the way," I muttered.

"What now?"

"Nothing."

"Jesus. You're being such a pussy. What the fuck happened now?"

I took another shot, the liquor burning a hole in my gut. "Fuck off."

He shook his head. "I'm not the one you're pissed at, man."

"Well, I can't exactly tell Dani to fuck off, now can I?"

Thor's lips twitched. *Dick.*

"I'm pretty sure Dani's heard worse."

"Not from me, she hasn't."

"Why? Because you walk on eggshells with her?"

"I don't walk on eggshells with her."

"Dude, you fucking do. You don't treat anyone the way you treat her."

Not tonight.

Fuck.

I hated that I'd lost my temper with her. Her words still cut me.

I tossed back the third shot, the Weed burning liquid fire down my throat. I slammed the glass against the wooden bar top, wiping the stray alcohol from my lips.

"We got into a fight."

"So what? Becca and I fight all the time." His tone of voice suggested an eye roll probably accompanied that statement.

"Yeah, you guys also bang all the time, too. It's a little different in this case, asshole."

"Why, 'cause you can't kiss and make up?"

I flipped him off.

"You're not really doing a great job convincing me you're a mature adult."

"I'm crushed."

"Do you want to know the truth?"

"Please. Enlighten me."

Thor shook his head. "You really are being a dick. Truth is, yeah, I think something's up with Dani."

"Really? I fucking figured that out when she bit my head off."

"Yeah, but *why* did she bite your head off?"

"If I knew that, do you really think I'd be standing here?"

"Did you ever think that maybe it bothered her to see you talking with those girls?"

"Yeah, I did." I ran a hand through my hair, impatience building inside me. I wanted to fix this, but I didn't know where to begin. "Maybe I hurt her feelings or some-thing. Maybe she thought I'd ditched her."

"Maybe she didn't like seeing you hitting on the other girls when she's used to all your attention going to her," Thor countered.

I froze.

"You think Dani is jealous?"

"Yeah, I do."

For a moment I couldn't speak, and then I voiced the thought that had been in my mind ever since I'd seen the look on her face. Hell, the question had been there for weeks now, lingering in the background, the fucking hope of it—

"You think Dani's into me?"

Even the words sounded strange coming from my mouth, but I clung to them now.

"She might be, yeah," Thor answered after what seemed like a fucking eternity. "Maybe she doesn't re-alize it, maybe it's a physical thing, maybe she really is into you. What the hell do I know? It's not as cut-and-dry as you guys being friends, and the more this shit comes up, the more things are going to be uncomfortable be-tween the two of you.

"Think of it this way: How would you feel if the roles were reversed and you had to watch her hit on some dude?"

As though someone had kicked me in the balls.

I stared at the empty shot glass, needing about four more to slide into oblivion. I didn't want to deal with this shit, didn't want to hurt her, didn't want her to hate me, didn't want to fuck this up. Everywhere I looked I was faced with the possibility of screwing this up with no way forward.

"What would you do if you were me?"

"You're really scraping the bottom of the barrel, asking me for advice, aren't you?"

"You're all almost married and shit. I figure you have to have learned something."

He was silent, and when he finally did speak, his answer shocked the hell out of me. "Maybe you should make a move. A small one. A move that's not a move. See if she responds."

"'A move that's not a move'? What the fuck does that even mean?"

"That you should do something that gives her an out in case she's not interested so you don't freak her out. Do I really need to spell this out? Aren't you supposed to be a woman-whisperer or something?"

"Or something."

"You're worried about Joker, aren't you?"

Joker. Dani. My heart.

I leveled him with a stare. "If something happened to you, and I made a move on Becca, how would you feel?"

"Considering I'd be dead, probably not much."

"You know what I mean."

He sighed. "If she lost me, I'd want her to be happy, and I'd want her to move on with her life. And if she did move on, I'd want to know that she'd moved on with a good guy, a guy who would treat her how I did, who would love her the way she deserved to be loved."

I swallowed, my throat dry. "I fucked up tonight."

"Yeah, you did. I'm guessing she did, too, though, to put that look on your face."

"She made a comment about me fucking around. I've never wanted her to see me like that."

"I get it. You want my advice? Give her some time.

Don't do anything before the deployment. Give her the chance to see where she ends up while you're gone. If she moves on and is happy, then there's your answer. If she's here when you get back, then go for it."

"You think so?"

"Yeah, I do." He jerked his head toward the entrance. "I'm going to take the girls home."

"Thanks."

I said good-bye to some people and caught a ride with one of the guys a few minutes after Thor cleared out. I got home, the whole drive spent thinking about what Thor had said, about Dani and the possibility that she might feel a fraction of what I felt for her.

I pulled out my phone and shot off a quick text.

DANI

I couldn't sleep. Every time I closed my eyes, I saw the look on Easy's face when I'd said what I did, imagined him back at his place right now, getting naked with some girl. And then I wondered what it would be like if he got naked with me, and the same panicky sensation I'd had earlier swept over me—waves of heat and the aching, restless feeling that had been humming through my veins all evening.

I hadn't had sex in over a year, hadn't had an orgasm in the same amount of time. When Michael had died, I'd closed up shop, boarded up the windows, and called it a day. But now . . . for the first time since he'd died, I wanted those things again, could imagine how good it would feel to slide my hand down between my legs, to ease the needy want building inside me—an orgasm to take the edge off. Maybe two.

My phone pinged with an incoming text message, jerking me from my fantasy. I grabbed it off my nightstand, staring at the screen—

I'm home alone. Nothing happened.

I had to read the words twice for them to sink in, but there was no denying the overwhelming sense of relief.

I had no claim to him, no right to make one, no idea what I even wanted, but for now I had to make things right.

I'm sorry for what I said. I wish I could undo the whole stupid fight. I didn't mean it. I don't see you that way. I'm so sorry.

I sent the text, my heart pounding as I waited for his response, praying he would forgive me.

He texted back immediately.

I know. Me, too.

Maybe it was best to leave things the way they were, to nip everything in the bud before I confused myself even more. Horny and emotional wasn't the ideal combination for sound decision-making. I could take the time he was gone to figure out how I really felt, if this crush or whatever the hell it was was a symptom of me being lonely, of us spending too much time together.

My fingers didn't get the message.

Can I come over to say bye tomorrow? I hate the way we left things.

He didn't make me wait long at all.

Yes.

TEN

EASY

I opened the door to Dani standing on my front step, wearing jeans and a black top, carrying a bag from my favorite cookie place and another bag I didn't recognize.

She smiled, a trace of hesitation in her eyes, last night's fight still lingering between us.

"I come bearing gifts. I know how much you love their sugar cookies even though you only get them like once a year, and you should have some of your favorite things before you leave." She held up the other bag. "I bought your favorite beer as well."

God, she was sweet.

"Thank you."

I opened the door wider, stepping back so she could come inside. As she stepped over the threshold her shoulder grazed me, the scent of her perfume teasing me.

I followed her into the kitchen, my gaze drifting to her ass more times than it probably should have. And fuck me, I was hard—*again*.

I leaned against the countertop, watching as Dani set the bags down and put the beer in the fridge. She turned back, holding a bottle out to me.

"You want one?"

I nodded, my throat closing up at the sight of her making herself at home in my kitchen. I had a fantasy of seeing her in the morning, wearing only one of my shirts, her long hair flowing down her back, a smile on her face, her legs bare . . .

Dani handed me a beer, our fingers brushing each other, her skin's caress enough to have my dick jerking against my zipper. I shifted; if the whole thing wasn't so pathetic and sad, I would have laughed. I didn't think I'd ever been so hard up, not even when I was in high school.

I grabbed a bottle opener, opening the beer, and passed it to her. "Here."

She hesitated for a second and then took the bottle from my hand. "Thanks."

I reached forward, my arm brushing against Dani's side, grabbing another beer and repeating the action, taking a long gulp.

We stood across from each other, drinking our beers in silence. God, this was awkward.

I took a deep breath. "About last night—"

"I'm sorry," she blurted out at the same time. A strand of hair fell forward and she pushed it back, revealing the slightest hint of pink across the curve of her cheek.

I gripped the bottle tighter, telling my hands to behave, not to reach out and stroke her skin. I shifted again, adjusting myself when she looked away.

Fucking torture.

She began talking, her lips calling to me, and I devoured her with my eyes, losing myself in the simple pleasure of seeing her in my kitchen, of pretending it was *our* kitchen, that she was mine.

I'd done that so many times over the years, gone somewhere in my head where it was safe to feel this way about her, where I wasn't damned for wanting, loving one of my best friends' wives. As though that excused what I'd always known was so wrong. Even when it was hard to really and truly believe it was wrong since everything about her felt so fucking right.

I heard snippets of what she said—she'd realized I was upset last night—but I couldn't concentrate beyond committing the sight of her to memory, holding the pieces of her close so I'd have them to keep me company in the months apart.

And then I realized she'd finished talking.

"Easy?"

I forced myself to concentrate on her words and not her beautiful green eyes, soft pink mouth . . .

Her tongue darted out to wet her lips and I got a little light-headed.

Right.

"It's fine."

The expression on her face suggested she wasn't buying it for a second. Hell, neither was I. But I couldn't exactly explain to her why I'd been so upset, why her words had struck such a chord with me. Not without giving her the rest—she held my heart and always had.

But because I was hopelessly, stupidly in love with her, I found myself telling her the truth—or as close to it as I could get without sending her running for the hills.

"I wasn't trying to get laid last night."

Her cheeks colored. She'd definitely heard worse hanging out with fighter pilots for years, and at the same time, I'd always attempted to keep that side of my life away from her, had hated when the other guys gave me shit for my sex life in front of Dani.

"Totally not my business." If possible, she turned even redder. "I shouldn't have even joked about it last night. I'm really sorry."

I shook my head. "It's not your fault; I'm not upset with you. You were fine."

My gaze dropped down to her lips—

Christ, I wanted to kiss her.

"I would have rather spent the night talking with you than getting laid."

Disbelief filled her gaze. "Easy—"

"I mean it; I wanted to spend the night hanging out. I'm sorry things got complicated."

"Why didn't you?" she asked.

"Why didn't I what?"

"Why didn't you hang out last night?"

"Because I was an idiot. I'm sorry."

Silence settled between us.

Dani fumbled with the handle of her bag, not meeting my gaze. She hesitated, as though she wasn't ready to go, but she didn't make an effort to speak.

I set my beer down, taking a step toward her, trying to read the emotions swirling around her.

I stopped a foot away from her, reaching out and lifting her chin so she stared into my eyes.

My heart clenched at the sadness there.

Thor's words ran through my mind again. Was he right? Was she jealous? I tried to search her gaze, to figure out why she looked at me now as if she was in pain, and what I could do to make it stop.

"Are you okay?" I asked.

She took a deep breath, her lips trembling, and nodded.

"Not convincing."

"I know," she whispered. "Sorry."

I dropped my hand, taking a step back, fighting the urge to take her into my arms and draw the sadness out of her.

She held my gaze. "I'm worried about you."

I froze.

"I'm sorry. It's stupid. You've been flying for years, and you're really good, and the deployment probably isn't even a big deal to you anymore, but . . ."

But her husband had been safe and experienced, and really fucking good in the jet, and she'd still lost him.

"I'll be safe."

"I know."

I could hear the doubt there, mixed with fear.

"I'll be safe. Nothing's going to happen to me."

It wasn't a promise I was really qualified to make; on any given day, anything could go wrong when we flew. That was part of the high, the roll of the die you took each time you went up in the air. I wasn't risky with my life, but I'd always approached the whole thing with a level of nonchalance I couldn't summon right now. I'd never had a reason to worry about coming back before.

Now I did.

DANI

I couldn't get my bearings, fear and lust muddling my head. Could he sense how things had changed between us? The nervous, edgy energy that seemed to pulse around us?

I wondered what it would be like to press my lips to his neck, inhaling his scent, to lay my body against his and lose myself for a bit.

Down, girl.

"I should probably let you go so you can get some rest."

Easy nodded, his gaze inscrutable. As well as I thought I knew Easy, there always seemed to be pieces of himself he didn't share with me, parts that were locked away tight. At face value it seemed like what-you-see-is-what-you-get with him, but the more you looked, the more you realized how much lay beneath the surface.

Like right now.

And suddenly, I wanted inside. He'd seen me at my worst, watched me fall apart and struggle to put myself back together again, had a front-row seat to the most vulnerable parts of me. And all I got were glimpses of him, glimpses that hinted at something deeper, more, before he slammed the door in my face. I wanted to peel back that layer, wanted to know what was going on in his head right now. It didn't seem fair that he'd seen all of me—well, all except *this*—and yet he still had secrets, still had things that were off-limits, even to me.

I took a step closer, and then another, a knot growing in my stomach. I didn't know exactly where I was headed, but I hoped I'd find out when I got there.

I stood up on my toes, wrapping my arms around him. He was so big, so solid against me, and I held on tight, not sure I was ready to let him go.

"Be safe," I whispered. "Promise me."

He didn't answer me, not with words at least, but his

body jerked against mine as he nodded, as he lifted his arms and his hands settled on the small of my back.

A tear trickled down my cheek, then another. It was crazy—I'd been through so many deployments over the years, but this one was terrifying. I'd peered under the bed, and saw the monster, and now my worst fears weren't some abstract possibility that made me sick with worry. They were real, and they'd happened, and I couldn't bear the thought of losing Easy, too.

My body shook as I cried in his arms, as I inhaled the scent of his cologne, as I pressed myself against him, trying to memorize the shape and weight of him, trying to mentally prepare myself for the possibility that I'd never see him again.

He likely thought I was insane, was probably now wondering how the hell to handle the crazy, crying woman in his arms. He didn't hug me back, had gone still as a statute, his arms fallen down to his sides. His heart pounded against my chest, the ragged sound of his breathing filling the room.

I dropped my hands from his neck, wiping at my face, trying to calm the emotions pushing their way to the surface. I took a step back, but before my heel hit the floor, his hands rested on my waist, the small of my back, catching me, anchoring me.

"I'm sorry. I didn't mean to cry all . . ." My voice trailed off as our gazes locked.

He staggered me.

There was no wall now. Only emotion. So much emotion—raw and naked, staring back at me—more than I knew what to do with. I wanted to touch him, to calm the storm in his gaze.

I swallowed, my heart tattooing a wild beat in my

chest, my fingers drifting to his face as if of their own volition, until I held him in my hands, my fingertips skimming his cheekbones, his eyes fluttering closed.

"Easy."

It was more plea than anything else, a search for understanding, an attempt to figure out what I wanted, to master the emotions churning inside me. I moved closer to him, wanting the steady presence of him to surround me, needing comfort and to comfort, and knowing I'd find both in his arms. I rested my forehead against him, the height difference between us enough that I nearly fit under his chin.

"Will you keep in touch while you're gone?"

He nodded against my forehead. "Yeah."

His voice had gone husky and hoarse, and I couldn't help but think whatever I was experiencing, he felt a bit of it, too. Good-byes became a hell of a lot harder when you feared they'd be final.

"I'm going to miss you," I whispered, tears clogging my throat.

For a moment he didn't answer me, and then he did, his words muffled by his lips brushing against my hair as he pressed a kiss to the top of my head. "I'm going to miss you, too."

I wrapped my arms more tightly around him, silence descending around us as we held each other. His mouth grazed my forehead, pressing softly there, soothing.

Except it didn't soothe.

Instead, the strangest thing happened. It started in my stomach—a twitch, a flutter, so light I initially dismissed it. But there it was again—a whisper, so gossamer thin I almost ignored it a second time. Until it spread.

Slowly, the flutter grew, a butterfly using its wings for the first time, hesitant at first, and then stronger, surer, taking flight in my body, moving through my limbs until suddenly I was crackling with it, and I didn't even know what it was. It was the beginning of what I'd felt last night, and yet it wasn't. It was more. So much more.

It was resurrection.

I opened my mouth to speak at the exact moment Easy tightened his grip on me, gathering me against his tall, muscular frame, and then the feeling simply exploded, the flutters inside me turning to a weakening of my knees and a tremor that racked my body all the way down to my toes as he adjusted me so any question I might have had about whether he felt the same way, too, was answered for me.

He was hard. Rock hard. *Easy* was hard, throbbing, big, pressing into me.

I began to fear the flutter would send me into cardiac arrest.

I took a step back—in my mind, at least. But my body? My body stayed right where it was. For a beat. And then another, until I wasn't content to stand there, and I found myself leaning into him, my breasts rubbing against his pecs, my nipples pebbling between us. The throb between my legs intensified and I could feel myself growing wetter, feel that pull, that ache—

His grip on my hips tightened, and for one agonizingly long moment, I wasn't sure if he was going to hold me close or push me away.

His mouth left my forehead, the skin there heated from his breath, from the fire burning inside me. His lips rubbed against the curve of my cheek, his nose grazing my skin, his touch featherlight in a motion that teased another tremor from my limbs, and a line of goose bumps over my skin.

My heart hammered as his mouth slid down my jaw, his lips inches from mine. He paused there, so close our breath mingled, our bodies fused together, and suddenly, I had the answer to the questions that had been plaguing me, knew exactly what I wanted from him.

I wanted him to kiss me.

He shuddered against me. "Dani."

My name was a whisper falling from his lips as my body screamed for more.

I couldn't take it anymore. I tilted my head an inch, a fraction of an inch, putting my mouth on a direct path with his, as I pulled down on his neck, rocking my hips forward in an unmistakable invitation. In a plea.

And then his mouth came down on mine, hard, and the flutters took flight.

ELEVEN

DANI

He kissed me. *Easy* was kissing me. Right now. The truth of it—the *novelty* of it—hit me like an electric shock. Or maybe it was the way he kissed me—breathless kisses that pulled me into him deeper and deeper, my fist reaching out and grabbing his shirt, hauling him toward me, his heart pounding beneath my fingers.

An alarm screamed in my ears, a siren of what-the-fuck-are-you-doing that might as well have been accompanied by a flashing red light.

I summarily dismissed it.

His tongue invaded my mouth, tasting me as though he coveted every part of me, as if he wanted to mark me as his. My back hit the wall, his hands in my hair, hard body pressing into me, the feeling both alien and surprisingly right. My body had already accepted what my brain struggled to process, and then my mind went blank.

His hands were so clever, nimble long fingers I could easily imagine working their magic behind the stick of a jet or making a lucky woman come. He stroked me softly, reverently, the pads of his fingers gliding over my body as though he were trying to learn the shape of me. My hands found their way under his shirt, touching the planes of his back, his skin warm and smooth beneath my palms. His lips left mine, trailing down to the curve of my jaw, his face buried in the crook of my neck as his cock throbbed between my legs, as his teeth grazed my flesh. A shiver slid down my spine, my nipples pebbling.

Easy released me as abruptly as he'd kissed me, whatever this was between us operating in fits and starts that left me unable to catch my stride. Or my breath.

I closed my eyes, not quite ready to face what I'd done, not even sure what that was. He'd kissed me. And yeah, I'd kissed him back, but in this moment the salient fact seemed to be that he'd kissed *me*. How long had that been going on? Was this a result of us hanging out more lately? He'd always had a reputation in the squadron, but I'd never noticed his interest in me. Had I missed it? Did it matter if it had been there before or if it was here now?

I opened my eyes, my heart pounding, my body already protesting his absence, wanting to close the distance between us.

Easy stared back at me, his face pale, his eyes wide. His lips were swollen, a red mark on his neck I'd apparently given him somewhere along the way. His shirt was rumpled and disheveled from where it lost a battle with my hands in the fight for skin. And it was impossible to miss that he was still hard.

"Fuck."

He looked away, the oath falling from those beautiful lips sending another tremor through my body. It sounded so harsh, so male coming from his mouth, and suddenly,

I wanted him to give me the rest. I wanted the brash fighter pilot who turned swagger into a verb. I wanted to lose myself in tonight. It had been so long, and I was tired of feeling as though I'd died, too, nothing in front of me but fifty-plus years of being alone. I wanted to be touched, kissed, held. I'd deal with the guilt later. In this moment, I just wanted Easy.

"Dani, I'm sorry, I—"

I took a step toward him, and then another, my legs shaking as I erased the distance between us. Three steps. Three steps that might as well have been a mile.

He didn't speak. As soon as I took that first step toward him, his mouth slammed shut, his body tense as though he was holding himself back. His eyes—

I faltered on the last step, my gaze locked with his. It was as though a mask had been torn away and suddenly I stared at a stranger. We'd been friends for years; how could I have missed this? How could I have not seen that he looked at me as though—

I didn't even know how to classify the emotion in his eyes. I wasn't sure there was a word for it. At least not one that came to me now. But he'd put a feeling to it when he'd kissed me, and I wanted the feeling again. Needed it.

I reached up—God, he was tall—and laid my palm on his cheek, my fingers skimming his cheekbone. I studied him—the bone structure that would have made a male model envious, the blue eyes that looked so utterly ravaged, the full mouth that had a hint of a pout that the guys gave him so much shit about, the dark blond hair that always seemed to be a touch too long, an inch out of regs. He was the same Easy I'd always known, and yet he wasn't. He'd somehow become someone new and I saw him for the first time, as someone other than my friend.

"Dani . . ."

Had he always said my name like that?

My hands moved to his neck, stroking the skin there as he shuddered against me, his chest rising and falling as he took a deep breath and then another. I stepped into his body, inhaling the scent of him. His heart pounded between us, his mouth tempting me.

Neither one of us moved as we stayed together, locked in an almost-embrace, adjusting to this shift between us, to this new sensation that had sprung up unbidden. His hands found their way to my hips, settling over my hipbones, not quite holding me to him, but not pushing me away, either, his fingers moving in little circles over me. He stood there in limbo, waiting for me to make the next move, offering me his body, all the want inside him that stole my breath away.

So I took it.

I stood on my toes, tugging his head down, making him meet me halfway so I swallowed the breath that passed between his lips, and then his tongue slid in next, and whatever invisible leash had been holding him back finally snapped, and I got a glimpse of Easy in all his unfettered glory.

It. Was. Glorious.

He pushed away from the wall, his hands coming to my waist, lifting me up as though I weighed nothing at all. My legs wrapped around him instinctively, my body rocking forward as he pulsated between my legs, hard and heavy. His hands came to my ass, holding me up, squeezing, while his mouth unraveled me.

God, he could kiss.

Our tongues tangled as I rubbed myself over him, my body turning greedy. His mouth left my lips, and then he grazed my neck again, his tongue sliding over the skin, leaving goose bumps in its wake.

My ass hit the counter, and he laid me down, his hands that had been so hungry now turning gentle. The cool granite hit my back and I looked up at the hanging pot rack above the kitchen island and then the man before me.

Ohmigod.

Easy stood in front of me, staring down at me, that look in his eyes again. And then his fingers grazed my knee through the denim, drifting higher, higher, stroking the inside of my thigh, sucking the air from the room.

"I want you naked."

His words had a bite to them, a bite I felt as keenly as though he'd put his mouth between my legs. I didn't have a response beyond lifting my hips in invitation.

A ragged breath escaped his lips.

His fingers found the button of my jeans, my heart fluttering, his knuckles grazing my skin in a move that had me biting back a moan. I was sensitive, so sensitive everywhere, the year of celibacy taking a toll on me, my body ready to combust if I didn't come soon.

He undid the button, dragging the zipper down, hurtling us over the edge.

You're going to have sex with Easy. You're having sex with Easy.

I lifted my hips another inch as he pulled my jeans down, yanking them off my feet—I'd lost my shoes somewhere between him lifting me up and setting me on the countertop—a groan filling the silence as he slid his palm over my thong, as his fingers drifted lower and discovered the wetness seeping through silk. Whatever shyness I might have had disappeared as the sound hit me, as his thumb ghosted across my clit.

I grabbed the hem of my shirt, sliding the fabric up over my stomach, over my breasts, and then it dropped to the floor, and I lay on Easy's kitchen island, dressed in a bra and underwear.

He swallowed, his Adam's apple bobbing, drawing my attention to his tanned skin, and suddenly I wanted him naked more than anything. Wanted more of the hint I'd gotten the day I watched him paint and what I'd seen in his swim trunks.

I sat up, his palm still inches away from my clit, resting there, branding me. It would take a woman with greater willpower than I possessed to walk away from Easy without him leaving a mark.

I reached out and tugged on his shirt, lifting it up, revealing the six-pack I'd seen before. He had to finish the job, yanking the shirt off his shoulders, because as soon as I saw his body, I leaned forward and put my mouth on him.

He shuddered the second my lips connected with his skin, inches away from his belt buckle. I inhaled his scent, rubbing my mouth against the muscle there, the throb between my legs growing more intense with each moment that passed. His hands found my hair, rubbing the strands between his fingers. My heart clenched. This was sex and yet I was old enough to know this wasn't some casual hookup or one-night stand. I'd loved him as a friend before, and now we'd added lust, sex into the equation, and I didn't know where we'd end up.

Easy's hand cupped me, tilting my head so our gazes locked.

I blinked, needing to break the connection, wanting to get back to the point where we put our mouths on each other. This wasn't a night for trying to figure things out; it was a night for letting go.

I leaned back, ducking my head and averting my gaze, getting a little bit lost in the view in front of me. He really was beautiful. So, so beautiful.

I didn't realize I'd said the words aloud until I looked up and saw the flush settling over his cheeks.

Something about it, knowing I'd evoked such a reaction in him, spurred me on.

He stood still as a statue while I took my time exploring him, my hands stroking, caressing, feasting. He reached between us, pulling me to the edge of the counter and spreading my legs so that when he stepped forward, he was right where I wanted him. And then his big body arched over me as he pushed me back down on the granite, taking control, his fingers moving to my bra, sliding the hooks out and pulling the lace from my body.

My bra hit the ground as his lips closed over my nipple.

The pull of lust was instantaneous, the sensation of his mouth . . . Holy hell, he had moves, orgasm-inducing moves. My hands threaded through his hair, holding him close while his tongue broke me apart and put me back together again, while I arched my back, as my eyes fluttered shut, and I gave myself over to the incredible ride that was Easy.

EASY

In all the years I'd been in love with Dani, all the dreams I'd had about her, all the times I'd been with a woman and her image had taken root in my mind, I'd not once considered that she might want me. Not like this. I hadn't fathomed that she would come apart in my arms, her nails digging into me, her hips thrusting against me. I was fairly sure I'd burn in hell for this later, but right now, I couldn't resist a shot at heaven.

This was a dream I never wanted to wake from. Her fingers tugged at my hair as I sucked on her, as my tongue laved her tight nipples. She moaned, her hips jerking toward me, and it took everything I had to hold myself back, the need to be inside her eclipsing all else.

My hands slid down her torso, fumbling when I reached the waistband of her thong. I broke away from her, my fingers still on the silky fabric, my chest heaving as I struggled to breathe.

Our gazes locked as I stared down at her, as the absolute fucking beauty of her registered with a punch to the chest.

I opened my mouth to speak, to give her an out, her name hovering on my lips when she answered the unspoken question for me.

She sat up, wrapping her arms around my neck and pulling me toward her, her nipples rubbing against my chest, her mouth unraveling any resolve I might have had.

"Tell me to stop," I begged, needing her to be sure, needing to know she wouldn't regret this, that I wasn't taking advantage of her grief, that she wanted me as badly as I wanted her.

"Don't stop," she whispered, her voice ragged with need. "Whatever you do, don't stop."

Fuck it. This was happening.

I had her thong off a minute later, my heart hammering in my chest, Dani in all her naked glory spread before me—pale skin like silk, soft curves that were more understated than I normally went for yet were absolutely perfect.

She was absolutely perfect. Mine for the night.

I leaned forward, wrapping my arms around her, cradling her against my chest. She left a trail of kisses across my pecs as I carried her to the bedroom.

I set her down on the mattress, my heart clenching at the sight of her there. How many times had I imagined her here? Dreamed of her? Now she was here, and all the fantasies I'd had about her vied for attention. I hovered over her, my hand on the inside of her knee, my fingers idly tracing the smooth skin there, my eyes eating her up.

Her hair was spread out over my pillow, her mouth swollen from my kisses, her skin pink in all the places I'd touched her, kissed her, sucked on her skin. Her nipples were tight and flushed, her chest rising and falling rapidly. She was close. So close. And suddenly I wanted nothing more than to watch Dani come, for her control to shatter.

There were so many fantasies I'd had about her over the years, and because this was apparently my chance at them, I drew it out, starting with my head between her legs, my hands spreading her open, my mouth over her clit, the taste of her on my tongue. As soon as I put my mouth on her, her body bucked beneath mine, her hands grabbing my hair, pulling me closer, sighs and moans escaping her lips.

I'd always loved going down on a woman; there was something about giving pleasure that made you feel like a god. But with Dani?

Fucking incredible.

DANI

Oh my God. Oh my God.

There were no words; I was so far gone I could barely think. I was going to come, and considering it had been over a year since I'd had an orgasm, this one was going to be pretty life-changing.

It built inside me with each stroke of his tongue, with his breath on my clit, his lips rubbing over my sensitive flesh. His teeth nipped at me, playful and so fucking hot, and a rush of heat flooded my body, my skin sensitive, the sensation building under the surface.

And then it hit. Hard. It was as though a year's worth of frustration and quiet built to a screaming crescendo as my body bowed, my neck thrown back, and I rode the first wave. And holy hell, what a wave it was.

He didn't let me go, ravaging me with his mouth, swallowing shudder after shudder, laving my swollen flesh. When the tremors subsided, when my body finally came back to me, my eyes fluttered open and my gaze locked with Easy.

The look in his eyes said it all. For tonight, I was his.

He stroked between my legs again—once, twice—sending another tremor through my body.

"Too sensitive," I gasped.

A wicked smile covered his lovely mouth, sending

another flutter through me, and then his big palm slid between my legs, pushing them apart as he settled his body against me.

He felt good—large, strong, so fucking male—and I reached down, pulling him toward me, my nails raking down his back, settling at the base of his spine while he groaned against me, his face buried in my neck, his teeth scraping my skin.

The head of his cock brushed me, sliding across my wetness, rubbing over me, grazing my clit, sending another spark through me. He groaned again, stroking back and forth, creating a delicious friction that had me throbbing, my legs falling open, wider, taking him into my body. I grabbed his biceps, pulling him toward me, needing, wanting him closer, inside me.

He entered me with a smooth thrust, his body surging forward, stretching me, filling me. He didn't move; he stayed there, fully seated, and something shifted—the realization that we'd reached a turning point in our relationship, that we could never go back to the way we were. A moment of panic hit me, a moment that took me away from him and back into my own head, which right now was a scary place to be—and then he began to move, erasing the fear and doubt, and nothing else mattered.

He took my hand, linking our fingers as he thrust in and out in a delicious slide, our bodies slick with sweat, as he made us one. His lips found mine, his kiss sharp, savage, taking more than it gave, building me up only to tear me back down in a delicious loop that invaded every part of me.

Everything—our clasped hands, the roughness of his kiss, the way his body fit with mine—felt right. And now, more than anything, I needed it to be casual, unremarkable. I didn't want to feel the greedy possessiveness running through me as I stroked the hard planes of his back, as my legs locked around his hips, pulling me closer to him.

I didn't want the word "mine" running through my head like a chant that gained momentum with each thrust, as his fingers tightened around me, as we shared the same breath.

He shifted, the angle of his hips changing, and then he hit a really good spot, and I moaned, writhing beneath him, my control shattering as I came again. Easy increased his pace, his hips pumping, body shuddering. His lips left mine, his head buried in the curve of my neck once again, his teeth sinking into the skin there, hard enough that he'd leave a mark, holding on to me as he came.

I rode out his release, coming down from my own, my arms wrapped around him as sanity soon began to filter in, forming tiny hairline cracks that erupted over me.

We'd had sex. We'd actually had sex. He gave me not one, but two amazing orgasms. And then I caught sight of it—resting against his back, next to a red mark where my nails had scored his skin—the glint of my engagement ring, the diamonds on my wedding band staring back at me.

I choked back a sob.

Slowly, I released him, my hands falling to my sides, my heart pounding. He slid out of me and the cool air hit my body, bringing with it the harsh reality of what I'd done, the line I'd crossed.

The bed dipped and I heard him walking to the bathroom to get cleaned up, but I couldn't make myself look at him, worried I'd fall apart if I did. I stared up at the ceiling instead, the image going blurry the longer I focused on it.

I was a virgin when I met Michael; had only ever been with him. That I could no longer say that was another loss, a piece of him I'd never get back. I couldn't deal with seeing Easy, couldn't even begin to think of what I'd say to him.

He was deploying tomorrow. I couldn't say good-bye, couldn't face him, but more than anything, I couldn't face myself.

I ran instead.

TWELVE

DANI

The drive home passed by in a blur, my mind struggling to come to grips with what had happened, with the irrevocable shift in my relationship with Easy. Numb inside, I clung to the void, fairly certain if I did let myself feel, if I really faced the fact that we'd been together, that I'd had sex with one of Michael's closest friends, I'd fall the fuck apart. I'd thought I had a crush on Easy, had known I was attracted to him, even when I didn't want to be, but somehow I hadn't imagined we'd end up here, that it would have been as intense as it was—that my body would feel so worn out and electric, a dull ache between my legs.

How was I supposed to face him now? How did we go back to the friendship we'd had? Were we supposed to pretend it hadn't happened? That he hadn't been inside me, his hands and mouth all over my body? Maybe that was normal for him; maybe one-night stands were supposed to be left in the rearview mirror, treated as little more than bumps in the road. I was so out of practice, I had no idea where to even begin.

I made it home, and the moment I stepped over the threshold, it hit me—the sensation that I had returned as someone entirely different than the person who'd left it. I stripped out of my clothes, my limbs surprisingly sore. My cheeks heated as I saw the marks on my body from his mouth, his hands. And then my gaze drifted to my fingers, to the rings on my left hand once again, and the world shifted beneath my feet.

A sob escaped, one I'd held in since I'd left Easy's, followed by another, guilt and grief piercing the veil that had kept my emotions at bay. My legs crumpled and I hit the ground, my arm braced on the edge of my bed for support. *Our* bed. Mine and Michael's.

Even as some rational piece of my brain attempted to find solace in the notion that I hadn't technically done anything wrong, it still felt like a betrayal of the vows I'd made when Michael had placed the wedding band on my finger.

We'd promised 'til death do us part, and while I'd always known I could lose him, that his job might take him away from me one day, I'd always envisioned death to be gray hair and grandchildren by our side, had imagined whichever one of us went first, the other would fade away until we could be together again. But there were no grandchildren together, no weddings where we'd beam with pride as our children walked down the aisle, no days when he would look at me and tell me I was still beautiful even as my face was covered in lines, no nights when we would look back at the memory of the life we'd lived together and smile. There was only me. Alone. The gaping, yawning void of a life spent without him. And the memories we'd had together, the short life we'd lived, were now tainted by this night and what I'd done, as though I'd taken a sledgehammer to our marriage and shattered it.

I didn't know if it was that I'd moved on, feeling like I'd left Michael behind, the moments when he'd simply slipped out of my mind, when I'd forgotten him, if it was the sex, or even worse, if it was who I'd been with, the sensation that I'd betrayed Michael, that we'd *both* betrayed him.

And then I felt another pang, for Easy and the fact that I'd simply fled, and worry that he was as screwed up about it as I was.

I considered texting him but I didn't know what to say. I'd thought about going to see him off tomorrow, but now I couldn't imagine how uncomfortable a face-to-face would be, and the last thing he needed was the distraction before he deployed.

I twisted my rings around my finger, each turn a knife stabbing deeper and deeper into my heart.

EASY

She'd left.

It was as though she'd never been here at all, like it had all been a dream, but no—

I stared at the empty bed, the rumpled sheets, the indentation in the pillow where she'd laid her head. I could still smell her perfume on the sheets, bore the marks from her mouth and nails on my body, and she'd fucking fled, as though I was some one-night stand she was too ashamed to face afterward.

Fuck.

I'd had one-night stands, had sex better forgotten the next morning. Hell, I'd been the one to sneak out so many times before; there was probably some poetic fucking justice at play here, but right now all I knew was she'd fled after the best night of my life.

I sank down onto the edge of the bed. As much as it had hurt to want her and not have her, the only thing that hurt worse was having her and learning that it meant nothing, that I was little more than an interchangeable body and an easy orgasm, that she didn't really want me.

And even worse, I'd crossed a line I'd sworn I would never breach, in doing so betraying a man who I respected and missed.

I barely slept, the memory of Dani in my bed a constant loop I couldn't shake. I considered texting her, typed out a message over and over again only to lose my nerve every single fucking time.

I could drop a bomb without breaking a sweat, had been to war, nearly died more times than I could count, but she was the scariest thing I'd ever faced, my feelings for her sending me into a spin.

As fucked up as everything was between us, as much as I hated the way she'd left things, as fucking guilty as I felt, I wanted to see her again, wanted some chance to make everything right between us. What if she wasn't here when I got back? What if I'd trashed the friendship we'd developed?

My head spun with questions and doubts, but the truth

was, I wasn't ready to face the possibility that I'd lost her for good.

I'd intended to nap during the day, but I couldn't get my shit together. She'd left her mark on my room, on me, and I couldn't erase the traces of her no matter how hard I tried. I finally ended up taking one of the "go" pills the flight doc gave us, already dreading tonight's flight. Spending hours cramped in the jet while we flew across the ocean, not getting to do anything cool, wasn't anyone's idea of a good time, and these flights were always the worst. Sometimes we'd play trivia games with the tanker guys who refueled us in the air, doing whatever we could to stave off the mind-numbing boredom. I was leading a six-ship tonight, the guys in my formation fairly young wingmen. I needed to have my head in the game.

By 6 p.m. I gave up on any hope of hearing from Dani, came to terms with the possibility that I'd irretrievably screwed everything up. Maybe it was for the best if the house sold and she moved on, if we lost touch, if I let her go.

I got my bags together, throwing stuff in at the last minute as Noah arrived at the house to take me to Bryer so I wouldn't have to leave my car on base while we were gone.

"You ready?" he asked in greeting.

I nodded, for the first time feeling like I really was. Flying always made sense, and for three months my life would narrow to the jet, to the mission, to doing what I'd spent my days training for.

"How was it at Charley's after I left?" Noah asked once we'd settled into the car.

"Fine."

"Thor mentioned some shit went down with you and Dani."

If he only knew.

"What, do you guys chat before bed every night?" I asked, staring out the window as we headed toward the base.

"Something like that," he replied, his tone wry. "So?"

"I don't want to talk about Dani."

"Is everything okay?" he asked, concern in his tone.

Not even fucking close.

"Just keep an eye on her while you're here, okay?"

"Did something happen?"

If there was anyone I trusted, it was Noah, but there was no fucking way I could tell him this. Not when it was Joker's wife, not when we'd all seen the year she'd had, how she'd struggled to move past her grief. I didn't want him to think I'd taken advantage of that, and at the same time, I didn't know how to explain that we'd had sex.

"Just keep an eye on her. If she needs anything, that sort of thing."

His gaze slid to me. "I thought that was your deal."

"Not anymore."

"What happened between you guys?"

"I don't want to talk about Dani, okay? Promise me. If anything happens to me while I'm gone, I want to know she'll be taken care of."

He was silent for a moment, and I wondered if he'd push, but then he nodded. "Of course. I got it."

We drove in silence, and I found my mind drifting again, to the memory of her mouth, her body, how amazing it had been when I'd thrust inside her, when she'd clenched down around me, surrounding me in her tight heat.

My hand clenched in a fist.

We got to the squadron as the sun was setting. The plan was for us to take off at night. Twenty-four of us were flying jets over; an advance group had already gone ahead earlier in the week to set up for the squadron to arrive.

"You sure you're fine to fly?" Noah asked.

Flying was the one place where I didn't feel completely and totally fucked. Thor had struggled in the cockpit after Joker's death, had been plagued with PTSD for nearly a year now. For me, it was the opposite. When I was in the jet, everything made sense. I'd never forget that day, never forget the sound of Joker's voice on the radio, and everything that had come after, but when I was up there I felt the closest to him; I could make sense of all the shit in the air that I couldn't wrap my head around on the ground.

"Yeah. I'm fine. I'll see you when you're back from Korea."

He gave me a nod and a slap on the back, never one for drawn out good-byes, and then I grabbed my bag for the travel pod, most of my stuff already on the way over on the main body flight. I saw Thor and Becca, their arms wrapped around each other, watched sleepy kids in pajamas say bye to their dads in the squadron parking lot. As far as deployments went, this one was the shortest we'd had in a while, but a year later the memory of losing Joker was still too fresh, tension in all the families as they said good-bye.

I tried not to, but I found my gaze scanning the crowd, looking for her, found myself checking my phone one more time, only to come up empty.

Maybe it was better this way.

I walked into the squadron, exchanging hellos with a few people. I made my way to the jet and stuffed my remaining bags into the travel pod, my mind already transitioning to the flight ahead, switching focus, leaving everything else behind me.

I headed to life support, grabbing my G-suit, harness, helmet, and pubs bag. I put on my survival vest for the ocean crossing and headed to the vault to get my classified materials. I made my way to the desk and got my step brief, the last-minute information I needed before stepping to the jet. The weather looked iffy, high winds and low ceilings, leaving no doubt that the flight would be a bitch.

Six of us walked out to the flight line, helmets in hand, our boots hitting the concrete in a chorus of thuds. No one spoke. The jets loomed ahead under the sunshades against the backdrop of a pink and orange sky, the sun getting ready to set. I did my walk-around, making sure everything looked good, exchanging a few words with the crew chief.

Showtime.

I stepped onto the jet's ladder, my hands gripping the metal as I hauled myself up, my heart pounding as the adrenaline began to rev inside me. I hung my helmet bag on the inside of the jet and then I swung my legs into the cockpit, hoisting myself onto the seat, adjusting myself.

I strapped in, and I shook the crew chief's hand as he wished me a safe flight and stepped away, taking the ladder off the jet. I went through my verification checklist, the interior of the jet growing dark as the sun slipped away, the night quiet around me as I began setting up my cockpit for the flight across the ocean, all thoughts of

Dani gone. These movements came naturally now, a calming rhythm to preparing for the sortie.

I began talking to the crew chief on the radio, setting out all the important papers I needed on my kneeboard. I turned on the battery, powering the channels, switching on the main gen. A low hum sounded, lights flickering inside the cockpit. I put my helmet on, my oxygen mask hanging down.

I looked at my line-up card, checking my watch, waiting for the start time—

The sound of six jets starting up filled the night, a puff of smoke emerging from the jets around me. We pushed to idle, and the noise got louder, an orange glow emanating from the jets. The cockpit vibrated, the roar of power rushing between my legs.

My engine gauges came alive, swinging clockwise, lights turning on as I ran through another checklist, making sure everything was working properly. I pushed up the throttle, the jet rocking forward a bit. I tested more systems, a low hum starting in my veins. I turned on the avionics power, loading my flight data into the jet's computer, and then I was running through the rest of the checks, making sure everything was working as it should be.

I called ops and checked in, signing off with the squadron motto—

"Aces High."

The crew chief gave me the pull-chocks symbol and then I owned the radios, flashing my crew chief the hand signal as I lead out the taxi of six Wild Aces heading to the runway, our jets lit up. We paused, getting armed up by the arming crew, turning our lights off. I breathed into my mask, the hum building inside me like a crescendo, the beginning of an incredible high sparking. Then, in reverse order, from six to one, the jets turned on their lights, letting me know they were good to go.

It was time.

I called the tower, waiting to be cleared for takeoff, arming my seat, flipping switches—

I taxied the jet, the runway mine, lining up, pushing up my throttle and checking the instruments. I rotated the throttle outboard and pushed forward, lighting the afterburner, the thrust of it a kick in the pants as the jet quickly accelerated. We hurtled down the runway, five jets following my lead, and then I was climbing away, leaving Oklahoma, and Dani, behind me.

THIRTEEN

EASY

The first two months of the deployment went by in a blur of sorties, dropping bombs, strafing enemy targets on the ground. I was on the night train, sleeping during the day, flying most nights, collapsing into my twin-sized bed every morning, my body worn-out and exhausted.

I worked for eight weeks straight with only three days off, and then finally at the eight-week mark our squadron commander, Loco, took pity on us and gave us a weekend off.

I used the time to catch up on much-needed sleep and to connect with family and friends back home. I pulled up Skype on my computer, a trickle of sweat running down my neck in the Afghani heat. Oklahoma in the summer wasn't exactly pleasant, but there was something about Afghanistan—the bright sun, the sand—that turned you to glass. I'd been burning up for two months now, going a little bit crazier each day, exhausted and worn out, ready to get out of the desert and go back home.

Before, home had been wherever my squadron went, a traveling caravan I could pop up and take down in conjunction with the Air Force's needs. Now home was a person I'd left behind, and I thought of her constantly no matter how hard I tried not to. It was impossible to focus on the mission when my personal life was such a mess, when I didn't know what she wanted from me, or how she was doing, or how she felt after that night.

Dani sent care packages to the squadron every couple of weeks, and it hadn't escaped my notice that each contained my favorite things, stuff I hadn't even realized she'd picked up on. Each time we opened the packages, I fell impossibly more in love with her, wondering if she was trying to send me some message in the granola bars, packets of energy drinks—hence the phone call to Jordan.

She answered after a few rings, her voice breathless.

"Hey, it's Easy. Is this a bad time?"

"Easy! No, of course not," Jordan answered. "Wait, let me put Julie down in her crib."

Rustling sounds filled the line and then Jordan came back on.

"How are you? How's the desert?"

"It's fine," I responded automatically, answering her questions and making small talk for the next few minutes, the whole time gathering up the balls to ask about the one person I desperately wanted to hear was fine.

Finally when we'd caught up and it was safe to switch topics, I asked about Dani.

"She's good," Jordan replied.

Come on.

"Has the house sold?"

"No, it hasn't."

"Relieved" didn't quite cover how that made me feel.

"Is she doing okay?"

"Yeah, she seems good. She went back to Georgia for a few weeks to visit her family."

"Did she have a good time?"

Jordan laughed. "Um, maybe you should call her. I mean, yeah she had a good time, but I wasn't with her or anything . . ."

"Sorry."

"No, it's okay. But I'm trying to figure out why you're checking in with me and not Dani."

"I was just curious. I wanted to make sure she's okay, that she's happy . . ."

Jordan's tone sobered. "She's okay. I'm keeping an eye on her and she's fine. I promise."

Somewhere inside me, the knot in my chest loosened a bit.

"Thank you."

"No problem."

I swallowed. I wanted the rest of it, even as I feared her answer, even as I had no right to it.

"Is she—" My voice cracked. "Is she seeing anyone?"

Silence filled the line, and in those moments, I told myself I was fine with her moving on with someone else, fine with what happened between us meaning far more to me than it had to her. At least I'd had the one night.

"She's not seeing anyone," Jordan answered, pity in her voice.

Thank God.

It wasn't much to go on, but I needed the thread of hope to cling to in order to carry me through the next month, until I could go home and see her again, before I could face what would happen between us.

DANI

Two months crept by; the house didn't sell, I found myself still in Oklahoma, missing Michael, and thinking about Easy way more than I should have. I regretted missing the chance to say bye to him before he deployed, that things were left the way they were. And now I worried about him constantly, afraid something would happen while he was gone, and I would never get a chance to see him again, to speak to him again.

The sex had been beyond incredible, and I cared about him; I always had. But I didn't know how those two things mixed together—like bacon-flavored chocolate— good separately, questionable when joined. There were limits to what I had inside me, to my ability to have or want anything more than pieces of someone. If I could compartmentalize our relationship, somehow put us into boxes, sex and everything else, that was one thing . . .

But I was worried. Worried things between us could get too messy, that the connection with Michael already made this so, so wrong . . . and not in some forbidden, tantalizing sort of way, but rather in a way that made me cringe every time I looked in the mirror, as though I might as well have a scarlet letter on my forehead.

And whatever thoughts he had about the whole thing remained a mystery—he didn't call, didn't write, and the days stretched on and on.

I sent the guys care packages, torn between the desire to write Easy and each time chickening out. Despite how awkward things were between us, during the day I found myself missing him and at night I woke from vivid dreams of his mouth on mine.

Noah had gone back to Korea for his final month there, and I spent more time with Jordan and the baby. I didn't tell her about Easy—*couldn't* tell her about Easy—but she shared updates with me that she'd heard through the grapevine from Noah, and even though I worried about him daily it helped to hear he was okay, to feel that connection with him, however tenuous it was.

The thing about boxes was that when you filled them, bursting to the seams, things snuck out, pushed and prodded their way to the surface and no amount of shoving could get them back inside.

I went to Jordan's halfway through the week, tired of my own company, of the doubts and questions running through my mind. And more than anything, I went for the news of Easy she gave me each time we spoke.

"So how have you been?" Jordan asked as we sat next to each other on her couch, the baby asleep in the next room.

"Good. You? Excited for Noah to come back?"

She grinned. "You have no idea. I can't believe it's only a couple weeks away."

He was due back two weeks before the Wild Aces returned from Afghanistan. Not that I had a countdown or anything.

We talked for a few minutes about Noah's return and then I summoned the courage up to ask the question that had been in the back of my mind since I arrived at her place.

"Have you heard anything from the guys downrange?"

Have you heard anything about Easy?

"Noah's talked to Thor a few times. He seems to be doing well."

"That's great."

My stomach pitched and rolled, nerves rumbling around. I waited a beat, and when she didn't say anything else, I couldn't resist.

"How about Easy?"

"He's good. I actually talked to him a couple days ago. He asked how you were doing."

"Really?"

"Yeah, he was a little worried about you." She shot me a curious look. "Have you guys talked since he left?"

"No, not really." I tried to keep my voice and expression vague, even as I wanted to know more . . . What he'd asked, if he'd said anything about me, if she had any clue as to what had happened between us. There had been so many times I'd wanted to tell her, had needed to talk to someone, to try to explain and understand how we'd gone from friends to something else entirely, but each time the words stuck in my throat.

"Is everything okay with you guys?"

"Yeah. It's fine." My throat got really dry. "So what did he ask? Why do you think he was worried?"

"He asked how you were doing, if you were still in Oklahoma, if the house had sold, that sort of thing."

"What did you tell him?"

"That you were fine." She hesitated. "He wanted to know if you were seeing anyone."

Did he really care?

"What did you tell him?" I repeated, the words not coming as smoothly as normal.

She shot me a suspicious look. "That you weren't. You aren't, right?"

"No, of course not," I squeaked, another ball of nerves rolling around in my stomach.

"Okay, well that's what I told him. If you guys had a fight, you should talk about it. Things are obviously strained between both of you and neither one of you seems happy about it. You've been too important to each other to lose that."

If only it were that easy.

"It's complicated," I murmured.

"Well, whatever it is, he obviously misses you."

"I miss him, too," I admitted.

She was right. Easy and I were friends, were too important in each other's lives to let sex screw up the connection we had. We were adults, and yeah, it was awkward, but we'd talk about it and move forward. We had to. I wasn't ready to throw away our friendship because of one night, spectacular though it was.

"Then talk to him. There's nothing you guys can't get past."

"Thanks for the advice."

"No problem. Whatever it is, you guys will work it out." She yawned, the rest of the words disappearing behind her hand. "Sorry. I haven't been sleeping much with the baby. It's not the company, I promise."

"No worries. I don't even have the excuse of being a new mom and I'm tired all the time. I've been thinking about switching up my vitamins, or eating more protein, or something, because by the end of the day, I'm ready to fall asleep. I caught a cold last week and even though the symptoms are gone and I'm not contagious or anything, I haven't gotten my energy back."

Jordan yawned again. "Ugh. That's the worst. Maybe you should go to the doctor and have it checked out. You could be anemic or something."

"Yeah, I might. I've been a little dizzy lately, too."

Concern filled Jordan's gaze. "Do you want me to go with you? I don't mind."

"No, I'm fine, but thanks. If it doesn't get better in another week, I'll see the flight doc. It's probably allergies or something."

"Be careful with the dizziness. I got so dizzy one day when I was pregnant I almost fainted. Luckily Noah was there, but I worry about you by yourself if you're feeling that bad. You can always call me if you need something."

"Thanks, I really appreciate it."

That was the thing about the wives—we stepped in and helped one another when we needed it, when we were left behind. We were a sisterhood of sorts, connected by an unbreakable bond. We celebrated birthdays together when we would otherwise be alone, marked anniversaries when our husbands weren't here with us. We were family; while the pilots formed their bonds in war, ours came from keeping everything together while they were gone.

"How long have you been feeling bad?" Jordan asked.

"A couple weeks, maybe? Not long."

"Are you PMSing? I get light-headed before mine's about to start."

"Maybe." I tried to think back to the last time I'd gotten my period. I'd never had much of a regular cycle—yet another reason why Michael and I had struggled so hard to get pregnant—and after he died my cycle had nearly disappeared entirely, popping up at the most random times. I'd gone to the doctor only to be told it was likely stress and grief, and I'd lost more weight than I should have thanks to the stress and grief.

How long had it been?

I half listened as Jordan kept talking, pulling out my

phone and checking my calendar, trying to figure out the last time I'd written it down.

April. So if I'd had a normal cycle, I should have gotten my period in May. But I didn't have a normal cycle . . .

"Dani?"

I jerked my head up, struggling to focus on Jordan, white noise rushing through my ears.

"Yeah?"

It was probably a nutrition thing. After Michael died I'd hated cooking for myself, spent far too many dinners eating cereal . . .

"Are you sure you're okay? You look really pale."

We hadn't used a condom . . .

It was crazy. I was being crazy. I'd been married for seven years, spent a large chunk of them trying to get pregnant, only to have one miscarriage. I was reproductively challenged. There wasn't a chance.

And there was no way I would be able to relax until I knew for sure.

"I'm really sorry, but I'm not feeling great after all. I'm going to head out."

"Are you sure?"

I nodded, my heart pounding. I was overreacting, letting my mind spiral, but I couldn't help it. Until I confirmed what I suspected, that it was anemia or diet, or something totally mundane, calm would be a pipe dream.

I said bye to Jordan, and then I was driving to the drugstore, replaying that night, trying to calculate the odds of a thirty-one-year-old woman getting pregnant from one night—one time—of unprotected sex.

When I got to the store, I headed down the feminine-products aisle, my head ducked lest anyone recognize me, feeling like all eyes were on me anyway. My fingers shook as I grabbed the box, experiencing a sense of déjà vu and a pang in my heart at the memory of the last time I'd done this and the baby I'd subsequently lost.

I checked out with the pregnancy test—okay, tests—with all the subterfuge of a back-alley drug deal. The drive home seemed to take forever, fear gnawing at me, mixed with something else I wasn't ready to name.

If I were pregnant, this thing with Easy would become so much more complicated; impossible, really. I'd always imagined being a mother with Michael by my side, had this image in my head of baking cookies at holidays, and family dinners, and smiling proudly as we watched our kid play a pumpkin in the school Thanksgiving play. Being a single mother wasn't part of the plan. Then again, neither was being a widow.

A part of me, a part that grew with each moment that passed, wanted to be pregnant. So badly. It was such a long shot, and yet now that it was just me, it might be my only chance. Maybe it was selfish to want a baby when I couldn't give it the stability I'd always imagined, but right now the kernel of hope, the possibility of it, was enough for me to cling to even as I knew the best thing was for it to be negative.

I skimmed the testing instructions, fumbling with the packaging. I went through the motions, and then I sat there waiting, staring at that little stick. My hands shook.

A minute passed as I waited for the digital reading to finish, the test flashing that it was still processing.

How long did this take?

Bile rose in my throat.

The minutes stretched on and on, each time I checked

the screen the stupid test-processing message stared back at me, and then it wasn't anymore.

Pregnant.

I blinked at the word, convinced I'd hallucinated it, that I was reading it wrong, that I was dreaming.

Pregnant.

Ohmigod.

My legs gave way and I sank down to the floor, my back against the wall, my palm on my stomach, hovering over the life that was there, the life we'd created. My baby. Easy's baby.

Pregnant.

The first tear trickled down my face, and then another, my body shaking as I sobbed, as my emotions bubbled over until I didn't know why I cried or what I cried for.

I was overwhelmed and scared, and through all of it, shining bright, piercing me with surprising intensity, I was happy, so happy. Laughing as I cried. Already in love with the life inside me.

Pregnant.

Would the baby be a little girl? A boy? Would it have my green eyes or Easy's blue ones? My auburn hair or blond hair like his?

It was bittersweet. The image of the child I'd carried in my head changed now, its features shifting from the ones I'd always imagined it inheriting from Michael. We'd wanted a baby so badly, spent so many nights lying in bed imagining the kind of parents we'd be.

I had no clue if Easy even wanted to have kids.

Would he be happy or scared? Would he want to be involved in the baby's life or would he be happy to take a more hands-off role?

I didn't know.

I wanted to have faith in him, in us, wanted to believe things would work out between us, but right now we were rolling down a cliff, and I didn't know where we'd end up. Our night together wouldn't remain a secret, would become something public, something I would have to face.

Life had become infinitely more complicated.

Pregnant.

I sat there with my hand splayed over my stomach, running through a mental checklist of all I needed to do—doctor's appointments and prenatal vitamins—calculating my due date, trying to figure out how I would make this work. And in the back of my mind constantly was Easy, and the knowledge that I would have to tell him eventually, even as I struggled to come up with a plan, and I worried about how he would respond.

FOURTEEN

DANI

I scheduled my first doctor's appointment after going through five home pregnancy tests, each one telling me the same thing.

I was definitely pregnant.

Despite the positives, the small changes I began to notice in my body, I was relieved when the doctor confirmed the pregnancy and told me the baby was doing well. My earlier miscarriage was in the back of my mind constantly now, and I was afraid to get too attached to this baby, to go through the same pain. With each day that passed, though, I grew a little more confident, a little more secure, and when the doctor told me he didn't think there was any reason why I couldn't have a healthy pregnancy now, I felt a overwhelming sense of relief.

I refrained from buying anything for the baby until I made it through the first trimester, some superstitious part of me wanting to get over that first hurdle, but I occupied my time making lists and planning for what I needed to buy. I checked out a giant stack of books from the library, filling in the gaps in my knowledge that I hadn't gotten the first time around.

I spoke to the baby constantly, each day falling more in love. I dreamed about it—sometimes a little girl, other times a blond-haired boy with a wobbly smile—imagining this tiny person curled up inside me needing to be kept safe.

During my first pregnancy I'd been sick often, my entire body aching in one way or another. This time around was completely different. I was tired during the day, and my breasts were growing at an alarming rate, but otherwise I felt good. There was no morning sickness, no dramatic mood swings. Despite the circumstances and all the unresolved issues, I was happy. So, so very happy.

"You look like you're better," Jordan commented as I stepped over the threshold to her house and gave her a quick hug, wondering if she would notice the differences in my body, the weight I'd put on. I didn't have a bump yet, but I kept staring at myself in the mirror, wondering when my stomach would pop. Wanting it to.

I grinned. "I am. Thanks."

"I'm about to put Julie down for her afternoon nap. Do you want to hang out in the nursery for a bit?"

"Sure."

I sat with Jordan while she fussed with the baby—she really was adorable—watching as she put her in her crib for her nap, the whole time wondering if I would get my stride, if I'd be able to figure out how to be a mom. The books I read all talked about parenting styles, and the importance of getting your kid into the right preschool, and how old was ideal to learn a foreign language, and I was somewhere back at the beginning, still adjusting to this change, still trying to figure out how I would answer some basic questions: Where would we live? Would I end up doing this alone? How would I tell Easy?

I followed Jordan out to the living room when she finally got Julie to go to sleep.

We sat down next to each other on the couch, the ceiling fan whirring to life overhead.

"She's beautiful."

Jordan gave me a tired smile. "She is. She's such a sweet baby, too. Just not a good sleeper."

"Is it hard to get her to go to sleep?"

"Hard to get her to go to sleep, hard to get her to stay asleep, hard to get her to sleep more than a few hours." Jordan made a face. "It's as if she's afraid that if she does sleep, she'll miss out on something exciting."

I laughed. "You can't argue with that. Well, if you ever need me to help, I'm happy to watch her so you can nap or something."

"I really appreciate the offer, and I definitely might take you up on it. My mom's coming to stay with me for a bit next week, but it's been difficult with Noah gone."

"How are you doing?"

She shrugged. "In some ways it's easier than it was before in the sense that it's not just me; now I have the baby to take care of, so that keeps me focused, distracted. At the same time, now it's harder because I have the baby to take care of and if I thought I was tired during pregnancy, tired with a baby is a whole other ballgame."

A thin thread of panic filtered through me as I wondered if that was the future before me—life as a single mom. I wanted to tell myself I could do it and do it well, but I'd also have been lying if I didn't admit part—most—of me was scared.

"Enough about me, though. What's going on with you?" Jordan asked. "Anything new?"

Only a secret that was now somewhere between the size of a green olive and a prune.

I opened my mouth to tell her everything was fine, but suddenly I couldn't do it anymore. I hadn't told anyone about this, not my family or friends, and it was this big secret bursting inside me that I didn't want to keep anymore. Jordan knew us both, and she was one of the least judgmental people I knew. If I could trust anyone to keep my secret, it would be her.

"I need to talk to you."

Worry clouded her gaze. "What's wrong?"

I didn't even know where to begin, merely that I wanted to say it, wanted to get her advice on how to handle this. Easy was home in two weeks; I couldn't put the truth off much longer.

"You know how I was hanging out with Easy a lot before the guys deployed?"

"Yeah. Does this have anything to do with why you guys haven't talked in a while? And why he was asking about you when I spoke to him a couple weeks ago?"

I nodded. "We got close. I mean, we always were close, but I guess we got closer."

"Okaaay." She dragged the word out as though she wasn't sure what she was going to get when she reached the other side.

"The thing is, the more time we spent together . . ." This was the hard part. I was a thirty-one-year-old woman; sex shouldn't feel so illicit. But I was a thirty-one-year-old *widow*, and somehow that seemed to make the quintessential difference.

I swallowed.

"I had sex with Easy."

Silence descended around us. I stared down at my hands, afraid of what I might see lingering in Jordan's expression.

"You had sex with *Easy*?"

I nodded.

"Easy?" Jordan squeaked. "Our Easy?"

My Easy.

"Yeah."

"Ohmigod."

"I know."

"Ohmigod," she repeated.

I couldn't tell if it was horror or shock, or some combination of the two; she stared at me as though she didn't know how to respond to the bomb I'd just dropped. Being a widow meant people handled you as if you had "Fragile" stickers stamped all over you and I could tell that was coming into play here, shaping her responses, making her hold back her words when honestly I wanted the unfiltered response, wanted a glimpse of how everyone would react to this before I had to start telling the people who would really be rocked by the news—my parents, Michael's parents.

"Are you guys together?"

"No. No. Nothing like that."

Jordan opened her mouth and then closed it again, clearly grasping for the right thing to say.

"Okay. I'm going to need you to start at the beginning."

"I had sex with Easy. That is the beginning. And the middle and end."

Okay, so maybe that wasn't all of it, but given how blown away she seemed by that fact alone, I wasn't sure I was ready to give her the rest.

"How? When?"

I shot her a look. "Seriously? How?"

She laughed. "You know what I mean."

"It was the night after their send-off party. We'd gotten into a fight and I wanted to smooth things over before he deployed so I went to his place to apologize and say good-bye. We were there, and I went to give him a hug, and then somehow the hug changed, and the next thing I knew, we were having sex."

She stared at me, unblinking.

"It's bad, right?"

"I don't think it's bad." Comprehension dawned in her eyes. "Oh."

There it was. It had hit her that having sex with Easy meant I'd screwed my dead husband's best friend.

"You shouldn't feel guilty."

I gave her the look again. "Would you feel guilty?"

She bit her lip. "Okay, yes, I see where you're coming from, but this is a special circumstance. You shouldn't feel bad about it."

"Well, I do, but unbelievably, that isn't even the most complicated thing. It gets worse. Well, not worse, but—"

Her entire expression changed. "Oh God. He told you, didn't he?"

Huh?

"He didn't want you to know he loved you. He worried it would make things awkward, and that it was disrespectful . . . And no one else thought it was right to tell you. I mean it wasn't our secret and . . ." Her voice trailed off. "I didn't ever think he'd act on it. He said he'd never act on it. I never imagined you'd be interested in him."

It was the word "love" that did it. It stunned me into

silence, drying up all the words inside me, creating a chokehold on my heart, cutting off my breath.

"What are you talking about?" I sputtered.

"Easy."

What?

"What do you mean he loves me?"

Like a friend.

She had to mean like a friend.

Jordan looked guilty, her voice strained. "He loves you."

She said it as though it was a commonly accepted truth, when I still wasn't sure I'd heard her correctly.

"Easy?"

What?

"Yeah. Isn't that what you meant when you said things were more complicated?" Her voice rose. "Please tell me that was what you were talking about."

Nausea rolled around in my stomach. "No. It wasn't."

Panic filled her gaze. "Oh, fuck."

"Jordan—"

"Please don't tell him I told you. He didn't want you to know. Ever."

They'd talked about this? Actually talked about him and me? How did that conversation even go?

How was work today?

Good. I think I'm in love with Dani?!?!

"Easy doesn't love me. That's ridiculous," I sputtered. She had to be mistaken. He'd meant he loved me as a friend, and she'd misunderstood the whole thing. "We had sex. Maybe he's attracted to me, but that doesn't mean he *loves* me. You know how Easy is with women."

Women who were beautiful and sexy, young and free,

not old widows who'd given their heart away nearly a decade ago.

Jordan bit down on her lip.

"What?"

What else could she not possibly be telling me? What else was there to say? I'd thought *I* had the bomb to drop.

"You don't get it. He really loves you."

"I think you're overstating the sex."

"I'm not talking about you guys having sex. He told me he loved you. Everyone knows he loves you. This isn't about you guys having sex one night. This is more."

I couldn't feel my legs, couldn't fucking breathe.

What was she talking about?

"When?"

"When, what?"

"When did Easy tell you he loved me?" My voice rose at the end, hysteria sinking in.

Jordan's eyes widened. "Last year."

"Last year?"

This wasn't happening.

I choked on the words. "As a friend?"

"No, definitely not as a friend. He's in love with you." Her tone gentled, compassion in her eyes. "Dani, he's been in love with you since the first moment he saw you."

I couldn't breathe.

Could.

Not.

Breathe.

All this time. *Years.* He'd been one of Michael's closest friends for *years.* He'd been there for me when I'd lost the baby. Had held me close when Michael died, stood next to me while I struggled to speak at the memorial service, staring out at the sea of people waiting expectantly for me to make some sense of my loss, to put a spin on it, as though Michael's heroism made the absence of him bearable, when all I'd wanted to do was crawl into a ball and die. But I hadn't. All the moments in the past two years when I'd struggled, Easy had been there—laughing with me, smiling at me, carrying me through the hard times. And I'd never known, never even suspected.

Memories hit me one by one—the way he looked at me, the sound of his voice saying my name, the touch of his lips against mine. All the little things he noticed about me, the way he made sure I had my favorite things.

Easy loved me.

So much.

So much it terrified me.

"Why didn't you tell me?" I was drowning in the memories. "You knew this whole time?"

Tears swam in her eyes. "You were married."

He'd loved me when I was with Michael. His best friend. I couldn't breathe.

"You were so happy with Michael," Jordan continued. "Easy knew you didn't feel the same way about him. Knew nothing would happen between you guys . . ."

Her voice trailed off and what she didn't say lingered between us, impossible to ignore.

And then your husband died.

I couldn't take any more. It was too much, the pieces of my life shifting and rearranging, until suddenly I didn't recognize anything. Couldn't recognize myself. All the things I'd known to be true weren't anymore, and suddenly every memory I had of Easy, of Michael, of me, was tainted by this secret he'd kept and by the night we'd spent together.

"I'm going to be sick."

I made it to the bathroom before I doubled over, my body heaving. Jordan came behind me, holding my hair away from my face, and then for the second time in our friendship I simply crumpled on the floor, her arms enfolding me as the sobs racked my body.

I wasn't sure if it was the pregnancy hormones, this latest bomb, or the guilt that battered my body, but I was utterly wrung out. I couldn't even make sense of what I was feeling, didn't understand the emotions pummeling me, mixing together to create a giant snarl I couldn't untangle.

I'd loved my husband. I still loved my husband. My marriage hadn't been perfect, but we'd been happy. So happy. And somehow this change—the baby, the realization that while I'd been with Michael, Easy had loved me—felt like I'd lost him all over again.

"I'm pregnant."

I'd envisioned telling Easy first—hell, I still couldn't quite come to grips with the reality that I was in this position to begin with: unmarried, pregnant, wearing another man's rings on my finger. Did Easy even want kids? Would he want to be involved? Was that what I wanted?

Jordan froze. "Oh my God."

I nodded, wiping at my cheeks.

"It's Easy's?"

I nodded again.

"Oh my God. Does he know?"

I shook my head. "I need to tell him, but I don't know how to even start the conversation. Especially when he's deployed. And after last time . . ." I tried to push the fear out. "Until I'm through with the first trimester . . ." My hand drifted down, settling over the baby.

Jordan squeezed my free hand. "I know."

"How do you think he's going to take this?"

She took a deep breath. "I think he's going to be a little scared at first. And yeah, it's a complicated situation, but you can't think he'll be anything other than thrilled. He's going to love this baby so much. And for all that he seems like he isn't ready, he'll be a great dad."

"I don't want to hurt him," I whispered.

I couldn't bear it. Now that I knew how he'd felt about me all this time, now that I imagined what he must have gone through . . .

I ached for him.

"I know," she answered.

I didn't want to hurt him, and at the same time, I worried it was inevitable. That I couldn't give him what he wanted from me.

"I don't know what I feel. What I want. I love him like a friend. He's one of my closest friends. And yeah, suddenly there's this chemistry between us I never imagined. And now there's a baby."

But I didn't know if that was enough.

"I still love Michael."

Jordan's eyes welled up again. "I know."

"I'll never not love Michael." I clung to those words, both vow and plea.

"I don't think anyone expects you not to."

"I don't know where we go from here. I don't know how to act around Easy. Should I tell him I know how he felt—feels—about me when I don't have an answer for how I feel about him? Should we ignore the whole thing and just focus on the baby for now?"

"Well, first off, and most importantly, you have to tell him about the baby."

"I know."

"And he's going to want to be involved, so you'll need to figure out a way to make it work for both of you. You'll need to figure out how you're going to include him and what sort of relationship you want to have with him."

"Yeah."

"You're right; I would wait to tell him until he gets back from Afghanistan. It's not a conversation you want to have in a letter or e-mail. And the guys have enough on their minds. Wait until he gets back, until he's safe, and then tell him about the baby. It's only a few more weeks."

"And the rest?"

"How do you feel about the rest?" Jordan asked.

"Confused. Really confused. I don't know what I want or what I'm capable of, especially with another fighter pilot after everything I went through with Michael. And I don't want to lead him on or complicate things for the baby. I owe it to both of them to do the right thing. It isn't about me anymore."

"Then take the time you need. Don't rush it. You have a few weeks until they're back. Use that time to think about the kind of relationship you want to have with Easy. Use that time to adjust to this new change in your life, to the baby coming."

I nodded.

"You have to stop beating yourself up about this. I understand why you feel guilty, why you're confused, but considering everything you've been through, you really need to cut yourself a break."

I'd taken so much pride in my marriage; thanks to the frequent moving, and our inability to have kids, most of my adult life had been defined by being a wife. And I'd honestly been okay with it. It had been my job to support my husband, to serve in my own way. I worried I was abandoning that responsibility now.

"Do you think Michael would . . ."

I couldn't finish the question, wasn't even sure why I was asking it. I'd been his *wife*, had known him better than anyone, yet I needed someone else to say it, needed to hear something to absolve me of the guilt I choked on.

Jordan squeezed my hand again. "He would want you to be happy more than anything. You were an amazing wife to him; he would want you to move on with your life. Isn't that what love is? Wanting the best for the other person?"

"Even if that person is Easy? They were friends. Brothers. He was there when Michael died."

My heart hurt as I remembered the guilt on Easy's face when he'd landed, when the squadron had returned from the TDY in Alaska minus Michael. I'd known then that he would have traded places with Michael if he could have, but now I really understood what that must have meant for him, imagined how much he'd struggled over the past year.

"Michael would have wanted a good guy for you. Someone who would treat you the way you deserve to be treated. That's definitely Easy."

I couldn't disagree.

"He's always been there for me."

Jordan smiled. "Yeah, he has. And he'll be there for you now."

God, I hoped so.

Jordan's smile grew. "I can't believe you're going to be a mom."

I laughed through the remaining tears. "I'm so happy. And absolutely terrified."

"I promise you—we all are. You'll be amazing. And Easy will be a great dad. Really."

The crazy thing was, even as I was scared to hope this would somehow turn out okay, I could see him with our baby. *Our baby.*

"So you're what, two months along?"

"Yeah."

"How do you feel?"

I made a face. "My boobs are ginormous. I'm struggling to button my jeans and every day at five o'clock I have an overwhelming desire to take a nap."

Jordan laughed. "That's pretty much it. Have you been to the doctor?"

"Yeah, I had an ultrasound. Since I miscarried last time, they wanted to check and see if everything was okay with the baby."

"And everything looks good?"

I nodded.

"Did you go by yourself?"

"Yeah."

"You could have told me. I would have been happy to go with you. You shouldn't have to do this alone."

"I know you would have. I just didn't know how to say it."

"Have you told anyone else?"

"No."

"You haven't told your family?"

"No. It's awkward enough to admit I'm pregnant." I stared down at the diamond bands on my left hand. "Even worse, I don't know what to say when they ask me who the father is." I swallowed. "I don't want people to think there was anything going on before . . . when Michael was alive. I guess I'm not ready to deal with the questions or the whispers. It's bad enough that I feel as if I've cheated on him, even though he's gone, but I don't want his parents—anyone—to think there was something between me and Easy while Michael was alive."

Compassion filled her voice. "No one who knows you would think that."

"Yeah, but it looks bad."

"You shouldn't worry. It isn't anyone's business. You know the truth. The people who love you know the truth."

"I'm still worried it's going to hurt people. His parents lost a grandchild and a son, and now I'm pregnant with someone else's child. And one of their son's closest friends is the father."

"Yeah and you lost a child. And a husband. You deserve to be happy, Dani." She reached out and squeezed my hand. "You have to let this stuff go, okay? Trust me, it's hard enough to go through a pregnancy. You don't need the added stress. The baby doesn't need the added stress. Take care of yourself and the baby. The rest of it will work itself out."

She was right.

"I will."

"When are you going to tell Easy?"

"When he gets back from the deployment, I guess."

"I would tell him right away. It isn't something you can keep a secret for very long since you're going to start showing soon, and he deserves to hear it from you. He's going to be hurt if you keep it from him for much longer."

"I know. I will."

"It'll be okay."

God, I hoped so.

IFTEEN

DANI

A strange sense of déjà vu filled me as I stepped out onto the flight line, as I looked up at the sky, listening for the first sign of the jets. How many times had I stood here waiting for Michael? Now I waited for Easy, the familiar nerves tangled up inside me, my heart pounding. Except this time there was one notable difference. My hand drifted down to my stomach, my fingers splayed over the tiny bump that had grown in the past few weeks.

I'd settled on a loose maxi dress that provided the best chance of hiding the bump, figuring the last thing Easy needed was to land and immediately be faced with pregnant me. I'd planned on easing him into it, but now that I was minutes away from seeing him, I was having serious doubts about the whole thing.

"Take a deep breath," Jordan murmured. "It'll be okay."

She reached out, her hand finding my free one and squeezing. Noah stood next to her, their daughter in his arms, a tiny set of headphones covering her ears from the impending roar.

"What if he doesn't want to see me?" I murmured.

"That won't happen."

"The last time he saw me I snuck out of his bed," I hissed.

"Yeah, but you sent him care packages and stuff."

"A package of cookies and some disgusting-looking granola bars aren't going to mean all is forgiven."

He loved me and I'd walked out on him after sex. "Guilty" didn't even begin to cover it. At the time, I'd thought it was just a sex thing for him; if I'd known he had feelings for me, I would've handled things so differently, been more careful with him.

"It's going to be fine," Jordan said.

"How do you know?"

"I know Easy, and I know how he feels about you. Trust me, it's going to be fine."

Of all the emotions hitting me right now, "fine" wasn't anywhere on—or near—the spectrum.

And then we heard it—the sound of jets screaming through the sky. We all looked up, a squadron of families waiting to welcome our loved ones home.

Noah had mentioned Easy would be leading the six-ship formation, and I found my gaze searching for that first plane as I'd done so many times before, a different pilot in the cockpit now.

Despite the nerves raging through me, the uncertainty of how this would all play out, I couldn't deny I was excited to see him, that I'd missed him in the months we'd spent apart.

Going through the pregnancy without him felt weird; he was going to be involved in this baby's life, and I wanted him to have that chance, to share this experience with me. Complications aside, he was and always would be one of my best friends.

You're about to meet your daddy, I told the baby silently, my hand settling on my stomach instinctively before I remembered I was in public and only Jordan knew I was pregnant. I let my hand fall to the side, my fingers curling in a ball. I missed the connection between us, had grown used to the reassurance of the baby beneath my palm, even if it was little bigger than the size of a passion fruit.

When I was pregnant before, I'd been so excited, so happy, and I'd felt the same instant connection to the life inside me. But at the same time, while there had been some fears in my mind, I'd been so sure I would sail through the pregnancy, that we'd bring home a baby from the hospital at the end of all of it that I hadn't held on as tightly as I did now.

Love was different once you'd known loss. Now I held on a bit tighter, knowing all too well how it felt to have your heart ripped away from you.

I focused on Easy's jet, my body tense as he began his descent. The moments before the wheels touched the ground were always the most nerve-racking, the feeling that you were almost out of the woods, but not quite. Takeoff and landing were typically the most dangerous— not that you could discount the moments in the air.

Michael had died from spatial disorientation on a routine sortie while the squadron was in Alaska. "Spatial D," as the pilots called it, happened often; most times it wasn't deadly. Michael had become disoriented in the jet, thinking his position was different than what it actually was, and by the time he'd realized his confusion and tried to correct it, it was too late. His plane had crashed into the cold ground.

My heart pounded as Easy got closer, closer, and then his wheels hit the concrete, the jet's nose bouncing in the air, once, twice, and I exhaled, the tension and worry releasing at the same time a new set of concerns entered my mind.

Maybe I should have given him some notice before showing up here after we hadn't spoken in months. What if he didn't want to see me? Jordan said he did, but what if she was wrong or had misjudged the situation—

Jordan leaned into me. "Stop freaking out," she whispered. "It's going to be fine."

"Let's start walking over to the canopy," Noah called out over the loud roar of the engines as the next planes in the formation began to land.

I nodded, following Noah and Jordan on shaky legs.

The closer we got to the jet, the more the nerves built. What the hell was I thinking? I should have waited an appropriate time before coming to see him. Should have given him a heads-up or something.

And then the jet taxied into view and I got my first sight of Easy, and the nausea in my stomach gave way to something else—

Flutters. So many freaking flutters.

He had his helmet and mask on, his visor down, the jet's canopy surrounding him. I couldn't see his eyes, but I knew the exact moment when he saw me, watched as he turned his head, his focus on me standing next to Jordan and Noah.

I waited for it, waited for him to lift his visor, to drop the mask, waited to see the expression in his eyes, not sure what I'd find there. We stared at each other across the flight line, Noah and Jordan fading away, until it was just Easy and me.

I held my breath as he pulled his mask off, as he flipped up his visor and stared right at me.

Damn.

He looked good.

Really good.

My heartbeat kicked up, my skin going hot, and not only from the warm Oklahoma sun beating down on me.

Smile. Please smile.

I bit down on my lip, unable to look away from the sight of Easy, safe, home, and then my heart cracked open a little bit as his mouth curved and he broke into a smile, the one I knew so well, the force of it blinding, his eyes on me the entire time.

My hand drifted down, settling on my stomach, the move more instinctive than anything else.

That's your daddy.

EASY

She looked beautiful. So beautiful. After three months without Dani, I drank in the sight of her.

Her hair was longer than I remembered, shining red-gold in the sunlight, her dress billowing around her. I smiled at her and she smiled back, and suddenly nothing else mattered.

I'd been gone for months, had flown my ass off, my life narrowed to what I saw on the HUD, to the targets I focused on as though my life depended on it—to the guys on the ground who did depend on it. And now, I wanted this moment. Her, glowing, home. I wanted to pull her into my arms and surround myself in her embrace.

I didn't take my gaze off her as I sat parked in the jet, under the sunshade, waiting for the crew chief to bring the ladder.

She didn't look away, either.

Finally the jet's canopy opened up, and I climbed down the ladder, each rung taking me closer and closer to her. Somewhere in my periphery I was aware of the crowd around us, Noah and Jordan, guys from the other squadron welcoming me home. And at the heart of it, Dani.

I walked toward her, her smile wobbling a bit as though she fought back tears, her feet carrying her toward me until she met me halfway, and we came together, her body sliding against mine, my arms wrapping around her waist.

She buried her head in the crook of my neck, my skin wet from the tears that fell from her eyes, and I rested my cheek on the top of her head, brushing my lips against her hair, inhaling her scent, not sure who was anchoring who.

I wanted to kiss her. Badly.

I didn't.

I didn't know how she felt about everything, and even as I tried to ignore them, we had an audience. Let them think we were friends, although after the way we clung to each other, I doubted anyone thought that anymore.

I didn't give a fuck.

This was everything. The dream. Coming home to the woman you loved after going to war.

Maybe it didn't look exactly as I'd imagined it, but it was enough.

Her body shook as she whispered words lost somewhere against my body, as her lips skated over my skin.

"Shh," I murmured. "It's okay."

I stroked her back, tracing the ridges of her spine, tightening my grip on her, and I knew—

I wouldn't ever let her go again. Friends or lovers, we would always be in each other's lives. There were some bonds that were forged when you needed them most, unshakable connections that spoke to a shared history, an understood pain.

She soothed my aching spots, and, God, I hoped I did the same for her.

We broke apart finally, a pink flush covering Dani's cheeks as I stared down into her eyes, as my gaze fell to her lips.

Fuck, I wanted to kiss her again.

I settled for reaching out and taking her hand, linking our fingers together, tugging her forward.

"Will you give me a ride home?" I asked, my voice raw.

I wanted a chance to talk to her in private, without the curious gazes of a bunch of fighter pilots.

Dani nodded, her focus on me, a flush still covering her cheeks. I could tell she was uncomfortable, that she'd shown more of herself than she was used to. For as much as she let her walls down with me, she still clung to the image of impenetrable-stoic-Dani. She was close to Jordan, Noah, Becca, Thor, but she kept her inner circle tight, didn't want anyone to see anything she perceived as weakness, including her worry and grief.

I squeezed her hand. "We can get out of here soon. I need to take care of a few things first."

"Okay. I'll wait with Jordan and Noah. Thor's supposed to land soon, right?"

"Yeah." I checked my watch. "In about thirty minutes."

"Becca should be getting here then. I'll wait with them until you're ready."

"Okay. I'll be quick."

I hesitated. I needed to let go of her hand, needed to make my way into the squadron and take care of business so I could head home, but I didn't want to leave her, not even for a moment.

I took a step forward, hooking my free arm around her neck, pulling her toward me, burying my face in her hair again.

"It's so good to see you," I whispered. "I wasn't sure if you would be here; I was worried you would have left."

Worried I'd lost you forever.

I pulled back, releasing her slowly, staring into her green eyes, fighting the urge to lay myself at her feet.

Her gaze clouded and she swallowed, her tongue darting out to lick her bottom lip.

"I missed you, too." Her voice lowered. "You're probably tired, but can we talk later?"

My heart thudded at the words—"Can we talk later?"—pretty sure they'd never brought anything good in all of human history. Hell, I'd delivered them more times than I could count, usually followed by "It's not you, it's me" or something equally cliché. I tried to search her gaze, wondering if I'd see regret there, but was greeted by worry instead.

I nodded, leaning forward and tucking a stray hair behind her ear.

"Yeah. We should."

This time I did take a step away from her, facing the

other guys, exchanging quick hugs, ignoring the darting glances, the knowing looks.

When I got to Jordan, I expected to see the same burning curiosity stamped on her face, but all I found was a smile playing at her lips.

"Welcome home, Easy."

"Thanks."

My gaze settled on my goddaughter, looking adorable in a T-shirt with an American flag on it, red jeans, and a headset blocking her ears from the loud jet noise. She'd grown so much since I'd seen her last, and it was crazy to realize how much I'd missed since I left. I thought about all the guys who had families at home, who'd spent three months away from their kids. How had Noah done it when he was in Korea?

We walked toward the squadron en masse. The next cell of jets—Thor's cell—wouldn't land for a while. Someone had brought pizza and beer to the squadron, and Noah passed me a cold bottle.

God, I'd missed this.

When you were downrange, as we called it, you tried not to focus on what you were missing back home, on the people you ached to see, the life you'd seemingly pressed pause on. When you went to war, you splintered yourself into two—part of you so focused on the mission that eclipsed all else, the other part locked away, the part that felt, that missed, that loved. Without that clear boundary, the schism running through you, you ended up covered in hairline cracks until you eventually crumbled to dust.

I lost sight of Dani in the crowd as people greeted me, kids running around and screaming, the squadron descending into chaos. I managed to get through the greetings pretty quickly, dropping off my gear, tying up last-minute errands. When I walked back into the bar, I glanced through the crowd, searching for Dani—

I froze.

She stood near the bar, a smile playing at her lips, deep in conversation with Jordan and Becca. She leaned forward, laughing at something they both said, her hands gesturing widely as she made her point, her hair glinting in the sunlight. I stood there, watching her, the memory of the first time I saw her, the moment when I'd fallen in love with her, not even understanding what that meant. I hadn't understood then that the sliver of what I'd felt that day would lodge itself under my skin, shrapnel turned to a scar, infecting my bloodstream, running through my veins, until she became part of me, inextricably linked, her pain mine, the smile on her face answered in my heart.

I remembered the moment when she'd turned and looked at Joker, and suddenly I was catapulted back in time, watching a car crash in front of me, unable to look away as I realized what I'd instinctively considered mine would never be mine at all.

But this time, it was different.

This time she turned her head and our gazes locked, and I watched, unable to speak as she said good-bye to Jordan and Becca and began walking toward me.

"Are you ready to go home?" she asked when she was right in front of me, and I nodded, my throat and heart suddenly so fucking full.

She might not have realized it, but I'd been home ever since I'd stepped off that ladder and taken her into my arms.

She was my home.

DANI

Easy stared out the window as I drove him home, his gaze hidden by gold-framed aviators. I snuck glances in his direction, studying his profile, attempting to gauge his mood, trying to predict his reaction to the bomb I was about to drop on him.

He'd seemed happy to see me when he landed, and as awkward as I'd feared things would be between us, it hadn't been awkward at all. Rather, it had been the most natural thing in the world to wrap my arms around him and welcome him home.

He looked older now, worn, as though the months downrange had taken a toll on him. Michael used to come home like that, the weight of the world on his shoulders, and I'd always been the one to ease him back into normal life, to put a smile on his face and erase the lines of worry created by the responsibility of caring for the lives of an entire squadron and his determination to bring them all home alive. With Easy it wasn't quite the same, and yet

I could tell the months deployed had chipped away at him. I couldn't resist the urge to take care of him, even as I was about to add a whole other host of worries to his plate.

We stopped at a red light, and I tilted my head to the side—

Easy stared back at me.

"You keep looking at me," he commented, his voice a low drawl.

His tone was huskier, lazier, a hint of the Easy he'd been with every single woman but me. Whatever question still lingered in my mind of whether or not the sex had changed things between us was answered by the purr behind his words and the accompanying flash of heat.

He moved slowly, as though he was stripping the clothes from my skin, cataloging all the changes that had taken place in his absence. Could he tell my breasts were bigger, my hips a bit wider? Would he notice the barely there bump beneath my dress?

I tore my gaze away.

The light changed and I exhaled, trying to release some of the pressure pushing at me, turning my attention to the drive and not the way Easy's gaze had lingered over me when we were stopped, obscured by those dark sunglasses yet impossible to miss.

"You're quiet," he commented, reaching out and resting his arm on the headrest behind me.

I wasn't sure if he meant it that way or if it was merely a casual gesture, but it seemed like a move—one that, combined with the tremors from his voice, throbbed like a pulse between my legs, my body and mind at odds with each other.

I leaned forward, turning the A/C up, simultaneously

fighting the urge to lower the window and let some of the tension swirling between us out of the car. I wanted to move away from his arm, wanted to lean into his touch, wanted his fingers to reach out and stroke my hair.

Before I'd looked at Easy as anything other than a friend, I'd wondered what it would be like to be one of the women he pursued. I hadn't wanted him then, but I'd had a sort of morbid fascination with the stories I'd heard, with his reputation of having any woman he wanted. The face was a good start, the body even better, but what I hadn't understood was how he could look at a woman and seduce her without even saying a word, and when he did speak—

I swallowed, images of that night coming back to me. Yeah, Easy definitely had moves.

"I don't know what to say," I admitted, my fingers tightening around the steering wheel.

"How have you been?" he asked.

"Good."

Any answer I could have offered felt like a lie given the big secret between us. I almost blurted it out then and there, almost said the word "pregnant," but we were driving in the car, and I wasn't sure there would ever be a time when I wanted to have this conversation. I wished we could fast-forward through all the potential awkwardness and get to the point where everything magically worked out.

"Did you miss me?"

He asked the question casually, his voice teasing, even, but I heard the ache between those words—*Easy's in love with you*—and while I didn't want to lead him on, I didn't have it in me to be glib.

"Yes."

The word escaped in a whisper, the weight of it rocking me a bit. I'd missed the friendship we'd developed, but if I were really, really honest with myself, I'd admit I missed the rest of it, too. I'd had a taste of something so good it had shaken my foundation, and even though it had terrified me, a piece of me—a big piece—wanted to come back for seconds.

"I missed you, too."

My heart thudded as he spoke, as I read between the lines, recognizing the thread that ran through everything he'd ever said to me, all the love that had always been there pushing to get out.

He shifted, and I turned my attention away from the road in time to see him place his hand on my arm, moving lower—

I swallowed, forcing the words out. "We need to talk."

He froze, his fingers on my elbow. Slowly, one by one, he peeled them from my skin, erasing his touch.

"You regret what happened between us."

He delivered the words in a flat, unemotional tone, like a shield he'd thrown up to push me away.

"I—" I tried to come up with the right words, had spent the months apart searching for an answer to whatever questions he would throw my way and coming up short every time. I didn't regret it—not with the baby on the way, at least. And if there hadn't been a baby, if it was merely the two of us and one amazing night between us—well, I wasn't sure what my answer would be then, either. Maybe if he didn't love me we could have continued on. If it really had only been sex, things would be different. But it wasn't just sex, and it wasn't just my own fear that I would hurt him.

I wanted no part of his love, had no desire to be entangled in another situation where I could get hurt. He was a fighter pilot first. There would be deployments and nights spent alone. Birthdays, holidays missed. And always, there would be that lump of fear in my throat, that knot in my stomach, the one that had been on a constant low level with Michael and now had reached a paralyzing degree. I'd been through enough loss to last a lifetime, and I had no desire to add to my tally.

"It's complicated," I finally answered. It was a cop-out, but I had little else to give. "I want to talk about things, about what happened. We need to talk about it."

"So talk." His tone gentled, somewhere between the old Easy who'd always treated me with kid gloves, and this new Easy I couldn't quite get a handle on. "Tell me what's on your mind."

I'd always been able to talk to him about anything; the core of our friendship had revolved around a level of trust I didn't have with many people. He'd always been there for me, and it was unfair of me to think he'd bolt now. I owed him the truth, despite how nervous it made me.

I turned into a strip-mall parking lot, my heart pounding. Of all the ways I'd imagined telling Easy I was pregnant, it hadn't been this. I pulled into an empty spot, putting the car in park and turning the key in the ignition until the engine died. I took a deep breath, and then I shifted in my seat so we faced each other.

I reached out, my fingers grasping the metal frames of his aviators and sliding them off his face, my knuckles brushing against his cheekbones. He sat there like a statue, the only shift in his appearance a slight widening of his eyes. I needed the barrier between us down, needed to see his reaction, to gauge how he really felt when I told him about the baby.

"I need to tell you something."

Worry flickered in his eyes. "Are you okay?"

I nodded, took a deep breath, and let it all out.

"I'm pregnant."

EASY

Pregnant?

For a moment I wondered if I was having an out-of-body experience, if this was a dream I would wake from. I could have sworn she said she was pregnant, but the word eluded me, even as I reached out and tried to hold on to it.

"Pregnant?"

She bit down on her lip and nodded again. "Yeah."

I couldn't—

Pregnant?

"It's yours," she added, a thread of—fear, worry, emotion, regret?—my stomach clenched—entering her voice.

Pregnant?

I tried to formulate a response, my brain a series of short-circuiting emotions. That night—the sex between us—it had been so unexpected, so far out of the realm of anything I'd ever imagined, that stupidly, irresponsibly, I hadn't even considered protection. That was a one-off for me, but I hadn't had sex after my last regular clean exam and in the moment, Dani getting pregnant had been the furthest thing from my mind. After, I had thought about it, but I hadn't wanted to pick at what was obviously a sensitive subject for Dani; I'd figured with how hard it had been for her to get pregnant with Joker—

Oh fuck. Joker.

I didn't know how to describe feeling like the worst person on earth at the exact moment you got one of the greatest gifts you'd ever received. Actually, I did.

I was a thief. A thief who'd stolen his best friend's dream.

"I—" I ran a hand through my hair, realizing I was shaking. I tried again to find the right words, to say something, but each time I thought I had what I wanted to say the words simply came up short, everything inside me inadequate in the face of the child we'd made.

We were going to have a baby. *Dani* was going to have a baby.

Our baby.

The memory of holding her in the hospital while she cried after the doctors told her she'd miscarried hit me and I felt a pang of fear unlike anything I'd ever experienced before. Was this pregnancy safe? Was she at a higher risk of miscarrying?

"Do you feel okay?" I blurted out.

She blinked. "Umm, yeah. Tired, but that's supposed to be normal."

"Okay. Good. And you're healthy? Have you been to a doctor? Is the baby okay?"

She reached out and squeezed my hand. "I have. I'm doing well and the baby's great."

I racked my brain for anything I could think of that was pregnancy-related, only to discover unsurprisingly, my knowledge was sparse. What did Noah tell me about Jordan?

"Have you, uh, been getting sick?"

"Like morning sickness?"

I nodded.

Her eyes widened. "You want to talk about morning sickness?"

I released her, running my hands through my hair.

No, I didn't want to talk about morning sickness, but right now morning sickness seemed to be the safest topic of all the ones we could choose.

I closed my eyes, my head in my hands, trying to get my bearings. Did this mean she wanted to try having a relationship? Did she want me to be involved in the baby's life? I couldn't imagine not being there, didn't want to miss out on the moments little and big—our child's first steps, watching cartoons on the couch together on Saturday mornings, teaching the kid how to throw a football, lifting them up into the seat of the jet—

We were having a baby.

I looked at Dani, really looked at her, imagining her body changing, seeing her swell with my child. The image changed and I saw our baby on her lap . . .

I'd thought I loved her before, hadn't been able to imagine loving her more than I already did, but that love paled in comparison to how I felt about her now, to how I felt about our child—

She took another deep breath. "Look, you probably never saw yourself here, and if you don't want to do this, if you don't want to have kids, I'm fine with doing it on my own. I want this baby. So much. I can be a single parent, and still give our child an amazing life. I don't want you to feel pressured or resent me—"

Wait. She thought I wasn't happy?

I was shocked, but I was definitely happy.

"I do. Want to have kids. Always have."

Especially with you. I want to have a baby with you more than I've ever wanted anything in my entire life.

"I'm sorry." I took a deep breath. "I just— I'm just trying to catch up. But yes, I want to be involved in the baby's life. Absolutely. Of course."

Did she really think I was an asshole who would abandon his child? Abandon her?

"You don't have to say that," she mumbled, twisting the diamonds around her finger, refusing to meet my gaze.

My heart clenched at the sight of Joker's rings on her finger.

"I want to be there for you and the baby. I can't promise I'll get everything right at first—I'm a little out of my depth here—but I'll get it. What do you need? What can I do to help?" My voice cracked. "How are we going to do this?"

The fingers on her ring stilled. "We're going to have to figure it out as we go along."

She was right, but for the first time in my life I didn't want to take things as they came, had no idea how to even do that. I knew nothing about kids, had no clue how to be a father or a husband or any of that shit. Hell, I'd barely been a boyfriend. Did she want that? Did she want us to be a family? I couldn't get a read on her, and if anything, the rings on her finger seemed to answer the question for me.

"What do you want?"

I struggled to push the words out, to pretend I merely wanted her answer when really what I wanted more than anything was to hear our night together had meant something to her, that this baby meant something to her because it was *ours*, that I meant something to her, that we had a future together.

She hesitated for a beat. "I want to do the best thing for this baby."

"Me, too."

I also wanted to do the best thing for her, wanted to make sure she was happy, that she had nothing to worry about. I wanted to take her into my arms and make love to her, wanted to place my palm against her stomach over the baby we'd made, wanted to fall asleep with my arm around her, her body tucked into the curve of mine. I wanted a lifetime of things I worried would never come to be.

"The best thing right now is for us to figure out how we're going to co-parent, how we're going to raise this baby." Dani's cheeks turned pink. "What happened between us . . ." She trailed off. "I think we should just be friends for now."

Friends.

How would we raise a baby as just friends? Would she meet some guy one day and would he end up being involved in my child's life? What if he was an asshole? Dani wasn't likely to pick a jerk, but still.

I nodded as though I agreed with her, like her words didn't cause an ache inside me, as if I hadn't spent the last three months imagining the feel of her beneath me, wishing there could be more with her, that I would come home to an announcement that she'd changed her mind and we had a chance together.

My throat was drier than the fucking Sahara as I forced myself to answer. "Okay."

The look of relief that flashed in her eyes was another punch to the gut.

"I have a doctor's appointment coming up. It's a big one—we can find out the sex of the baby. Do you want to be there?"

The dryness was immediately replaced by the boulder

that rolled in, and suddenly I worried I was going to lose my shit. In the span of ten minutes I'd gone from a single guy to a guy with a baby on the way, and now this baby was going to become a boy or a girl, shift from abstract concept to flesh-and-blood child, and fuck, there were still so many questions swirling around in my head, so many unknowns.

"Yeah. I want to be there."

Dani nodded, and I didn't miss the relief in her voice. "I'll text you the appointment details."

"Thanks."

I wanted to be at all her appointments, didn't want to miss a moment in this child's life, especially in the wake of all the moments I'd already missed in her pregnancy.

She looked down at the floor and I racked my brain to come up with something to say, a million questions running through my mind. I needed to get one of those books on having kids. Maybe Noah had one—hell, I probably needed to talk to him and ask him all the things I had no clue about. I wanted to be there for Dani and the baby, wanted her to know I was someone she could count on, but she couldn't lean on me when I had no clue what I was doing.

She hesitated again. "We're going to be okay, right? As parents?"

"Of course," I answered with way more confidence than I actually possessed.

Dani I wasn't worried about. My own skills were the ones I questioned—not my resolve, but random things like whether or not I'd know how to hold the kid the right way, and whether I'd be able to change a diaper, and what I was supposed to feed it. Weren't they supposed to eat liquids first or something?

"Do you promise that whatever happens, we'll always be a team?" Dani asked, tearing me away from my trip down the rabbit hole. She bit her lip. "Like, we won't end up in family court arguing about custody or something?"

Surprise filled me. "Is that something you're worried about?"

That had never even entered my mind. Should I get an attorney? Did she have one?

"No. Yes. I don't know." The strain in her voice tugged at my heart. "It's so complicated. And I'm sorry I didn't tell you earlier; I didn't want to stress you out when you were deployed."

I nodded. "I'm not angry with you. And if it's okay with you, we can sort this stuff out on our own. I trust you."

Tears welled up in her eyes. "I trust you, too."

"Then we have nothing to worry about."

"Are you scared?" she asked.

"Yeah. I think that's natural, too."

She sighed. "Me, too."

I reached between us, taking her hand, linking our fingers together, bringing them to my mouth, my lips brushing over her knuckles.

"I promise you, no matter what, we'll give this baby a good life. You're going to be an amazing mom, and I have a lot to learn, but I'm going to spend every day of my life working on being a great dad.

"Things are complicated; this isn't the way you envisioned yourself having a baby. But I promise you—we'll make this work. I don't want you to worry about anything other than staying healthy and taking care of our kid."

"Thank you," Dani whispered, tears sliding down her cheeks.

"Hey." I released her hand, swiping the tears away with my thumbs. "No more crying. We got this, okay?"

She nodded, her voice shaky. "Okay."

"Are you getting tired? Do you want to take me home and get some rest?"

It was almost eight now, and I didn't want her driving at night if she was tired. If I could have kept her and the baby in a protective bubble, I would have.

My stomach clenched as I remembered that day in the hospital—

I couldn't bear losing this baby, too.

"Yeah, if you don't mind, I might go home and go to bed. It's been a long day." She offered me a weak smile. "Do you want to come over soon? Tomorrow, maybe? I'll totally understand if you'd rather take a few days to get acclimated to being back."

"Tomorrow sounds perfect."

Dani dropped me off at my house and I paused to set my bags down in the living room before jumping into my car and heading over to Noah's. Dani had mentioned Jordan knew about the baby, so the cat was out of the bag, so to speak. Besides, he was my oldest and closest friend, and considering he'd just been through a pregnancy with Jordan, he'd understand these feelings inside me better than anyone. I sent him a quick text before I left the house to let him know I was coming over, and then I was on my way, my conversation with Dani playing on a loop the whole drive.

Noah met me at the front door with a beer, and we both headed to his back deck.

"So how does it feel to be back?"

There was no time to beat around the bush; I'd already lost three months.

"Dani's pregnant."

"Excuse me?"

He gawked at me, speechless.

"She's pregnant," I repeated, taking a long pull of the beer.

Noah's face was ashen. "Fuck, man. I'm sorry. I had no idea. Who's the father?"

I swallowed, choking on the beer, my body shaking as I coughed.

Shit.

I'd definitely violated some unwritten bro code here, and if anyone was going to call me on it, it would be Noah.

I wiped at my mouth, my heart pounding as I gave him the rest of it.

"The baby's mine."

I still couldn't quite get used to saying it, thinking it, even as a rush of pride hit me every single time I savored those words—pride and shame vying for the lead until pride simply took over and smoked the regret by a mile.

Noah jerked back, shock in his gaze. "What? When? How?"

"Seriously?"

"You know what I mean," he sputtered.

I did, and as much as I wanted to talk about the baby, I didn't want to talk about me and Dani. Not that there even really was a "me and Dani." In the past we'd shared about women, but this was different.

"Let's say it happened, and leave it at that."

He looked at me as if I'd lost my mind. "You've been in love with her for years, and you drop this bomb, and I'm supposed to act like it's no big deal?"

"No, I'm not saying it isn't a big deal; I just don't want to talk about it. It's complicated. Really fucking complicated. We aren't in a relationship, and she doesn't know how I feel about her, and I don't want her to know."

"Why?"

"Because she's pregnant with my child and she's still wearing Joker's rings on her finger. Because she already lost a baby once, and she doesn't need to be worrying about this shit. I don't want her to focus on anything but our baby right now, and I really don't want her stressed or more afraid than she already is. I'm worried if I tell her, things are going to become uncomfortable between us really quickly. She needs someone she can lean on, and I want her to know she can lean on me, that I'll be there for her no matter what."

"And you don't think it would be easier to do if she actually knew how you felt about her? That you *love* her?"

"No. Telling her I have feelings for her would be one of the most selfish things I could do. This isn't about me; it's about our baby and it's about Dani. She made it pretty clear she didn't want to complicate things between us, that her focus right now is our child, and I'm going to respect that. I love her, and she's the mother of my child, and if doing the right thing means I stand by her that's what I'm going to do. I don't need to be someone in her life in order for her to be the most important person in mine. We're having a baby together. We'll always be connected."

Noah shook his head.

"What?"

"I can't decide if that's the most romantic fucking thing I've ever heard or if you're an idiot."

I flipped him off for old times' sake.

"Dude, seriously—like I didn't watch you make an ass of yourself with Jordan."

He returned the gesture. "Yeah, but I got the girl."

I took another swig of beer, staring out at the darkening sky. "And I guess right now that seems less important to me than what Dani needs."

Silence filled the space around us until finally Noah spoke.

"And what about you? What do you need? What about sex? Are you telling me you're going to abstain from now on? That you're going to have a platonic relationship with her and save yourself?"

He would probably die if he realized how long it had been for me; if you took out the night with Dani, and didn't count the times I got myself off to the memory of that night with Dani, I was practically abstinent.

"This shit is going to blow up," Noah continued. "There's no way she isn't going to figure out what you feel for her. You don't think she at least suspects it considering the two of you had sex?"

"I don't know what she thinks, just that we're going to have a kid, and I need to figure out how to be a dad." I shot him a pointed look. "I came here for parenting advice, not for you to bust my balls about how I'm fucking up things with Dani."

"Sorry."

I shook my head, some of the anger filtering out of me. I hadn't meant to lose my shit with Noah, but this had been bottled up inside me since Dani told me about the baby, and as hard as I'd tried to keep it away from her, I needed to let loose with someone I trusted.

"No, I'm sorry. This thing has fucked me up a bit, and I'm doing my best to wrap my head around it, but—"

"It's a lot."

"Yeah." I took another gulp of beer, wishing it were something stronger. "I'm happy about the baby, obviously. The idea of having a child . . . with Dani . . ." I swallowed, my chest suddenly tight, a stinging sensation behind my eyes. I cleared my throat. "I don't know what she wants, though. Not about us, but life. If her house sells, is she planning to leave Oklahoma? How are we going to raise a kid together if we're living in different places? What if the Air Force sends me overseas for my next assignment? I don't want to end up seeing my kid a couple times a year." The pressure got tighter. "What if she meets some guy? What if she remarries?"

"You need to talk to her about it, then. I get that you're still processing everything, and you don't want to upset her or stress her out, but you guys are going to need to figure out a custody plan. You're going to have to figure out how to make things work so you give your kid a stable life. Trust me, as soon as the baby's here, you aren't going to want to be away from it." His voice turned rough. "It was horrible being in Korea without Jordan and Julie. The whole time I wanted to be here, with them; I felt like I was missing out on everything. You don't want to miss out on your kid's life."

"Yeah."

It was hard enough for the married guys—they spent more time away than home, missed bedtimes and birthdays in the face of twelve-hour workdays and deployments. I'd seen pilot after pilot get out of active duty because it wasn't conducive to married life. And the divorced guys?

I'd watched guys break down in the bar because they hadn't seen their kids for months; shared custody arrangements were a bitch with our lifestyle. I didn't want to be one of those guys—marginalized in my own kid's life.

I was silent for a beat, staring at the dark sky, trying to get my bearings, to readjust to the notion that suddenly my life looked a hell of a lot different from anything I'd ever imagined. I couldn't deny I'd spent a good chunk of my life doing whatever the hell I wanted, never having to worry about anyone else. But now there was a baby who would depend on me, and then there was Dani . . .

"I can do this, right? I'm not going to fuck up and ruin the kid for life or something?"

I mean, really, what the hell did I know about being a dad? I was a fighter pilot; "fuck" was pretty much a noun, adjective, and verb in my vocabulary and I used it liberally. What if the kid was fluent in cursing by the time they hit kindergarten? What if they hated me because I missed out on all the important moments in their lives? What if Dani felt like I let her and our kid down?

Sympathy and understanding shone in Noah's gaze as he slapped me on the back, his voice gruff. "You'll be fine."

"Were you—?"

"Utterly terrified?" Noah finished for me.

I nodded.

"Yeah, that comes with the territory. When Jordan told me she was pregnant, I was thrilled, but scared, too. I worried about her getting good medical care, about us being apart when we decided for her to come back to the U.S., worried I'd miss the baby's birth, that I'd do a shit job at being a birth coach. And the thing is, Jordan was scared, too. It helped to talk about things, to figure it out together. I'm sure Dani's worried about how everything's going to come together, and the best thing you can do for the both of you is to talk this shit out."

"You're right. I didn't—" I ran my free hand through my hair, frustration coursing through me. "Maybe we should have talked about it more when she told me. I didn't know what to say, and more than anything, I didn't want to say the wrong thing."

"Don't be too hard on yourself. She dropped a pretty big bomb on you, and it's understandable for it to take a moment for you to adjust. Take today to deal with it. Tomorrow go see her and start figuring out how you're going to make this work."

"Yeah."

I drained the bottle of beer, my mind still reeling from how much our lives were about to change.

Noah shook his head, a wry smile on his face. "I can't believe you're going to be a dad. I'm happy for you, man. It's complicated, but you're going to be great. So will she."

I exhaled, not realizing until now how much I'd needed to hear those words.

"Thanks. That means a lot. The whole situation . . ." My fingers tightened around the bottle. "It's weird. I'm happy about the baby, but at the same time I feel guilty for being happy, and then I feel guilty for how fucked up I am about the whole thing." I swallowed. "He wanted a kid with Dani so badly."

His voice turned solemn. "I know. I get the guilt—imagine how Dani feels."

I had. The part of me that had pretty solidly fallen out of fucks to give was ready to tell anyone who passed judgment on us where they could shove it. But the other part of me that had respected Joker still struggled with feeling like I'd somehow dishonored his memory. And because it mattered so much to Dani, it mattered to me. At the same time, I didn't want our kid to be something we were ashamed of, or a secret to be hidden away. I was proud, so fucking proud, and there was no way I wanted my son or daughter to think for one moment I didn't love them.

I set my bottle down on the deck railing, sitting down on the wood steps leading to the yard.

"I know how hard this is for Dani. She's not ready to tell people; she's worried about what they'll think, about how it looks."

"Are you worried about that?"

"No. It's different for her. She was his wife—the face of his death, the woman who spoke at the podium, who they mentioned on the news. She feels a responsibility to his memory, as if she's his legacy or something, as though he's alive in her. I'm worried she thinks she let him down, that she hasn't done a good job of keeping him alive."

My voice cracked. "I get it, because I know how she is, but at the same time, I hate that she's living her life for someone else, that she's a living memorial to Joker. She loved him and it doesn't bother me; I want her to always have that memory, but I wish she could let go for a bit so she could take care of herself more. He loved her so much. He wouldn't want her to spend the rest of her life in mourning; he'd want her to live."

"Have you tried telling her that?"

I shook my head. "I don't know how to talk about Joker with her now. We were friends before we slept together, but now I feel like we've complicated everything between us."

"What do you want? Take Dani out of the equation;

forget about your guilt with Joker. Don't worry about what you think is best for everyone else or what you think you should want. What do *you* want?"

It was so simple, and so utterly complicated at the same time.

"Dani. I want Dani. I want us to be a family. I want her to be my wife."

"Then stop being such a fucking pussy and make it happen."

I shot him a wry look. "Just like that?"

"Just like that. I've never known you to not go after what you want. None of this would have happened if she wasn't attracted to you. I never pushed it before because I didn't think she felt that way about you. But clearly she does. And you guys were already best friends. That's a pretty good start to a relationship. You'll be good for her; you can make her happy. Hell, you already have. Prove it to her."

$\mathcal{S}$EVENTEEN

EASY

I slept for a few hours after I left Noah's and then I was up, scouring the books I'd borrowed from Jordan.

An hour into it, I was even more confused than I had been. Who knew kids were this complex? I'd figured I had to work on feeding it and keeping it alive, making sure it was happy and didn't turn into an asshole. But no. There was all this stuff about parenting styles and sleep training, and if I'd thought learning to fly the F-16 was tough, this was fucking unreal.

I grabbed my cell, dialing Dani's number, remembering my conversation with Noah last night. I wasn't going to push, had meant what I said about not putting pressure on Dani, but I fully intended to be there for her, to show her we could be more than friends, to prove I was the right man for her and the baby.

She answered the phone right away.

"So are we going to be authoritarian or indulgent parents?" I asked her.

Laughter filled the line.

"You're reading parenting books."

"I am, although I gotta admit I don't know if they're making any of this clearer. Did you know this sleep training thing was such a big deal?"

"I'd like to say yes and pretend I did, but honestly, no, not really. Where did you get the books?"

"I borrowed them from Noah and Jordan."

"So you told him?"

"Yeah, I did. He didn't know; I guess Jordan never mentioned it to him."

"How did he handle the news?" Dani asked, worry in her voice.

"He was surprised, but supportive. Really supportive. He's happy for us, and he's excited to play Uncle Noah."

"Good." She exhaled. "I was worried."

"I know, but I promise it'll be okay. Do you trust me?"

"Yeah."

"Then don't worry."

Silence filled the line.

"Dani?"

"I'm nodding."

I grinned. "Good. So on this parenting thing—can't we put the kid to bed when it's tired?"

"You would think, right? Apparently it needs sleep training and a schedule."

"And some magic beans?"

She laughed.

"So I'm not the only one totally baffled by this?"

"Nope."

"Thank you. I was beginning to think there was something wrong with me," I teased. "So how are you feeling?"

"Good." I heard the sound of sheets rustling on the other end of the line. "Just waking up."

God, the mental image of her in bed had my dick twitching. I swallowed, fighting the rush of arousal and the urge to reach down and fist my cock.

"Did you sleep okay?" I croaked, stifling a groan.

"Yeah, I did. Before I was pregnant I could get by on five hours of sleep, but now I have to have eight or I'm a mess the next day."

"What do you have planned for the weekend?" I asked, trying to get my mind out of the gutter.

"Not much. Taking it easy. I'm starting to get to the point where I want to look at baby stuff, but at the same time I'm a little wary to start this early."

I couldn't blame her after the last time she'd been pregnant and the miscarriage she'd suffered. She'd said everything was fine with the pregnancy, but I'd definitely feel better about it after going to her doctor's appointment with her.

"Can I come over today? To hang out? Maybe talk a bit."

A pause filled the other end of the line. "I'd like that."

"Awesome. Is there anything you want me to bring over? Pickles? Ice cream? Sprinkle donuts?"

She laughed. "Have you been reading up on pregnancy cravings?"

"Yeah, maybe a little bit. Seriously, though, is there anything you want?"

"Barbecue chips."

I grinned at how quickly she answered me and the eagerness in her voice.

"Done. Anything else?"

"No, that's it. I'll let you know if I come up with anything else. Thanks."

"No problem. See you in a bit."

I hung up the phone with Dani, already reassured. I'd meant what I told Noah—I wanted this to work between us. The best way to make that happen was to do everything I could to make Dani happy and comfortable, to take care of her and the baby. Food runs were the easiest thing in the world.

I jumped in the shower and got dressed in record time, already excited over the prospect of seeing her again. I'd tried not to dwell on how much I missed her while I was deployed, worried if I did the three months would simply be unbearable, but now I was back and she was in my life, and I wanted to savor every moment together.

I left the house and drove to the closest grocery store, the car windows rolled down, rock music blaring. I'd missed driving when I was downrange, missed the freedom of getting into my car and going wherever I wanted, missed having a Saturday to myself. As much as I loved to fly, it was nice to not have a mission ahead of me, to sit back and enjoy the fresh air.

I bought Dani a couple bags of barbecue chips, not sure which was her favorite, and then I was back on the road, heading to her place. Ten minutes later I'd parked in her driveway and stood on her doorstep, chips in hand.

Dani answered with a smile, her gaze drifting to the shopping bags in my hand. "My hero."

I laughed, leaning forward and giving her a hug, inhaling the familiar scent of her, savoring the soft curves.

"Glad I could help."

She stood back, gesturing for me to cross over the threshold. She shut the door behind me and led me into the living room. I sat down on the couch while she went to the kitchen and put the chips away, my gaze running over the room, cataloging all the changes since I'd been here last.

"It looks good."

She sighed, sitting down next to me. "Thanks. I've done two price drops in the last three months, and it's still sitting here. I'm beginning to wonder if it'll ever sell."

"I'm sorry. The market's tough right now."

"Yeah, it is. It makes it harder to decide what I want to do. I was hoping to at least have an idea where I'd be living and have a chance to get settled before the baby came. I don't want to be nine months pregnant and in the middle of a move or something."

My stomach clenched at the idea of her and our baby moving. It was a distinct possibility, but I'd hoped we could come up with a better solution. I needed to put my "dream sheet" in and give the Air Force my list of assignment preferences soon, was due to PCS to a new base in ten months or so. Sometimes—rarely—you got the assignment you wanted. More often than not, you were shocked by where you ended up. Right now, making sure they didn't send me overseas seemed like the top priority. I had no clue if Dani's pregnancy would give me any options, but I'd do the best I could to see if they would accommodate a domestic PCS. But for now—

"You could always stay with me. I have an extra guest room and bathroom, so there's plenty of room. I want to help however I can."

She hesitated for a beat. "Thank you; it does help. It's nice to know I'm not going through this on my own."

"You're not. We should probably talk about this stuff.

It's complicated, but it would help us both to figure out what comes next."

"Agreed."

"At some point are you going to set up a nursery here?"

She nodded. "Maybe in the next few months? I guess if the house hasn't sold by then I'll hit pause on the whole thing and plan on staying until the baby's a few months old. Maybe the market will be better by then."

"That's a good plan. I can help you with the nursery if you want. Paint, that sort of thing."

"If it's a girl, I want to put a chandelier up. Maybe have a mural painted on her wall—a castle or a forest or something." Her cheeks flushed. "It's silly to make such a big change for a temporary room, but I saw these pictures online and they looked like something out of a fairy tale. If we have a boy, I saw these really cool vintage children's book covers that you can frame. I thought that could be fun."

Her words made me feel like part of the process, and I was no longer on the outside looking in.

"Those are great ideas." I cleared my throat. "So when's this doctor's appointment?"

"To find out the gender?"

"Yeah."

"In a little over two weeks. On the thirtieth at two. Does that work for you?"

"I'll be there. Can I pick you up and take you?"

She smiled. "I'd like that. Thanks."

"I can't wait to find out if we're having a boy or girl," I confessed.

Last night, I'd dreamed we had a daughter. She'd been so tiny, and she'd fit so perfectly in my arms. I'd been terrified to hold her, but Dani had stood next to me, her hand on my arm, and suddenly it was completely natural and so fucking *right*.

"Me, either. I've been dying to find out what we're having so I can start coming up with names, making plans . . ." Her voice trailed off. "*We* can start coming up with names," she corrected.

God, I felt that, too. I hadn't even thought about names, had figured that was more her arena than mine. I didn't want to overstep, but at the same time, I wanted to be a hands-on dad.

"It's cool. As long as you don't name the kid something horrible, I'm good."

"Define 'horrible'?"

I considered it for a moment. "No colors. Or fruit. And honestly, I'm probably not big on place names, either."

She grinned. "So I guess 'Kiwi' is out?"

"I'm going to pray you're joking."

"You'll never know, now will you?" she teased.

I shook my head, a smile playing at my lips.

Curiosity filled me. "What are you hoping for?"

"What do you mean?"

"Do you want it to be a boy or girl?"

"Honestly, I just want a healthy baby."

"Do you have any Spidey-Sense on what you think it is?"

Dani laughed. "I don't." She cocked her head toward me. "Okay, now I'm curious. What do you want it to be? Boy or girl?"

I shrugged. "I hadn't really thought about it."

Which was a little true, but also kind of a lie. I didn't really want to tell her the truth, not yet at least. The truth merely highlighted how utterly in love with her I was.

"Really? I'm surprised. I would have thought you would want a little boy."

"A boy would be awesome, really awesome. But honestly?" My gaze ran over her face, and the truth came out whether I was ready for it or not. "I want a little girl."

"A girl?"

I nodded. "Yeah." Embarrassment filled me, but I gave her the rest. "Maybe with your hair. That'd be cute."

A flush covered her cheeks. "Seriously?"

"Seriously." My voice gentled and I didn't bother trying to keep the emotion out. "A girl who looks exactly like you would be absolutely perfect."

Dani ducked her head, her eyes cast downward, the curtain of hair obscuring her expression. I wanted to reach out and brush the hair off her face, wanted to caress her skin. I wanted to kiss her so badly I ached.

There was something so intimate about this conversation, a connection between us now that we'd created a life together that hadn't been there before. We had a piece of each other that would stay with us always. Maybe it was some primal, biological urge, but seeing the woman I loved glow with my baby inside her bound me even more tightly to her. I wanted to get down on my knees and worship her, wanted to lose myself in her, wanted to come together, over and over again.

DANI

There was something about Easy that flipped a switch in me every single time; I was sleeping, and then he woke me up.

Hearing him say he wanted a daughter, that he hoped she looked like me, did funny things to my heart. I hadn't said it, but the truth was if we had a little boy, I imagined him with Easy's blue eyes, his gorgeous smile, his blond hair, and all his mischievous energy.

It was seriously adorable that he'd already started reading parenting books, and it was amazing to have someone I could talk to about the baby, to no longer go through this on my own. Talking to Jordan was awesome, and she'd been really supportive about the whole thing, but Easy's excitement matched my own, and it was different knowing we'd be in this baby's life permanently.

"Do you want to see the first sonogram picture?"

His eyes widened. "Yeah. Of course."

"I'll go get it; I'll be right back."

I headed into the kitchen, my hand on my belly, and grabbed the photo off the fridge. I walked back into the living room, holding it out to him, a rush of pride filling me.

The image in the picture already looked like a little person, it's head and belly prominent, little hands and legs just barely discernable.

His fingers trembled as he took the photo from my hands. He didn't speak. And then he looked up, emotion swimming in his gaze.

"I can't—" He cleared his throat. "I can't believe that's our baby. It's beautiful. Absolutely beautiful."

Tears welled in my eyes; I brushed them away. "I've probably spent hours staring at that picture. It's so incredible to see it like that. Apparently the baby is the size of a passion fruit now."

He laughed. "How do you know that?"

"There are all these websites that can track where you

are in your pregnancy and then they convert the baby's size to fruit sizes."

"Our little passion fruit," he mused. "What's next?"

"Next it'll be a lemon." I tried to give him my sternest look. "Do not make any bad puns."

Easy grinned, stirring another flutter in my heart. "I won't."

He hesitated. "Okay, dumb question, but what's it like?"

"Having a passion fruit inside me?"

A dimple popped out. "Yeah."

"A little weird," I admitted. "Cool, but weird."

"Is it uncomfortable?"

"A bit. Not too bad, though. As far as pregnancy symptoms go I've gotten pretty lucky. I'm tired, and a little nauseous, but I haven't been really sick. A few food cravings, but I haven't woken up in the middle of the night with an urgent need for pickles and ice cream. The aversions are stronger than anything. My grocery trips involve me going down the aisles thinking of all the foods I *don't* want to eat. My back hurts occasionally, and my feet have been strangely sore, but from the stories I've read online it could be way worse."

Those books were filled with horror story after horror story—hair in strange places, extreme pain, things coming out of your body. Each one freaked me out more and more, until finally I'd forced myself to skim the "body changes" sections. Let Mother Nature surprise me.

"If your feet hurt, do you want me to rub them?"

I blinked. He might as well have asked me if I wanted to spread margarine all over my body and then have him lick it off.

"I'll pass, but thanks."

He cocked his head, his eyes dancing with amusement as he studied me. "Why do you look like I suggested something utterly depraved? I offered to rub your toes, not suck them."

God, his voice sounded way too enticing saying the phrase "utterly depraved," even as I recoiled at the idea of his mouth anywhere near my toes. Other parts of my body, though . . .

"Feet are gross. And private."

He gave me a knowing look that said it all—he'd already been inside me; any barriers that might have existed between us had pretty much been eradicated the second he saw me naked.

"You know what I mean," I muttered, feeling my cheeks flush again.

"Come on. It's not a big deal. They're just feet. Put them in my lap." He wiggled his eyebrows, adopting a playfully wicked expression that knocked the air out of me.

Easy was lethal on a normal day, but when he played around, he was pretty much irresistible.

"No," I squealed, my protests growing fainter by the moment.

I mean, I'd gotten a pedicure a few weeks ago, but I wasn't sure I wanted Easy, way-too-good-looking-for-his-own-good Easy, to see my *feet*.

"You're being silly. Your feet hurt. You're carrying my baby." I didn't miss the pride that shone through his voice. "It's not a big deal for me to rub your feet."

This time he didn't bother waiting. Instead he grabbed my ankles, and before I could even catch my breath he'd slipped my flip-flops off. My toes curled instinctively.

He laughed. "This is really an issue for you, isn't it?"

"No. Maybe."

He laughed again, the sound rumbling around in my belly and sending a shock to my body.

"Relax."

Ah, hell.

His hands settled over my feet, the size difference between us enough that he covered me. He was merely touching my feet, but my body did exactly as he commanded, sinking into his embrace, my eyes fluttering closed as my head fell back on the couch pillow. He began rubbing my feet, his thumbs pressing into the soles, his fingers working their magic, and then I didn't need him telling me to relax because I was a pool of liquid, sinking into the couch.

"Oh my God." I bit back a moan. "Seriously, oh my God. Where did you learn how to do that?"

He grinned. "I work with my hands. I have this manual dexterity thing down."

A moan escaped. A tiny one. "Yeah, you do."

"Come on. How are you besides the sore feet?" he asked while another punch of lust hit me.

The rest of it was way too personal to share. My boobs were popping out of my bra, I had to pee every ten minutes, and I was horny all the freaking time.

"Okay, I guess."

"Does anything else ache?"

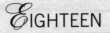

EIGHTEEN

DANI

God, that sounded dirty, and combined with the press of his fingers into my skin, it had my body responding. I shook my head, even though that was a ridiculous lie considering the pulse pounding between my legs. I wiggled from his grasp, tucking my legs underneath me, suddenly feeling warm.

"Thank you," I replied instead of answering his question, wondering if he could hear the undercurrent of need in my voice.

"Better?"

I nodded and lied, considering his touch had soothed one ache and ignited another. "Better."

He gave me another smile, and a shiver slid down my spine.

We'd moved into uncharted territory ever since we had sex and, on one hand, I wanted to be able to talk to him about the pregnancy, about how I felt. I missed the friendship we'd had before we'd slept together. But this *thing* between us had sprung up and changed everything, and I didn't know how to move past it, or through it, or whatever we needed to get to a point where I wasn't crawling out of my skin around him, my body on fire. I'd experienced flashes of it yesterday; now that he was sitting close to me, I couldn't deny those flashes consumed me.

Easy's gaze ran over me, and I couldn't help but wonder if he noticed all the changes in my body—the fuller breasts, exaggerated hips, the bump.

"I'm starting to show," I said, realizing as soon as the words left my lips how inane the comment was—he couldn't miss the changes in my body now that he knew to look for them.

His lips curved, his voice going husky. "Yeah. You are." His smile deepened and I was treated to a glimpse of how he ended up with all those girls at his feet. "It looks good on you."

I shouldn't have cared if he thought I looked good, but yeah, I did. My body was going through these crazy changes, and while half the time I felt more sexy and female than I ever had, the other half of the time I was a killer whale. And those feelings definitely turned on a dime.

"Thanks."

Easy's gaze settled back on the bump.

"Can I?" he asked, gesturing toward my stomach. His voice trailed off, the nerves there filling the space around us. God, this was screwed up. We were having a baby together, and yet the simple act of him laying his palm against my stomach felt like crossing a line—one we'd already crossed, yet now seemed desperate to avoid, as though we could jump back to the other side and pretend that night had never happened. Except it had, and the very real reminder lay between us.

I nodded, my throat tight, the words piled up there.

He loves you.

I heard Jordan's voice in my head, that same news I'd turned over and over again and couldn't quite make sense of. It was too big, too important. My world had been shaken enough in the past year, and considering Easy was my rock, I couldn't handle the possibility of losing that, too.

His hand settled on my belly, just above the tiny bump that had begun to show, his touch achingly gentle. I couldn't look at him and I found myself instead staring at the sight of his hand splayed across my shirt, those long fingers, I realized with a flush, that I'd been intimately familiar with. They'd been inside me. He'd been inside me.

Memories of our night together hit me. The feel of his mouth on mine, his hands on my breasts, his beautiful body looming over me as he thrust inside, filling me.

Hard muscles, slick heat, the scrape of his teeth against my skin, marking me.

I bit down on my lip, trying to fight the arousal pushing through, unbidden. I blamed the pregnancy hormones, and how good he smelled, and how close he was, close enough that if I leaned forward a few inches I could have my mouth on his.

I couldn't do this. We couldn't do this.

Even as my brain commanded me to move, my body responded to his touch, the heat from his palm, my nipples tightening, an ache beginning between my legs.

I didn't move; neither did he.

My gaze drifted higher, past his hand, wrist, those

tanned forearms with a sprinkling of hair that was so male. I swallowed, running over the impressive biceps until finally I reached his face, and the look there stole the breath from me.

I didn't know if it was the pregnancy or that I finally saw him, or at least, saw the way he saw me, but the look in his eyes . . .

I didn't know what to do with that look, wasn't sure I'd ever know what to do with that look, but that didn't stop me from leaning forward a hair. Okay, more than a hair.

His eyes widened, his gaze dropping down to my mouth, and suddenly my lips felt swollen, my skin feverish.

"Easy." It came out as a whisper, in a voice I didn't even recognize.

He really did smell amazing.

"Alex."

And his voice . . . holy hell, that voice. Had it always sounded like that? Did he use that tone with everyone or was it just with me?

Wait. "What?"

"Call me Alex." He reached out with his free hand, his fingers skimming my jawline, and the ache grew. "I want to hear you say my name. My real name. Not my call sign."

His fingers trembled slightly as they stroked my skin, and the tremor lit a spark inside me.

Something about the intimacy of calling him a name no one else used thrilled me.

"Alex."

He groaned, and his fingers moved higher, sliding through my hair, pulling me forward. He stopped when we were so close our lips barely grazed each other, our breath mingling. I waited for the rest, for him to kiss me, but he didn't. My heart hammered as he caressed my scalp, as he ran the strands through his fingers. God, it felt good.

My resistance collapsed.

I leaned forward another inch, the necessary inch, pressing my lips to his. I reached out, grabbing on to his biceps, holding on as my tongue slid between his lips and the taste of him filled me.

A girl could get addicted to this. To the shape of his mouth—those full, sexy lips—to the way he held me, to how big and strong his arms were beneath my hands.

I sucked on his bottom lip and another groan escaped him, the sound sending a surge of power through me. Last time I'd been swept up in the magnificent ride that was Easy. Now I wanted to take control.

I'd been worried about complicating things between us, and I still was, but there was something about seeing him again, listening to his enthusiasm about the baby—

I loved him. I always had. It hadn't been romantic before, I hadn't wanted him like this, but he'd always been someone I cared about. Now he was someone I cared about, trusted, loved—someone I couldn't keep my hands off of.

And because I loved him, because he'd been one of the most important people in my life for so long, I didn't want to hurt him.

"Wait."

I broke away, panting, my lips sensitive from his kisses. My body protested the lack of contact, even as sanity filled me.

I rubbed my mouth, as though I could clear my head and brush his kisses away.

"We need to talk about this."

He gave me an incredulous look. "Now?"

I nodded. "Especially now." My cheeks heated. "I jumped you before, but I meant what I said earlier; I don't want to complicate things between us."

His gaze shuttered. "We won't."

I'd always been honest with him, and if we were going to make any of this work, I couldn't stop now. I moved out of his embrace, standing, trying to put some distance between us for what felt like one of the most awkward conversations I'd ever had.

My heart pounded. I swallowed, not quite able to meet his gaze. The words came out in an awkward squeak. "Jordan told me you had—have—feelings for me."

It was so silent you could have heard a pin drop, and then an oath fell from his beautiful lips.

"Easy—Alex—"

"She had no right to tell you."

"She didn't mean to. We were talking, and she thought I knew, and it slipped out. She felt terrible about it."

"Jesus." He ran his hands through his hair, and I jerked my gaze away. This was too intimate, too raw, too potentially hazardous to my heart.

"How long have you known?" he asked.

I forced myself to look at him, the pain stamped on his face stealing the breath from my lungs. Why did this have to be so hard? Why did it feel like no matter what, one of us would get hurt? Why did the possibility of letting him into my heart terrify me so much?

"Not long. A month or so. She told me the same day I told her I was pregnant."

His jaw clenched, that wall back up again. "What did she tell you?"

"That you love me. You've always loved me." My voice shook as I forced the words out, widening the chasm between us. I swore I could actually feel him pulling away from me with each moment that passed. "Is that true? Have you always loved me?"

My words met moments of silence and then he nodded, and the look in his eyes suggested I was a fool for even asking, for not accepting it as gospel.

I swallowed, my voice suddenly so dry, my heart racing. I pressed the heel of my hand to my chest, my lungs struggling to drag in enough air.

"Since the beginning?"

"Since the first time I saw you."

I remembered that day—we'd been at the squadron bar, Michael and I. He'd been so excited to take command of the Wild Aces, so worried he would make a good impression, uncharacteristically nervous. It had been such a big moment for both of us; my career had taken a backseat to his, but I'd still felt like I was a part of his achievements, as though in some small way they were mine, too. I'd been there through the ups and downs, given him advice after a bad day at work, been the support he needed in order to serve his country. That day had made me proud of him, and of me, and looking back now it was crazy how much my life had changed, how the littlest moments that at the time had seemed to be nothing—Michael introducing me to Easy—turned out to be my future.

I took a step forward, and then another, reaching out and cupping Easy's—Alex's—chin until he met my gaze.

I grasped for the right words. "You shouldn't be embarrassed; I don't want things to be uncomfortable between us."

He made a frustrated noise. "That's easy for you to say. I never meant for you to find out like this. I didn't want to upset you, especially in light of everything else going on. I never wanted you to think I was somehow trying to undermine Joker when you were together—"

"I never thought that."

"But it changed things between us, didn't it? Tell me it didn't freak you out when Jordan first told you," he challenged.

"It did," I admitted. "It's still does a bit, but probably not for the reasons you think." I tried to gather my thoughts, tried so hard to figure out a way to explain to him how I felt without hurting him.

"You're one of the best people I've ever known. It's an honor to be loved by you."

He looked stung. "Is this some kind of pity thanks for loving you?"

"God. No. It isn't. At all. This is coming out all wrong." I took a deep breath, steadying myself. My hand slid down to my stomach, and his gaze followed, resting on our child. "It's my way of telling you it means something to me. That I think you're an amazing guy."

"This sounds a lot like you're trying to let me down easily. I don't want your gratitude, Dani. I haven't done any of the things I've done for you because I loved you; I did them because they were the right things to do. Loving you was extra."

He skewered me.

Couldn't he see what he did to me? See how much this mattered? How confused I was?

"I'm not trying to let you down easily. I'm trying to figure out how to handle this. I'm not saying it out of pity." It was as though we were speaking different languages, and I wanted him to understand me, but no matter how hard I tried I couldn't seem to find the words I searched for, the words I needed to ease the hurt inside him and show him he mattered to me as more than a friend. "You have to understand—I don't really know what I'm doing here. And it's obvious by now that I'm not very good at this, and our situation couldn't be any more complicated.

"I have feelings for you. I've always had feelings for you. They were different before, but somewhere along the way, these past few months, they've changed. I want you, and you're one of my closest friends. But the rest of it?" I took a deep breath. "I don't know if I'm capable of ever loving someone else again—not like that. I don't know if I can do this again. If I *want* to do this again."

I couldn't look at him as I told him the rest of it, the pieces I was ashamed of, that I hadn't shared with anyone else.

"Maybe I don't have a right to feel this way; nothing that happened was Michael's fault, but I'm angry. A part of me has been angry for a long time.

"He loved to fly, and the right thing, the thing a good wife should say is that he died doing what he loved and that makes it okay." I swallowed past the lump in my throat. "But what about me? He was my whole world, and then he was gone, and I was left with nothing. And everyone looked to me like I had to make sense of it, as though I could give his death some broader meaning, and turn it from a tragedy to some great heroic event.

"And Michael was a hero, absolutely, but what about the rest of it? The fucking bad luck of it all? Do you know how many times I wonder if things could have been different—what if he hadn't flown that night, if he'd taken off at a different time, if the upgrade to the F-16 had happened before that night, if he'd had the Ground Collision Avoidance System? It was an accident. A fucking accident that took my entire life away from me.

"In the span of a year, I lost my son and my husband. I'm all out of things I can lose."

"Do you know how badly I wished I could have traded places with him? That I could have spared you the loss?" Pain filled Easy's gaze. "I think about it all the time, too, remember the sound of his voice on the radio, the green explosion on my screen." His voice cracked. "That moment replays in my mind all the time. I wonder if I did something wrong, if I should have realized what was happening, if I could have stopped it somehow."

I brushed at the tears running down my cheeks. "You shouldn't. You did absolutely nothing wrong that day. None of you did. I'm angry, but I know—his death was an accident."

"I know," he whispered. "That doesn't make it easy to let go, though, does it?"

"No, it doesn't. I don't want to end up like that again. I don't want to—*can't*—spend my days and nights worrying you're not coming back like I did with Michael. I don't want my kids to always come second, and even though it makes me a terrible military wife to say it, *I* don't want to always come second. You'll love this baby, you'll do the best you can for both of us, but it's out of your control. The Air Force owns you. I don't want them to own me. I've given them everything; I don't have anything left to give."

Alex wasn't a guy like Thor, who could take it or leave it when it came to being a fighter pilot. Flying F-16s was who he was in a way that scared me, in a way I knew all too well, because no matter how much he said he loved me there would always be a piece of him I'd have to share, a part I'd never really understand that craved taking risks with an intensity that terrified me, that faced death on a daily basis and walked away unfazed. Losing someone I loved wasn't an abstract fear—it was real and it was hell, and I'd barely gotten out once—I didn't think I could do it again.

"If I weren't in the military, would we have a shot?" he asked.

"I don't know."

He took a deep breath. "You're scared. This life weighs the heaviest on the families, and you've already sacrificed more than anyone should ever have to. I could tell you I would give up flying for you, and I would, but I'm not sure that's the answer. Are you scared of being a military wife again or are you scared of losing someone you love?"

I didn't answer the question, but then again, I didn't have to. We both knew I was terrified.

"Flying isn't the problem. I could get in a car accident and die tomorrow. I could get cancer. My job's dangerous, but so is life. I can't live in fear on the off chance something might happen to me, and I don't think you should, either. It's easier said than done with everything you've been through, but you can't let your fear hold you back from taking chances, from living your life."

His voice thickened. "Joker fucking adored you. He would have done anything for you, and he wouldn't want you to live your life like you died with him that day. He would want you to be happy, and he knew life is too short to waste it being afraid to do what you love."

My voice shook as the tears ran down my cheeks. "I know."

"I get it if you don't want an asshole fighter pilot, and if it's my job holding you back—"

"It's not your job." The tears continued and I took harsh, racking breaths, trying to get the words out even as it felt like I was imploding. "I'm still angry, still hurt, still miss him all the time. I'm so scared at the idea of how I'm going to manage being a mom, much less the idea of starting a new relationship. I don't know what I have to give."

"Dani." Compassion filled Alex's voice and eyes, the look I'd seen so many times shining through with the same emotion that had always been there, the one I'd failed to recognize—love. So much love.

He got up from the couch and wrapped his arms around me, holding me tight, tucking my head beneath his chin in a move that now seemed so familiar, so us. I let myself relax in his embrace. His hands came up and stroked my hair, his lips brushing over the top of my head.

"It's okay. Things are complicated for you right now. I don't expect you to have all the answers or to know what you want between us. I understand how confused you are; believe me, I still feel guilty every time I think of Joker."

"Me, too," I whispered, the sound muffled against his chest.

He pulled back, holding me at arm's length, his gaze searching.

"If there's a chance we could be together, that this could work between us, then I'm in. You don't feel the same way I do right now, and I understand if you don't ever feel that way, but if you're interested in seeing if there could be more than friendship between us, then I want that, too. We can take things slowly, however slowly you need to."

I wiped at my face, embarrassment filling me at how much I'd fallen apart in front of him again. I wanted to be further along in my grief than I was, had finally reached the point where I accepted that there was no going back, that this was my life now. But now it felt like the future was too far away, any hope of happiness or normalcy out of my grasp.

"Why?"

He cocked his head at me. "Why what?"

"Why would you wait for me? You could have anyone you want, someone who doesn't have all this baggage. Someone who could be normal."

Understanding filled his gaze. "What's normal, Dani? Who doesn't have shit they're dealing with? I don't know what I 'could' have, just that I've only ever wanted you."

It was so like him to say exactly what I needed, to give me the sense that even though I was terrified I would fall, if I did, he would be there to catch me. If I could love anyone other than Michael, it would be him.

I wasn't scared about his job, and my fears and doubts had nothing to do with him. It was me. The thing about putting yourself out there, letting someone in, the catch with love was that it had the power to destroy you. Once someone was your entire world, you had something to lose. And I didn't know if I could survive another loss. Not after losing my son, my husband.

But Alex—something about the new name made me think of him differently, somewhere between the Easy I'd known for years and the man I was getting to know now—was right. I didn't want to live my life as though I'd died. And soon, it wouldn't only be my life—it would be my baby and me, and I owed it to both of us to let love have a place in my life. I owed it to both Alex and me to see if there was more here. I owed it to Michael to live, even as I couldn't quite get over the guilt about who I was taking this chance on. I told myself he'd loved Alex, and he'd loved me, and somehow I hoped he would want what was best for us.

I stepped off the cliff.

"I want to see where this goes."

He blinked. He didn't answer me. He stared, as though he needed to acclimate himself to the words, test them out, try them on for size. He looked like a man who'd won the lottery and couldn't accept his good fortune. He looked like mine.

"I'm taking you to dinner. A nice dinner," he amended. "If we're going to see where this goes, then we're going to do this right. I'll be over to pick you up tomorrow night. Does 7 p.m. work for you?"

And there it was—the shift from Easy to Alex, from the guy who deferred to me always, who had treated me like I was made of glass, to a different guy, one who wasn't afraid to take charge, who was at his best when he led. It was as though he looked at me like I was a woman now, not only a widow.

"Seven is perfect."

His lips curved, his voice filling me with warmth. "I'll pick you up then."

He leaned down and pressed a kiss to my cheek. "Will you walk me out?"

"Are you leaving now?" I asked, surprise in my voice.

I'd put the brakes on us having sex by wanting to talk, but I figured once we had talked, we'd pick up where we left off.

"I meant what I said. We're going to do this right. Next time we have sex, I want you to want it more than any fears or doubts in your head."

I cocked my head to the side. "'Next time'?" I teased. "You sound pretty sure of yourself."

"I am." He dipped his head, pressing his mouth to mine, his tongue sliding in as my lips parted. It was a fast kiss, but then again, he didn't need a lot of time. In and out, he knocked me off my feet.

As quickly as he kissed me he released me, leaving me staring up at him, staggered.

"See you tomorrow." He winked at me, and then he was walking out the door, swagger in his step.

I wasn't sure I was ready for this new version of him, but I had a feeling I was about to find out.

NINETEEN

DANI

"So you and Easy are going on a date? Tonight?"

I nodded, fighting back a grin at the unbridled glee on Jordan's face. "We are, and really, we have you to thank. If you hadn't told me how he felt about me, I never would have thought about us as a couple," I teased.

She groaned. "God. I still feel horrible about spilling the beans. How pissed was Easy?"

"In the grand scheme of things, not really. He seemed more embarrassed than anything."

"But it all worked out?"

"Hopefully. We'll see how things go tonight." I exhaled, my gaze sweeping over my closet, scanning the contents, wondering how the hell a girl accessorized for a sex god. "Seriously, I need help here. The pink shoes or the silver?"

I'd called Jordan in for an emergency pre-date summit, and really, more than fashion advice, I wanted moral support, needed someone to push me out of my nest.

I'd gone out earlier today and bought a new dress and two pairs of shoes so I had options, figuring everything about tonight called for a fresh start. I'd also binged on accessories and lingerie . . .

"I can't do this." I sank down onto the edge of the bed—the bed I'd shared with Michael—feeling like I was about to hyperventilate, panic pummeling me. I twisted my rings around my finger, holding on to Michael with everything I had. "Seriously, what was I thinking?"

Jordan sank down on the bed next to me. "Breathe."

I took a deep breath.

"What do you want here? Tough love or coddling?" she asked.

"Which do you think I need?"

"I say this because I love you—you need tough love. You need to forgive yourself. You need to let go."

I twisted the rings, the diamonds digging into my skin. She wasn't wrong, but forgiveness always seemed hardest when you were the one who needed it.

"You're beating yourself up about this, and you need to stop. It's a messy situation. I understand why you feel guilty considering Easy's friendship with Joker, but this isn't a situation where you left Joker for Easy or you cheated. Nothing is turning out the way you imagined it would, but all you're doing is trying to deal with the fucking awful hand you were dealt. You lost your husband. It's okay for you to be happy again. To love someone again. It's okay for you to let yourself.

"You guys didn't do anything wrong. It's messy, but so is life. You were an amazing wife to Joker. You have one of the biggest hearts of anyone I know. You can love both of them and not love either one of them any less.

You can be excited about the baby, about a future with Easy, and still mourn the child you lost, still love Joker."

"I just . . ."

Jordan nodded. "I know. You want to do the best thing, the right thing. But you are. Stop second-guessing yourself. If what happened has taught us anything, it's that life's too short for anything other than making the most of every single moment. You taught me that. Don't waste this shot because you feel guilty. You've had two amazing men love you with everything they have. That's a gift, Dani."

It was, and I didn't want to screw this chance up.

"Go out tonight; give Easy a shot. Give yourself a shot. I saw you fall when those officers came to your door, and honestly, in the last year I've seen you stay there, on the ground, covered in your grief. I've seen you afraid to walk, to open up that door and face the world. I'm not blaming you. I don't know if anyone could carry the weight you've been handed and not crumple. But you have a future in front of you that's so fucking bright. Don't throw that away."

I heard the truth in her words, and even more than that, I clung to the hope of them. I wanted this to work, wanted this chance with him.

"I won't."

I stood in front of the dresser, staring at my reflection in the mirror. Alex would be here in five minutes—somehow I knew he'd be right on time.

For the first time in a long time, I was happy with the reflection staring back at me. I didn't know if it was the baby or what, but I had that "glow" on my face. I felt it inside of me, too—

Hope.

I only needed one more thing.

I stared down at my hands, the sight of them so familiar, the rings I'd worn for so long becoming as much a part of my fingers as the lines and ridges, the bumps of my knuckles, the curve of my nails.

I tugged at the diamond engagement ring first, sliding the cool metal over my knuckle, off my finger, setting it down on the dresser. My throat clogged with unshed tears, but I continued, trembling now as I slid the eternity band off my finger, placing it next to the engagement ring. For the first time in nearly a decade, my left hand sat bare, the faintest of tan lines on my ring finger the only sign I'd been married.

There was a part of me that wanted to slide the rings back on my finger, that felt like I'd said a good-bye I wasn't prepared for, would never be prepared for. But I didn't. Instead, I opened my jewelry box, my gaze settling on a glint of silver—two broken wings.

Michael's wings.

When pilots pinned on their wings after they graduated pilot training, they took the pair and broke them in half, keeping one half for themselves and giving the other half to someone they loved. I hadn't known Michael then, but he'd given half to his mother, and on our wedding day, she gave that half to me. According to tradition, a pilot should never wear his first pair of wings, and for luck, the two broken halves should never be joined.

When a pilot died, the two halves were reunited to bring him luck in the next life. I liked to imagine that wherever Michael was, he soared.

I lay my wedding rings down next to his wings, a sob escaping.

"I love you. So much." I wiped at my cheeks. "And I miss you. Every single day. I hope you're happy. And you will always be in my heart. I will always love you." The rings and wings blurred in my vision. "I used to wish I'd died that day. When they came and told me, I wanted to die. I couldn't imagine living in a world without you. I still can't."

I took a deep breath, reaching out and running my fingers along the ridges of his wings.

"But now I have to move forward. I have to find a way to live without you." I took a deep breath. "I'm pregnant." My lips curved, even as more tears fell. "You know how badly I wanted to be a mom. And now the chance is here and I need to be a good mom. I need to give my baby a mother who isn't afraid to live, who isn't afraid to love.

"I've been holding on so tightly for so long, afraid if I loosened my grasp a little bit I'd lose you. But I won't. No matter what happens with Alex, I'll always love you."

I didn't know if it was my imagination, or standing in our bedroom, but I swore I could feel him behind me, his arms wrapped around my chest, my back against his front, holding me to him. And for a moment, I time-traveled; for a moment, a whisper of a moment, I had my husband back and all the love he had for me flowed between us, filling me with a warmth that took all my fears away.

I took a deep breath and then a step forward, out of his embrace, closing the jewelry box with trembling hands as the doorbell rang and Alex came to pick me up for our date.

ALEX

On Sunday, before my date with Dani, I had to go into the squadron to do some mission planning for my sortie Monday, and when I'd finished, I found myself walking to the grassy area next to the squadron where I'd gone so many times before to smoke a cigar with Noah, Thor, and Joker. When Joker died, we had a plaque planted in the grass to remember him exactly where he'd want to be—close to the flight line, the jets he'd loved, the squadron he'd led.

I sat down at one of the tables nearby, and it was almost as though I could feel him there sitting across from me, could still smell the Cohibas he'd loved to smoke. We'd sat out here for hours, getting drunk and talking about flying.

"I miss you, man. So fucking much."

I felt a little crazy talking to the air, but this had been building up inside me for so long, the grief and guilt a weight pulling me down, and I needed to get the words out. I didn't know if it would help, but being here, in a place we'd spent so much time together, it felt right.

My date with Dani tonight was a fresh start, a chance for us to see if we could have a future together. I had to say good-bye to Joker and to the guilt I still carried with me. I didn't want our lives to be constantly clouded by unresolved feelings; I wanted to remember him without the shame I felt now. So here I was, talking to the air.

I started with the thing that bound us together, the link we shared, because if he could hear me now, he'd want to know about Dani.

"She misses you. A lot. We all do." The knot in my chest tightened, but I pushed on, putting the words out there, imagining we were sitting across from each other, cigar smoke in the air, beers in hand, the faint sound of a Dos Gringos song lingering in the background.

"She's doing better, though. It was rough for a while, but you know how tough she is. You'd be proud of how strong she's been. So proud." I ran a hand through my hair, that knot growing bigger, squeezing my heart tighter.

"She's pregnant, man."

The words came out in a whisper that sounded like a scream. It was stupid; I *knew* he wasn't actually here, and yet this was a confession of sorts.

"It's mine."

I took a deep breath and continued on.

"I should say I'm sorry, but I can't, because this baby . . . I already love it. So much. And I'm sorry if I hurt you, but I can't be sorry about this baby. I can't be sorry about Dani."

I took another deep breath, the pain in my chest growing.

"Dani's healthy. She was scared in the beginning, but now she's in the second trimester, and a lot of her fear has gone away. She's so beautiful, man. She fucking glows.

"She's so excited to be a mom." My lips curved. "You know how she gets. She has all these lists and books. She's so determined to do this right, to be a good mom, and she's going to be amazing.

"I hope we have a little girl, that she has Dani's smile and her eyes. Well, Dani's everything, really."

Better her face than yours.

I grinned through the thickness in my throat, the tears welling in my eyes. "I'll give you that one."

Say the rest of it.

I swallowed. "I love her. I shouldn't, but I do. I don't know how not to love her. I've always loved her, always thought you were the luckiest guy in the world to be loved by her. She's amazing."

I know.

His voice sounded so real in my head—full of the same quiet confidence that had ensured we'd all follow him anywhere he led us. It was that same confidence, the reassurance in it, that gave me the courage to continue.

"I never wanted her to find out. Never wanted you to find out. All I ever wanted was for her to be happy, and she was so happy with you. She loves you. She'll always love you. I wouldn't ever try to take that away. I *couldn't* take that away."

I know.

"Her heart's so big, and she loves so much, and I don't know if she loves me, if she could ever love me, but I want a chance with her. A real chance for us to be a family. I gotta let go. I have to put the guilt behind me so I can be the man I need to be for Dani and our child.

"I miss you. Every day. You'll always be with me. Every time I'm in the cockpit, I wish you were up in the air with me. For a long time I wished I could have switched places with you, that you could have been there for her instead of me. But she needs me now. They both do. I'm going to do everything I can to make her happy. I promise. I won't hurt her. I'll make you proud."

Maybe I'd lost my mind. Maybe I needed to hear the words. Or maybe Joker really was out there somewhere, listening, watching over all of us. I didn't know what I believed anymore, only that I swore I heard him say—

Take care of our girl.

I wiped at my cheeks, my hands coming away wet.

"I will."

TWENTY

DANI

I opened the door to Alex standing on my doorstep, a bouquet of pink peonies in hand. Michael had always brought me roses, and I didn't think it was an accident that Alex had brought me something different.

He always knew what I needed.

"You look beautiful."

I smiled, suddenly a little shy. "Thanks. You look amazing."

He'd traded his usual uniform of jeans and a nice T-shirt for a pair of dark pants and a button-down shirt with the sleeves rolled, showcasing his impressive forearms. Seeing how amazing he looked, I was glad I'd gone shopping and bought a dress for tonight.

Alex stepped forward, giving me a hug, his lips brushing against my cheek. I inhaled the scent of his cologne, his aftershave, leaning forward a bit and pressing my body into the curve of his embrace. God, he felt good. Thank God for the other purchase I'd made this afternoon—the lacy pink bra and matching thong I wore under my flowered sundress. We'd agreed to take things slow, but it was hard considering I'd known him for years, he'd loved me forever, and we were expecting a child together. It was as though he'd been somewhere ahead of me all along, but suddenly I'd pressed fast-forward, and now I was caught up to where he was in real time.

I didn't want my fear to keep holding me back.

I took the flowers from Alex, and he followed me into the house while I found a vase in the kitchen and put them in water. When I'd finished, I looked up at him.

"Ready?"

His gaze bore into me, emotion simmering in his eyes.

"You took your rings off."

I looked down at my hand, feeling a momentary, instinctive spark of panic that I'd lost my wedding rings after years of seeing them there, and then remembering I'd taken them off. It would take a while to get used to. Change always did.

"I did."

He reached between us, rubbing his thumb over my bare finger.

"You didn't have to."

"I needed to. Maybe I'll do something with them later, but for now I need to move forward. I wore the rings more for myself than Michael. It was time."

He leaned forward, pressing his lips to mine, his kiss feather light. The remaining mass of nerves in my stomach dissolved. He pulled back, a smile playing at his mouth.

"Ready?" Alex held his hand out to me.

Yes.

I took his hand, linking our fingers, letting him lead me out the door and into his waiting car.

He drove us to the restaurant, our hands joined, a steady stream of conversation flowing between us. I'd imagined I'd be more nervous than I was, but it felt like two friends hanging out. Well, a friend I wanted to kiss and get naked with. And I thought about that a lot. But there were no awkward questions, no need to share our painful pasts. It was fun, the most fun I'd had since before he left for Afghanistan.

"So what's your favorite part of being back?" I asked as he drove on the interstate toward Bricktown. He'd made reservations for us at a French restaurant I'd never been to.

"You."

I smiled. "I can't be your favorite thing. Come on, getting to drink again? Eating normal food? Sleeping on a nice, comfortable mattress? Having A/C?"

"Still you."

I shook my head, unable to fight off the blush. "You know how to bring a girl to her knees, don't you?"

He laughed, the sound husky and low. "I don't know about that, but I'm not going to complain if that's the end result."

My body responded instantly, my mind going wicked, my nipples tightening, a low throb beginning between my legs.

Curiosity got the best of me. "You were holding back before, weren't you?"

"Maybe. A little. I didn't know what you wanted, didn't want to pressure you."

"And now?"

"Now that I know you want me, I'm making my move."

Considering how lethal he'd been before, I wasn't sure I had the willpower to withstand too many of his moves. And I didn't want to. I wanted it all.

"Good."

Alex's attention swiveled from the road for a beat, his gaze connecting with mine, and the desire in his eyes upped the volume on the arousal spreading through my body like wildfire.

His hand released mine as he turned his attention back to the road, and I watched, unable to tear my gaze away, as he settled his palm on the inside of my thigh. He kept it there for the remainder of the drive, as though we were more than two people on a date, the intimacy between us undeniable.

When we got to the restaurant, we parked and he got out of the car, walking over to my side and opening the door for me.

I grinned. "Who would have guessed you'd be such a romantic?"

I swore his cheeks turned pink.

"I want everything to be perfect for you tonight."

"It is."

He put his arm around me as we walked into the restaurant, instantly surrounded by soft music, linen tablecloths, white lights, and candlelight.

The hostess led us to a small table in the corner, and Alex held my chair out before sitting down in his own. I didn't know what I'd been expecting for our date, but somehow I hadn't counted on how smooth he'd be.

"What?"

I shook my head, a smile playing at my lips. At this rate, I'd be giddy by the time the night was over.

"You're knocking this date out of the park."

"Good. I was nervous," he confessed as a waiter came by and poured water for us.

"Me, too. I made Jordan come over and help me decide what to wear."

He shot me a wolfish grin. "You guys did a good job. You look phenomenal."

My heart pounded, and, God, it had been years since I'd flirted, but I couldn't resist. I wanted him to feel the same sparks exploding inside me.

"You should see what I'm wearing under the dress."

He froze, the glass of water in his hand halfway between his mouth and the table. He looked surprised, and then a gleam entered his eyes, and my heart fluttered.

"Does this mean I'm going to get to see what you're wearing under that dress?"

His tone was pure sex, and my body responded instantly.

"Yes."

"We're really doing this, aren't we?"

I nodded, my throat clogged with emotion. I didn't know if it was that we were already friends, or the attraction I felt for him, but this was right. Solid. There weren't any unwelcome surprises lurking around the corner—I knew him as well as you could know anyone, and at the same time, this shift in our relationship, the newness of it, at least, filled me with the kind of butterflies I hadn't experienced in a long time.

Alex's gaze held mine. "This isn't casual for me. I want to be up front with you from the start, want you to know that if we're doing this, my goal is that we'll end up as a family, my ring on your finger."

He must have read the look of panic that flashed across my face, because he continued—

"We can go slowly; I'm not saying everything has to happen right away. I want you to be comfortable. I don't want to push you for more than you're ready for. This matters to me; you matter to me, and I'm all in here. I'll wait however long I have to until you're there, too."

I blinked back tears, and then I leaned across the table, my lips brushing his.

I didn't hold back because we were in a fancy restaurant or worry someone might see us. I didn't care. I kissed him with everything I had, taking him by surprise and giving him all the passion and fire I had inside me until he was kissing me back with enough enthusiasm I was pretty sure the entire restaurant *was* watching us.

For the first time in over a year, my future looked good from where I was sitting, and I was actually excited for what lay before me. Jordan was right; life could fuck you over in an instant, but when moments like these flew past you, you had to grab hold and savor them, clutching them to you. And when a hot fighter pilot with a heart of gold told you he wanted a future with you—

You didn't pass it up.

ALEX

It was the best date of my life, every fantasy I'd ever had of taking Dani out obliterated by the reality.

She was funny, sweet, smart, sexy as hell. She was

everything I'd ever wanted, and somehow she wanted me. I spent most of the night wondering how I'd gotten lucky enough to have her interested in me, and the rest of it doing everything I could to show her how much she meant to me.

I'd loved her from afar before, but it was completely different now. I found new things to love—the little noises she made when I kissed her, like she was devouring a favorite pastry each time our lips touched; the way she would squeeze my hand at random points in the evening as though she was trying to reassure herself I was still there; the feel of her in my arms.

"Do you want me to take you home?" I asked as we walked outside of the restaurant. "Or do you want to come over to my place?"

I figured we were both uncomfortable with the idea of being together in the house she'd shared with Joker. It felt disrespectful in a way I wasn't sure I would ever get over; I'd left some ghosts behind, but there would always be moments when we'd both readjust, times in our relationship when there would be a third person involved.

Dani smiled up at me, leaning forward and pressing her lips to my cheek.

My heart hammered as I waited for her answer, as I hoped she wanted me as badly as I wanted her.

"Let's go to your place."

Thank God.

The drive flew by in a string of fantasies of what I'd do to her when we got back to my place, three months without her creating an overwhelming need inside me. By the time we reached the house my cock ached, desperate for release.

We held hands, silent, as we both walked toward my

front door, this moment between us a major turning point in our relationship. The first time we'd had sex, it had been a shock, something that had snuck up on me and knocked me on my ass. Now I wanted to savor every single moment, every curve of her body, every inch of skin. I wanted to linger over her until she cried my name.

I released Dani's hand in order to unlock my front door, my fingers fumbling with the key as nerves set in. I wanted all of her—not only her body, but her heart. I wanted to prove to her that things could be great between us, that she could be happy, safe with me. I wanted the promise of tomorrow with her.

When I saw she'd taken off her wedding rings, I'd felt the first shot of hope that she was ready to give us a chance, that she might be able to move on from Joker, might be able to love me. And now everything was on the line, and I really didn't want to fuck this up.

I opened the front door and Dani crossed over the threshold, her body brushing against mine with a soft caress. I sucked in a deep breath, the feel of her tits against my arm, her curves grazing my side making my dick twitch.

I closed the door behind us, taking a moment to drink in the sight of her, so beautiful, carrying my child inside her. I stepped forward, but she didn't move. She stood there staring at me, her breath growing more rapid, a rosy color spreading across her face.

"I love it when you blush," I murmured, moving forward another step. I reached out and brushed her hair behind her shoulders, exposing the swell of her breasts, swollen and larger than I'd remembered. I cupped them, running my thumbs over the fabric of her dress, her nipples tightening beneath the sweep of my fingers, her teeth sinking down on a lush, pink lip.

Another finger joined my thumb, tugging at those stiff points through the silky material, the motion earning me a moan from Dani that made me desperate to have her naked in my bed.

I leaned forward, picking her up in my arms as she laughed, the sound music to my fucking ears, carrying her into my bedroom between drugging kisses, her lips, teeth, and tongue devouring mine.

I set her down on the edge of the bed, sliding the strap of her dress off her shoulders, leaning forward and kissing the silky skin there, inhaling her scent, my teeth nipping at her flesh. I watched as goose bumps pebbled her skin. I repeated the motion with her other shoulder until both straps hung down her arms, her breasts nearly exposed as the fabric slid lower, lower—

I reached behind Dani and tugged at the zipper running down her spine, opening the fabric to the curve of her ass, stripping the dress from her body. She wriggled her hips, and I lifted the dress over her head until she sat before me in a pink lace bra and underwear, pink heels on her feet.

I groaned. "You look so beautiful. So fucking beautiful."

I shifted her forward, spreading her legs wide and kneeling down between them, my lips inches away from her glorious tits. I trailed my hands up the insides of her legs, stroking her.

I took my time, my gaze running over her body, the slight swell of her stomach, the way her thighs quivered. And then I couldn't take my time anymore, my need for her obliterating my ability to go slow. I pressed my lips to her stomach, to the bump, the life growing there, and then I moved up, trailing kisses higher and higher until I reached the front of her bra, until her breasts surrounded me.

I looked up at Dani, her lips parted, amusement in her gaze.

"I know; they're huge."

I grinned, reaching out to stroke the top of one breast, fingering the lace on the cup of her bra. "They are."

"I've walked into some male fantasy it's probably best I don't understand, haven't I?"

My smile deepened. "Babe, this is fucking heaven."

She arched forward as I reached back and found the clasp to her bra, basically pushing her tits into my face and rendering me momentarily dazed and incapable of speech. My fingers did the trick, releasing the hook, letting her bra fall from her body.

I opened my mouth to speak, but there were no words, only want and need churning inside me, pushing me to the brink. I'd always prided myself on making sure a woman enjoyed herself in my bed, had always considered sex an art, a skill to be honed like defensive BFM or strafing an enemy target.

With Dani, everything went out the window. I took my cues from the way her body responded to mine—her hands tugging on my hair, the little moans and sighs escaping from her lips, the way her body arched toward me as though she couldn't get close enough, as though she desperately wanted more. She'd asked me if I was holding back before and I didn't want to anymore.

"Take off your thong."

Her eyes widened at the command in my voice, but she did what I told her to, her fingers hooking under the waistband, stripping the fabric off her body until she sat naked on my bed, her legs spread.

Mine.

My mouth closed over her nipple and her nails dug into my back, legs wrapping around my waist as she rubbed herself over me. She tugged at my clothes, her fingers flying over my shirt buttons, but it was little more than a distant hum as I sucked on her, tugging on her nipple with my teeth, laving it with my tongue until it was a hard, red point, wet from my mouth. I admired my work for a moment, my cock aching, letting Dani push my shirt off my shoulders, helping her lift my undershirt over my head. When she'd finished, I dipped my head, capturing her other nipple at the exact moment when she shuddered against me, and my hand traveled down her torso, lower still, finding her wet and throbbing for me.

"Fuck."

I slid two fingers inside her, her body clenching down around me as I pumped in and out, as her arousal drenched my hand. Dani clung to me, writhing beneath my hands, rubbing herself over my fingers until I could feel the orgasm inside her building, her moans growing louder, her body hungrier. I increased the pace of my fingers, my thumb rubbing her swollen clit back and forth until she was thisclose to coming. Her nails dug into my shoulders as she shattered, her body bearing down on my hand, surrounding me in her tight, wet heat.

I pulled back in time to watch her riding my hand, her head thrown back, red hair streaming down her shoulders, her eyes at half mast as the orgasm racked her body.

I drank up every moan, every sigh that escaped her lips, until the tremors had subsided and her gaze met mine.

"I need you inside me. Now."

My hands flew to the button of my pants, tearing the zipper down, pulling my briefs off, my cock standing at attention. My clothes hit the floor, my shoes and socks removed in the fray.

Dani moved back on the bed, her hair spread out on my sheets, her gorgeous body on display. I crawled over her, nudging her legs to open more with my knee, settling myself right where I wanted to be, her wetness seeping onto my cock.

I rubbed the head over her clit, groaning at the delicious friction, at the way her back bowed in response, pressing her tits against my pecs, her nipples tight. I rubbed myself over her, moving slowly, dragging out my arousal and hers, determined to make her come again before the night was out.

Her eyes slammed shut, and she looked utterly gone, lost somewhere between the orgasm she'd just had and the one she craved, her body opening for me more and more, her hips telling me exactly what she wanted.

She moaned. "Alex."

That did it—the sound of my name falling from her lips wrecked me.

I guided the head of my cock to her entrance, feeding it into her body inch by inch until she covered me, and I surged forward with a groan, my hand fisting in her hair, pulling her head back.

Her eyes slammed open and our gazes instantly connected.

I thrust in and out, sweat pooling on my brow as she

clung to me, as my body slammed into hers, tilting my hips, adjusting my position until I found the right spot, the one that had her clawing at my back.

I lost track of time, of everything but her body and mine.

"I'm close," she whispered, hooking her leg over my back, changing the angle until I was even deeper. She groaned. "So close."

I increased my tempo, my fingers digging into her hips. She came fast and she came hard, her body bucking beneath mine. My balls tightened, pressure building at the base of my spine, and as she clenched down around my cock, my own orgasm came barreling toward me, my mind going blank as I found my release.

We both collapsed into a tangle of limbs, our bodies slick with sweat. Dani rested her forehead against mine, her lips brushing across my skin. I'd never been more at peace than I was at this moment, never felt more hope at the future than I did with her in my arms, our child between us.

"That was amazing," Dani murmured.

"It was." I reached out and pressed my finger over her lips. "You don't have to say anything; I'm not saying it because I want a response, or expect one, but because I've been waiting to say this to you forever—

"I love you."

DANI

I love you.

Alex's fingers traced the shape of my face, his thumbs rubbing over my lips, his touch achingly gentle.

"I will always love you."

I heard the vow contained in his words, heard it reverberate throughout his voice. It was the same vow he'd made to me more times than I could count in his actions, the looks he sent me, the touch of his hand, the warmth of his embrace. It was a vow I'd never quite understood, yet had relied on constantly. Little by little, moment by moment, he'd become someone I counted on. Someone I loved.

And suddenly I knew, like a new word I'd learned, a new facet of myself I simply accepted—

"I love you, too."

I hadn't planned on saying the words, hadn't even known I felt them, until they were there, inescapable and undeniable, as much a part of me as my legs or my hands. *He* was a part of me.

I didn't know what would happen next, didn't have all the answers, and I couldn't deny there was little that could be easy about this, but I wanted it. I wanted him. I wanted more of the friendship he'd given me over the years, the passion I'd found in his arms, the smile he put on my face. I wanted the family, and even as it terrified me, I wanted the shot at happiness. There wasn't anyone else I could imagine taking the chance with.

I'd been afraid from the beginning that if I let myself love Alex it would somehow diminish my memory of the love I'd shared with Michael. I'd thought of love as something to be weighed and measured, worried there wouldn't be room for both of them in my heart, that somehow there had to be one who was my all-caps, air-quotes great love.

But the thing about love was that it was infinite; it stretched and molded itself and filled up the empty spots inside. I loved them both, differently, with no regard for measures or guilt. With Michael it had come on strong with a look, a smile at the bar, and then I was hooked, completely and utterly his. With Alex it was a slow burn, something that snuck up on me unexpectedly, until he was there, in my head, in my heart, standing beside me, supporting me, giving me back a piece of myself I'd thought died with Michael. Giving me a future I hadn't dared hope for.

It was scary—loving someone so utterly and wholly that they became an essential part of you, inextricably bound. It was scary to put yourself out there, to descend into free-fall, especially when you'd already crashed and burned once before.

"Dani. You don't have to—"

"Shh." I quieted him with my finger on his lips, my heart pounding as I pushed on, as I took that critical step off the cliff, confident he was somewhere down there to catch me.

"I love you. I'm in love with you."

I didn't realize I was crying until his lips found my wet cheeks and he kissed the tears away.

"I want to be a family; I want to give us a shot at having a real relationship." I took a deep breath. "I don't know if I'm ready to get married again, not yet, but we want the same things. I'm serious about us, and I want to move toward the same future that you want."

"Are you sure? Just because we had sex—"

I grinned, feeling like my heart was so full it would burst.

"You're good, but not even you're that good. I love you independent of the sex. Well, maybe not independent," I amended, my voice teasing. "But no, you didn't just fuck me into love with you. It's been there for a while, taking root inside of me, spreading throughout. I've loved you in so many ways—my friend, my family, my lover.

"I'm still scared; I probably always will be. And it terrifies me to love another fighter pilot, but you're right—it isn't about your job. It's about me. It's about learning to love and loosen my grasp a bit. And it's about knowing the moments we will have together are worth more than anything that could come our way." I took a deep breath. "I don't want to miss out on this. I don't want to lose my chance at happiness with you."

His gaze swam with emotion, his eyes brimming with unshed tears.

"You won't regret it."

I leaned forward, accepting his promise and giving him one of my own.

"I know."

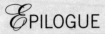

EPILOGUE

DANI

"Oh God, I can't do this."

A string of expletives ran through my mind as I fought to keep the words inside. Normally, I would have let the words fly, but I'd be damned if, after everything, my daughter's first moments were greeted by her mother cursing like, well, a fighter pilot.

"Just a few more pushes," the nurse encouraged, and I focused my attention—and ire—on her. Sure. It was "just a few more pushes" for her; she wasn't the one trying to squeeze something approximately the size of an oversized watermelon out of her.

I'd told myself I wouldn't lose it during childbirth, that I'd be Zen and calm, that it couldn't be *that* bad. The reality was both better and worse than what I'd imagined, easier in some ways and harder in others. Jordan had told me—or tried to, at least—but nothing, not even the many childbirth classes Alex and I had taken together, had prepared me for the real thing. I hadn't predicted the rush of emotions, the fear, how months and months of being pregnant would drag on until I was simultaneously ready for her to be here and equal parts terrified of the responsibility I'd have when she was here, of needing to protect this tiny, vulnerable baby from everything the world could throw her way.

I'd held my breath as I got past the point when I'd miscarried last time, as we reached every milestone in the pregnancy, spent more time than I cared to admit scouring the Internet for probabilities and percentages, for mathematical odds in our favor that said everything would be okay. The losses in my life had made me not take anything for granted and our daughter was no different. The doctors kept telling me everything was okay, that she was healthy and strong, but I wouldn't be able to breathe easy until I held her in my arms, until I stared into her eyes, until she felt *real*. Right now she was a dream, my greatest one, and I was terrified I'd wake from this life I'd carved out of sadness.

Another contraction hit me—harder than the last— rivulets of sweat raining down my face. Yeah, there was little glamorous or romantic about this. My teeth gritted as a cry escaped my lips.

Fuuuuck.

Alex squeezed my hand, his callused fingers rubbing against my skin. "We're almost there. I know you're tired, but you're amazing. So amazing. You got this. I'm here. I'm not going anywhere. Focus on me."

I turned my head, staring into his blue eyes, at the love swirling there. It didn't do anything to mask the pain; an epidural definitely would have been more effective, but there hadn't been enough time. Like her father, our baby girl played by her own rules and we'd gone from zero to sixty in no time at all.

"Oh my God!"

This time I couldn't hold back the litany of profanity, the pain unlike any I'd ever experienced.

"That's it," our doctor proclaimed. "I can see the head."

I gripped Alex's hand so tightly I half wondered if I'd broken a bone or two, and focused on his face, my gaze locked on his. I was aware of people speaking around us, of Alex saying something to me, but everything faded into the background, time running together as I pushed through the pain, the burning pain, and then—

A cry broke through the white noise rushing in my ears, a beautiful, healthy cry that suddenly took my world and spun it on its axis, shuttering time, that sound becoming everything. In an instant, my world changed and became something new again.

A tiny baby. A wedding band on my left hand, shiny and new, still unfettered by the nicks and scrapes that would appear over the years, the wear and tear of life, marriage, a military marriage.

Hope. Love. Joy.

"She's beautiful," Alex whispered, his voice cracking. "So beautiful."

Tears ran down his cheeks and it wasn't until I felt the wetness on my face that I realized I was crying, too—big, heaving sobs born of incredulous wonder and so much relief.

I looked away from Alex, my gaze falling onto the most perfect sight I'd ever laid my eyes on.

She was wrinkly and chubby-cheeked, her lungs getting a workout as she cried, her face scrunched up as she railed against the world for disturbing her slumber. The nurse placed her in my arms and I stared down at her, feeling as though I'd had an out-of-body experience, unable to believe she was here and she was really ours.

Hannah Marie Rogers looked up at me with big blue eyes—her father's eyes—and I fell in love. Head-over-heels in love.

"Hi." My lips curved into a smile, tears tumbling down my cheeks. "I'm your mama."

She blinked, her gaze locking on mine, and a look flashed in her eyes, her cries quieting, recognition steady between us.

I love you. I will always love you. My heart is yours.

"She recognizes your voice," the nurse said.

I nodded. I'd read how babies recognized the sounds they heard in the womb, but seeing it in my daughter's eyes, having that bond between us—

My life had been defined by so many moments—happy ones, sad ones—a knock at the door, a kiss, a glance.

"I think she does."

I turned toward Alex, lifting the baby in my arms slightly so he could get a good look at her.

"That's your daddy, Hannah."

His lips brushed the top of my head as he reached out and stroked her cheek, his cheeks wet, eyes shining.

"She's so beautiful. She looks exactly like you."

I smiled. "She has your eyes."

Wonder filled his voice, clutching my heart in a tight fist and sending it tumbling through my chest.

"Yeah. She does."

He wrapped his arm around me, our daughter between us, and in that moment, everything was utterly perfect.

"Can we come in?"

Jordan peeked around the door to our hospital room, a big smile on her face and Julie on her hip.

I grinned. "Of course."

She opened the door, revealing Burn, Thor, and Becca. The guys were still wearing their flight suits and had clearly just come from work. They carried giant pink balloons that read "It's a Girl" and lush bouquets of flowers.

"Easy's been sending like a million pictures, but it wasn't enough. We've been dying to meet her," Jordan added. Her gaze drifted from me to Alex. "Congrats, Papa."

His lips curved into a smile brighter and sexier than any I'd ever seen on him, the obvious pride blinding. "Thanks. She's sleeping in her bassinet."

Jordan handed Julie over to Burn and came over and gave me a hug.

"I'm so happy for you guys."

The tears—happy, exhausted, awed tears—that had been my constant companion these past couple days bubbled up again.

"Thanks."

She made her way over to the bassinet while I greeted the rest of the group.

"She's gorgeous," Jordan commented, staring at our two-day-old daughter. "Absolutely gorgeous."

She really was. I'd always liked kids, always wanted

my own, always thought they were cute, but there was something about your child that was everything. I'd read about this kind of love, had people tell me what to expect, and yet the power of it was so unexpected.

She was everything in my eyes.

They all made their way over to see her, the guys lowering their voices to keep from waking the baby. Burn gave Alex a hug and the look that passed between them— hell, the look on all their faces—

Burn held Julie cradled in his arms like she was the most precious thing to him. Her little head rested on his green flight suit, a spot of drool landing above the Wild Aces patch. Thor looked on with an indulgent smile on his face, the fighter pilot I'd seen slamming shots at bars mellowed to something else, this big, tough guy making faces at a baby.

And Alex—

I'd never seen him look happier.

Hannah stirred, a shriek coming from her bassinet, and before I could get out of bed and pick her up, Alex swooped down and scooped her up in his arms, his voice taking on the hushed tone he always used when he talked to her. Burn and Thor moved closer, Thor's fingers waving in the air at her as he began speaking in what could only be described as baby talk, a sound I never imagined I'd hear from big, badass Thor.

"God that's sexy," Jordan commented, a wry grin on her face. "Nothing like three fighter pilots reduced to mush by two babies."

Becca laughed. "Amen."

We stayed there, watching our men, snippets of their conversation filling the room, talk of flying and what Alex had missed at work interspersed with the occasional reference to the girls. Halfway through the conversation, Alex's gaze drifted to me, and he sent me a deeper smile, one that tugged at my heart.

"I love you," he mouthed to me.

"I love you, too," I replied, the power of those words overwhelming me, the love staring back at me filling me with peace.

My vision blurred, and something clicked inside me.

I'd never really understood why Michael loved to fly so much; never comprehended how he lived with the risks he took, how he could go up every time, knowing *this* time he might not come home. Eventually I learned to accept that it just was, that loving him meant loving every side of him, including the biggest part, the one that had me passing sleepless nights with worry or sitting next to a nearly packed suitcase on the floor, tears raining down my face as I smothered the sound of my sobs, as I faced another six-month stretch without him, another cycle of missed birthdays and holidays, memories we'd never make together.

With Alex, I accepted it because it just was. I'd been a fighter pilot's wife before; I knew the score. But I didn't understand it. Still. And if I were really honest, there was always a tiny piece of myself I kept ruthlessly locked away, that knew I'd never understand it.

Now I did.

It's a moment—a kiss at bedtime, a mumbled "I love you" in sleep, the sight of boots in your entryway, a much-awaited homecoming, a text in the middle of the day, a hug when you need it most. It's a million, tiny infinitesimal moments that fill your heart, that get you up in the morning and push you through the stupid fights, the nights filled with worry, the stress of daily life.

It's rolling the die and hanging everything you are, everything you have, everything you want on a moment, on love. It's having the courage to stand when you've fallen, and finding someone who will walk beside you, your hand tucked in theirs, when you do. It's the hope that pushes you through.

It's everything.

I'll never understand exactly what it is they find in the air, the adrenaline rush they chase every single time they go up, but I understand the *why* of it now, the passion that drives you to keep on, even when all your losses are stacked against you. I understand the risks they take, the terrifying, daunting risks for one moment of perfection—

For a little girl with chubby cheeks, copper-colored hair, and her father's blue eyes. For a man who loves you with every fiber of his being, who risks his life day after day for the things he believes in, for you. For a dream you clutch in your palm and protect at all costs—

I'm happiest with my feet planted firmly on the ground. But my heart—

It flies.

See where it all began in

FLY WITH ME

*Turn the page for an excerpt from the first
Wild Aces Romance by Chanel Cleeton
Available now from Berkley Sensation*

JORDAN

There was a time in a woman's life when she had to accept that wearing a headband made of pink—*glittery*—illuminated penises was too much. I couldn't put my finger on the number—and I definitely couldn't do it after my fourth tequila shot—but I figured that at thirty and still single, bachelorettes had ceased to be a fun rite of passage, and had instead become a wake-up call that if Prince Charming wasn't coming soon, I'd have to start exploring my options in the amphibian variety.

Of course, it didn't help that this was my sister's bachelorette—my cute-as-a-button, too-young-for-wrinkle-cream sister's bachelorette. Or that she was marrying my high school ex-boyfriend. I didn't care; I mean we hadn't been together in over a decade, but the fact that my future brother-in-law had once seen me topless added to the surreal feeling of the whole thing.

I took shot number five like a champ.

"I'm getting married!" Meg screamed for what might

have been the fifteenth time that night. Somewhere between dinner at Lavo and partying at Tao, this seemed to have hit her with a vengeance. On anyone else, it would have been annoying; on Meg, it was somehow still adorable.

At twenty-five, she was the baby of the family. A good five inches shorter than me, we shared the same blond hair and brown eyes. We both had curves, but on her, they were bite-size. I was a king-size—tits and ass that could put your eye out—not to mention the pink phalluses bobbing awkwardly on my head.

It had been Meg's idea to dress up, and I hadn't been able to disappoint her. So here I was, thirty years old, terminally single, wearing penises on my head, a hot pink barely there tube dress, and fuck-me Choos that topped me out at six feet. If I ever got married, I was so not doing a bachelorette. Or bridesmaids in hideous dresses. Or arguing with my fiancé over whether we'd serve filet mignon or prime rib. I loved meat as much as the next girl, but the drama surrounding this wedding had my head spinning, and I was just the maid of honor. If I were the bride? I totally got why people eloped.

My parents could do the big wedding with Meg. At least they'd get the budget option with me—if I ever got married at all.

Shot number six came faster than a virgin on prom night.

I wasn't really even tipsy. I could definitely hold my liquor, but this was Vegas, and everything about tonight screamed excess, and as depressing as it was to be the eldest, even worse, I felt like the mother hen to the group of three Southern girls ready to make the Strip their bitch. It was time to up my game.

I rose from our table and headed over to where Stacey and Amber, my sister's friends from college, were dancing, determined to kick this feeling inside of me's ass.

When I'd look back on this evening, and it would play in my mind on repeat for months to come, this would be the moment. *Freeze it. Remember it.* How often could you say that you could pinpoint the *exact* moment when your life changed?

I could.

If I had anyone to blame for the wild ride that came next, it was Flo Rida. Because as soon as "Right Round" came over the club speakers, my tequila-fueled body decided it needed to move. It was the kind of song you couldn't resist the urge to dance to; it made normal girls want to grab a pole and let loose. Okay, maybe just me. But it felt like kismet, like the song played for me, to breathe life into my sad, old self. So I danced, pink penises gyrating and flickering, hips swaying, hair swishing, until my world turned upside down.

NOAH

"Dibs."

I took a swig of Jack, slamming the glass down on the bar.

"You can't call dibs, asshole. There are four of them."

Easy shrugged with the same nonchalance that had earned him his call sign and made him lethal behind the stick of an F-16. He lulled you into thinking he was just fucking around. He never was.

"Are you saying I can't handle four chicks?"

"I'm calling bullshit on that one."

The guy got more pussy than anyone in the squadron, but a foursome was ambitious even for him.

"Fifty bucks," he offered, knowing my pathological inability to back down from a challenge.

"Fuck you, fifty bucks. You can't bang four chicks."

Easy's eyes narrowed in a look I knew all too well.

"Watch me."

We all gave him a hard time for being a princess because his face was a panty dropper, but he could throw down like nobody's business. Lately, though, this shit had been getting darker and darker. We'd broken off from the rest of the group, Joker had gone back to the hotel to call his wife, and now Easy was drinking like he wanted to die.

The Strip had seemed like a good idea four hours ago, but I was tired and now I just wanted to collapse in the suite we'd booked at the Venetian. I'd flown four sorties leading up to today, each one more demanding than the last. Today's double turn had topped me out at six flights this week, and my body definitely felt it. I was tired, my schedule screwed six ways to Sunday, and right now I was far less concerned with getting laid than I was with getting more than five hours of sleep.

Our commander, Joker, was on my ass for the squadron to perform well at Red Flag—our international mock war held at Nellis Air Force Base in Vegas. As the squadron's weapons officer, it was my job to make sure we were tactically the shit. Babysitting F-16 pilots with a hard-on for trouble? Not in my job description. It was really sad when I was the voice of reason.

Sending a bunch of fighter pilots to Vegas for work was basically like putting a diabetic kid in a candy store.

We got as much training done as we got tits and ass. And considering we pulled fourteen-hour workdays? That said something.

"It's a bachelorette party," I ground out, the subject already hitting way too close to home.

The flash of pain in Easy's eyes was a punch to the nuts. Shit. It was worse than I'd thought.

"Screwing around isn't going to change things," I added, trying to keep any judgment or sympathy out of my tone.

If it were anyone else, I would have minded my own business; but it wasn't anyone else, it was *Easy*. He'd been my roommate at the Academy, gotten me through pilot training when I'd struggled, flown out to Vegas when I'd somehow graduated from weapons school.

Easy threw back the rest of his drink. "Be my wing-man for ten minutes. I won't go after the bride. Then you can leave."

I'd been ready to leave an hour ago.

"You owe me for the twins in San Antonio," he reminded me.

Shit, I did.

"Ten minutes."

He nodded.

I turned my attention to the group of girls dancing; they looked young and already well on their way to drunk. I was definitely calling in my marker at a later time.

At thirty-three, I was getting too old for this shit. Most of the squadron was either married or divorced, Easy and I among the few single holdouts left.

It wasn't that I was opposed to marriage. I'd thought about how it would feel to land after a deployment to a girl who'd throw her arms around me and kiss me like she never wanted to let go, instead of landing to my bros carrying a case of beer. Hell, I saw the way guys climbed out of their jets, their kids running toward them on stubby legs, looking like it was Christmas, their birthday, and a trip to Disney World all rolled into one.

Even a fucker like me teared up.

I wasn't Easy; I wasn't trying to screw my way through life. I wanted a family, a wife. But I'd learned the hard way that not many girls were willing to stick around waiting for a guy who was gone more than he was around, who missed holidays and birthdays, who came home for dinner some nights at 11 p.m., and other nights not at all. It was hard to agree to moving every couple years, to deployments that stretched on and on, to remote assignments, and *Sorry, honey, this one's a year, and you can't come.*

I got it. It was a shit life. The kind of life that sliced you clean, that took and took, stretching you out 'til there was nothing left but fumes. But then there were moments. That moment when I sat in the cockpit, when I was in the air, up in the clouds, feeling like a god. When the afterburner roared. The times when we were called to do more, when the trips to the desert meant something, when we supported the mission on the ground. The times when we marked a lost brother with a piano burn and a song. I couldn't blame Easy for needing to let off steam, the edge was there in all of us, our faithful companion every time we went up in the air and took our lives in our hands.

We flew because we fucking loved it. So I guessed I already had a wife, and she was an expensive, unforgiving bitch—

Fortysomething million dollars of alloy, fuel, and lube that could fuck you over at any given time and felt so good when you were inside her that she always kept you coming back for more.

JORDAN

As the soberest one in the group, I noticed them first. To be fair, they were pretty hard to miss.

A loud and more than slightly obnoxious bachelorette, we'd run into our share of guys tonight—preppy polos and leather shoes with tassels—some single, some married, all looking like they'd served a stint in suburban prison and were now out in the yard for good behavior. They had that wide-eyed overeager look, as though they couldn't believe their luck—*Look at the shiny lights on the sign. Did you see the ass on that girl?*—and Vegas was their chance to make memories that would keep them company when they were coaching Little League or out buying tampons for their wives.

These two were something else entirely.

They walked toward us, and I stopped dancing to enjoy the show. They didn't look like anyone had let them out for good behavior, or like Vegas was their grown-up amusement park. They looked like this was their world, and they carried themselves like fucking kings.

One was tall and lean, his face—well, fuck, there was no other word for it—he was beautiful. Tan skin, full mouth, blue eyes. Dark blond hair that begged for a woman to run her fingers through. Great hair. Perfect hair.

I admired him for two point five seconds, and then he ceased to exist.

The other one was not beautiful. He didn't have pretty hair, or long lashes, or any shit like that. I wasn't even sure his features really registered all that much before he was just there, standing in front of me, and everything else in the club disappeared.

Dark hair. Dark eyes. Tan skin. Sexy mouth.

He was tall—in my heels we were nearly even, which was saying something considering I was a few inches off of six feet and wearing a wicked pair of Choos. He was broad-shouldered and definitely built. He wasn't dressed up—I doubted this guy even owned a polo—but he rocked his jeans and T-shirt. An expensive-looking, enormous watch that appeared capable of coordinating missions to the moon flashed on his wrist.

His gaze ran over me, his mouth curving as his survey ended at the top of my head. I reached up to see if my hair was out of place and got a handful of something else instead.

My cheeks flamed. The penis headband. *Shit.*

I dropped my hand as though I'd been scalded.

Act cool. Pretend you didn't just grip the base of one of the giant pink phalluses currently bobbing on top of your head.

His lips curved even more as he gave me the full punch of his amusement—gorgeous white teeth and a laugh I wanted to cloak myself in.

He kept coming until his body was a breath away from mine. He was big enough that he blocked out the club around us, the scent of his cologne sending a little shock between my legs. I didn't know what it was about that masculine scent, but some primal part of me that probably harkened back to days when men roamed around bare-chested carrying animal pelts on their shoulders liked it a hell of a lot. His head bent, his dark hair nearly brushing against my blond strands. I got a glimpse of his tanned neck, barely resisting the urge to bury my face there and inhale more of his delicious scent.

I wasn't much of a romantic—not with my track record, at least. I didn't believe in love at first sight, but *lust at first sight*? That was a thing definitely happening all over my body tonight.

"Please tell me you aren't the bride," he whispered in my ear, his lips teasing the sensitive skin there.

I shivered, basking in that voice. It was gravelly, and growly, and I was pretty sure I was drenched.

"I'm not the bride."

Our gazes met, his eyes darkening as soon as the words left my lips in a move that had me sucking in a deep breath, my lungs desperate for air. I didn't know if it was the loud music, or the late night, or the tequila coursing its way through my body, or the stilt-like heels, or the fact that my ovaries exploded as he engaged all of my senses, but either way I was feeling more than a little light-headed and fighting the temptation to reach out and grab on to one of his impressive biceps to hold steady.

He smiled and I might have had a mini-orgasm.

"Thank fuck."

Thank fuck, indeed.

He reached out, tucking a strand of hair that had escaped behind my ear. His hand grazed my cheek as he released me and I swayed toward him.

I wanted to lick him, and bite him, and do all kinds of naughty things to that gorgeous body. Multiple times.

"What's your name?" he asked, interrupting my fantasies.

"Jordan." I held out my hand to shake and then froze, my hand halfway there. *Smooth. You're in a nightclub, not a freaking business meeting.* To say it had been a while since I'd dated was a massive understatement. Plus, I'd have been lying if I didn't admit I had blindingly horrible moments of awkward even on my good days. I pretty much lived in extremes. I either totally rocked it or epically failed, with very little in between.

His mouth quirked up as he held out his hand. "I'm Noah."

Well, now I knew the name I'd be calling out in my dreams.

Our palms connected, his hand warm against mine. I waited for him to let go, already mourning the loss of his touch. But he didn't. He just stood there, holding my hand in the middle of the club, staring at me like I was not alone in these feelings.

"It's nice to meet you," I squeaked. *Really nice to meet you.*

The song changed and the club grew frenzied around us, and then he was pulling me toward him and I was dancing, Noah behind me, his big hands on my hips, fingers laced with mine, his body moving against me.

Yes, please.

For such a tall guy, he had good rhythm. *Really good rhythm.* I loved dancing, but I was more of a dance-alone or with-friends kind of girl. Most guys were pretty terrible dancers, and I hated having to try to match my movements to theirs, unable to let the beat of the song take over. Noah wasn't like that at all. He molded his body to mine, letting me set the pace.

And by the way he rolled his hips against my ass, he definitely had some moves.

Holy hell.

His hand drifted up my side, gathering my hair, fisting the ends. Arousal pulsed between my legs, the beat steady, strong, a slow ache. He pulled me back toward him, his hard cock pressing against my ass. A tremor ripped through my body as his fingers grazed my nape, tracing the skin there, my nipples tightening beneath the thin fabric of my dress. My body felt overheated, the music and alcohol flooding my senses. Around us, people danced, bodies rubbing against each other, mouths tangling, hands roaming. It was that point in the evening when inhibitions lowered, and it was Vegas—it was a night for letting go.

Head bent, his arms wrapped around my torso, the curve of my breasts brushing against his muscular forearm. Another tremor throbbed between my legs. His lips grazed my neck, brushing over the sensitive curve where it met my shoulder. I bit back a moan.

More.

I leaned into him, reaching out, our fingers threading together, our hands joined. His body behind me called to mind other images—of me naked, on my hands and knees, while he drove into me.

He was easily the hottest guy I'd ever seen, and tonight was quickly ranking up there with one of the more memorable evenings of my dating life.

His hold on me tightened and another mini-spasm wracked my body.

I turned in Noah's arms, my breasts grazing his chest. His hands moved lower, grabbing my ass, hauling me toward him, his gaze on my mouth.

I'd never been happier of my single status than I was now.

NOAH

Dibs had flown out the window. I didn't know which girl Easy wanted, didn't care. This one was mine.

I feasted on her mouth. She tasted like tequila and mint, her lips soft and plump. Her tongue wreaked havoc on my sanity.

I'd kissed my fair share of girls; drunken kisses in dark club corners weren't anything new. But this—this was mind-blowing.

The second I touched her, she lit up. Her hands pulled on my neck, her fingers threading through my hair, tugging on the ends, yanking me toward her as though she couldn't get close enough. My hands cupped her ass, squeezing her through the thin fabric, loving how she squirmed against me, rubbing herself over my jeans and my hard cock.

She was sex in heels, the kind of body that was all curves, made for a centerfold. The beauty mark just above her upper lip took hot to an all-new level.

I released her mouth, kissing my way down her neck, my teeth scraping her flesh, my dick jerking with the moan that escaped her lips. I nipped her, running my tongue over her skin, the taste of her swirling in my mouth. Jordan gripped the back of my head harder, her body begging for more.

No question about it, not only was she sexy as hell,

but she liked to play. I'd just hit the motherfucking jackpot.

I shifted so I was behind her again, my hands on either side of her hips, our bodies swaying in time to the music. The girl was gorgeous—long blond hair, big tits, curvy ass, long, shapely legs shown off by the sexiest pink dress. Absolutely gorgeous. And the second our gazes had locked across the club, her brown eyes had looked at me like I was her favorite meal and she wanted me for breakfast, lunch, and dinner.

Done.

My hands moved higher, pulling her tighter against me. Her neck arched, her head tipping into mine, and one of the pink penises hit me in the face again.

I grinned. Fuck, she was cute.

"Babe, gotta remove the headband. Don't need pink dicks in my face."

Jordan turned to face me, locking her arms around my neck. Her cheeks turned a soft shade of pink and she nodded.

I'd always had a weakness for blondes, and this girl had incredible hair. It fell down the center of her back in a mass of loose waves and curls. I set the headband on the table, my gaze on hers the entire time.

At some point we'd stopped dancing, and now we stood in the club with our bodies plastered together, her arms around my neck.

I stroked her hip, pulling her even closer. We danced for a long time, moving from song to song, our bodies matching each other's rhythm like we'd been dancing together for years. I'd been exhausted, and with one kiss she breathed new life into me.

I leaned down, my lips inches away from her ear, struggling to be heard over the loud music.

"Do you want to get out of here?" I asked, her answer suddenly feeling like everything.

I hadn't come out looking to get laid, had honestly been about to call it a night, but the second I saw her, my plans for the evening became whatever put me in her orbit. I didn't know where this was headed, but right now I was happy to follow her anywhere.

She nodded, and a knot tightened in my chest as she linked hands with me and I led her off the dance floor.